SUBURBAN GOTHIC

Also by Brian Keene and Bryan Smith:

URBAN GOTHIC by Brian Keene
THE FREAKSHOW by Bryan Smith

A NOTE FROM THE AUTHORS

While this novel is structured as a standalone story, it also serves as a sequel to both *Urban Gothic* by Brian Keene and *The Freakshow* by Bryan Smith. While it is not necessary for readers to have a familiarity with either of those books, we recommend that you read them at some point to further increase your enjoyment.

SUBURBAN GOTHIC

Brian KEENE

Bryan SMITH

deadite press

DEADITE PRESS
833 SE Main Street #342
Portland, OR 97214
www.deaditepress.com

An Eraserhead Press company
www.eraserheadpress.com

ISBN: 978-1-62105-315-6

Printed in the USA.

This book is dedicated to Keith Giffen...

ACKNOWLEDGEMENTS

Our thanks to Rose O'Keefe and Deadite Press; Paul Goblirsch and Thunderstorm Books; Alex McVey; Xander Harris; M.J. Withers; Dot-Com Intelligence; Sick Of It All; Dustin James and Church of Disgust; Jeremy Wagner and Broken Hope; Richard Christy and Charred Walls of the Damned; Ryan Harding; Mike Lombardo; Jeff Burk; Paul Synuria; Tod Clark and Mark Sylva.

"Folks in the suburbs don't know each other. They go to work. They come home. They go inside with their families. Maybe they know their next-door neighbor, enough to nod at him and shit, maybe exchange some pleasantries—but for the most part, they can't tell you who lives down the street, or the name of the family three houses down from them. All they know about each other is what their neighbors are driving and which political sign they had in their yard during the election. That's all."

—Perry Watkins, URBAN GOTHIC

"This place…it's diseased somehow. It's been dying for a long time. For centuries. And that's why the freaks are slowly and subtly worming their way into our world. They want to leave this tainted place behind and claim our world as their own."

—Mike Garrett, THE FREAKSHOW

PROLOGUE

They hid in shit and piss the first night, sheltering themselves in the reeking, decrepit sewers beyond their subterranean tunnels, cowering in the slimy, steaming wetness of Philadelphia's accumulated waste and filth, while a fire raged above them, engulfing the only home they had ever known.

Scug spent most of that first evening searching for survivors. Jax and Gax had helped him (although it was really only Jax, since Gax was nothing more than Jax's asymmetrical conjoined fetal twin—a tiny, scabrous pink head poking out of the flesh between Jax's shoulder and chest). They'd left the cyclopean Curd behind to guard the children, knowing the little ones would be safe with him while they braved passageways now filled with tear gas and smoke and heat and men with guns. Curd would shred anything that came near the little ones and paint the walls with whatever was left.

By dawn, the house above had been reduced to smoking, glowing cinders, and more men began to pour into the tunnels beneath the wreckage. Their shouts and footfalls echoed in a bewildering cacophony. Police and first responders came armed with lights and equipment and more guns. So many guns.

Scug returned to his family and took count of the huddled group. In addition to himself, Curd, and Jax/Gax, they'd found Klavo the mute dwarf, and the twin sisters—Gretch and Slava. The latter had suffered several gunshots and eventually succumbed to the trauma, dying there amidst the shit and piss. They'd also rescued seven misshapen little ones, including an infant with stubs for limbs and another with flippers and a third that was more spider than humanoid. Another of the rescued children was Noigel's offspring, Lorok. Jax and Gax had found the baby hidden inside the chest cavity of a dead policeman, mewling and suckling at a severed artery that had no blood left in it. That brought the number of children to thirteen, which was a lucky and powerful number. Scug couldn't take any joy in the symbolism, however. He was too distraught. Their family was decimated—hunted, hounded, butchered, and burned into oblivion. Scug wanted to rage. He wanted to go topside and rampage through the city streets, cutting and stabbing, disemboweling and decapitating, spilling innards and bathing in blood, slaughtering every living thing in his path until the sidewalks were as red as the anger boiling inside of him. But he could not. No matter how strong his need for revenge, his only focus right now had to be their survival. The nineteen of them were all that was left—thirteen young ones plus Jax and Gax, Curd, Klavo, Gretch and himself. If they died, the family bloodline died with them. And that could not happen.

Revenge—slaughter—would have to be delayed. The family's survival was paramount. It was his responsibility.

Curd looked at him expectantly. "Noigel?"

Scug shook his head. "Dead."

"Noigel is dead? But…nothing can kill Noigel!"

"Well, something sure did."

"How? You're sure, Scug?"

"I said it, didn't I?"

"He lives through his offspring," Jax said, turning his attention to one of the infants "We will raise Lorok to honor his father."

Klavo drew in the dirt with his finger.

Jax frowned. "I cannot read that."

Gretch grinned. "He's saying that when Lorok is bigger, Curd can teach him the ways of smashing heads."

Grunting, Curd turned back to Scug. "What about the Trash? Any of them left?"

"The Trash were all still down in the pit. Water got hot from the fire. They were boiled alive."

"It's just us?" Jax asked.

Scug nodded again.

Gax began to weep from Jax's shoulder.

They remained hidden beneath the city throughout the day. None of the search crews ventured far enough into the sewers to find them. While they waited for an opportunity to escape, Curd butchered Slava's corpse and fed her to the children to keep them quiet. Gretch took her sister's third index finger as a keepsake. Scug and the others fashioned weapons from her bones. The work made Scug think of Noigel's massive warhammer, constructed from a granite boulder and an iron pipe. He wished he had it now. Of course, even if he had access to it, he wouldn't be able to lift the weapon. None of them would. They weren't strong enough.

When they were finished, they ate as well, joylessly devouring what was left of Slava and building up their strength for what was to come. Then they waited, hiding while the men searched the tunnels. Each time one of the intruders got close, Scug resisted the urge to kill. It would have been so easy to do, and so satisfying to feel the hot spray of blood, and to feel their insides slipping and sliding beneath his fingers. But he had bigger responsibilities now.

On the second night, Scug led the group through the sewers until they came across an exit far removed from the rest of the city and, one by one, emerged into the safety of darkness. They found themselves standing in a dilapidated industrial park. The cracked concrete buildings were covered with graffiti and leaned crookedly, their sagging roofs dipping down. Trash covered the pitted pavement. The sky was thick with clouds and pollution, obscuring the full moon, and streetlights were sparse. A police siren wailed in the distance, then faded. It was soon replaced by a car alarm. Eventually, silence returned.

Clutching a crude knife made out of Slava's arm bone, Curd surveyed the area with the lone eye affixed in the center of his face. A cool breeze caressed his smooth, bald head and rustled the hair sprouting out of his cauliflower ears.

"What now?" he asked.

"Now?" Scug shrugged. "We start over again. Find a new place to live."

"Here." Jax's voice was deep and somber. "We could live here, Scug. Inside these buildings."

"Not here," Scug replied. "There are too many people. More people every day. Too much of a chance at being found. We need to get out of the city."

Curd's expression turned to fear. "But we have always lived in the city."

"Yes," Scug nodded. "We have. For generations. Hundreds of years. But the city is different now. We can't stay in Philadelphia anymore. We have to leave."

"And go where?" Jax asked.

Scug pointed into the darkness. Far ahead, headlights flashed on the highway.

"The suburbs," he said. "We're moving to the suburbs."

Jax nodded. From his shoulder, Gax gibbered in excitement.

Scug turned to Curd. "That okay with you?"

"The suburbs." Curd's broad gash of a mouth slowly split into a grin, revealing sharp but rotten teeth. "The food is better there."

Scug laughed, and then turned to the others. "Klavo? Gretch? The suburbs sound okay with you?"

Klavo grunted, which was the most he could manage since he'd been born without a tongue, but his eyes mirrored agreement.

"I always wanted to see the 'burbs," Gretch said. "They have stores. Shopping malls. I've seen them in the catalogs. Can we get stuff from the stores? Can we go shopping?"

"We can," Scug told her. "But we'll have to get settled first. Find a place to live."

"Where?" Jax asked.

Scug ignored the question. "Round up these young ones and let's head out. We'll need to find a place to hide again before morning."

They walked into the night.

"Speaking of stores," Scug muttered, "that reminds me. I'll need to make myself a new dress."

Gretch pulled a scab from her knee and popped it into her mouth.

"And some man-chews," Scug added. "I could really use a man-chew right now."

ONE

Eleven years later…

As a new member of the Boseman-Kline commercial realty team, Michael McCafferty had been on the job less than three months and his current portfolio wasn't exactly filled with desirable properties. The top-drawer stuff was reserved for the more senior members of the firm. Those were properties located in prosperous areas—large, beautiful buildings that typically housed fine-dining restaurants, advertising agencies, public relations firms, and digital content providers. Even in the midst of the Covid-19 global pandemic, they rarely sat vacant for more than a month or two.

Meanwhile, Michael was expected to sell things like a decrepit old gas station that had sat empty for so long that the big sign out front, now half-covered in vines and faded from the sun, displayed a per-gallon price of gas from just before the 2008 financial recession. His portfolio also included a roadside motel that looked like something out of a noir filmmaker's fever dream of the 1950's. He'd been pitching it to potential buyers as something that could be renovated in a retro way that might appeal to hipsters. The problem was that any renovation of that roach-and-rat infested dump would have to be fucking extensive. Burning it down and rebuilding from scratch might be easier.

The most disappointing item in his portfolio was the Westgate Galleria, a massive indoor shopping mall that had opened in 1977. For decades, it had been a popular Central Pennsylvania destination, a place where suburban adults spent entire days running up debt on their credit cards while their kids wandered around in packs, occasionally causing headaches for the rent-a-cops who provided security.

In his early forties, Michael was just old enough to remember the heyday of such places, before online retail sent malls like the Westgate Galleria into an inexorably slow death spiral. He'd put in his time as a mallrat during his teens back in the 90's, haunting Spencer Gifts and the vintage arcade and hanging out with his friends in the food court. Going to the mall was fun back then, in those days before smartphones became ubiquitous. People were addicted to their goddamn tablets and phones, kids and adults alike. Everywhere you went, people stared at their screens like zombies. Real social interaction was a quaint thing of the past—just like the shopping mall. After all, why bother driving to the suburbs to tramp around a giant mall when, with a few clicks of a button, you could buy everything you needed? It was no wonder that places like the Westgate were slouching toward obsolescence.

Michael shook his head as he steered his black BMW convertible into the massive parking lot outside the mall's south-facing entrance. His train of thought made him feel like an irascible old man yelling at those damn kids to get off his lawn. Things changed. The world moved on and progressed. Nothing remained the same forever, even things that had once seemed monolithic and essential. He was as guilty as anyone when it came to living life via smartphone. He upgraded to the newest iPhone every year, just like all his colleagues. He used social media to find clients and sell properties every day. Every date he had been on in the last two years was arranged via Tinder, Match, and other online dating services. In truth, he wouldn't turn back the hands of time even if he could. He liked how things were now, the advances in technology and the infinitely greater levels of convenience that came with them.

And yet, he couldn't help lamenting how those same advances were negatively impacting his job. Many years ago, the Westgate would have been a prime property. Now, it was a shit sandwich—an albatross around the neck of any realtor unlucky enough to be assigned it. How many years had this place sat unoccupied? How long had it been a tumor festering among the body of Boseman-Kline's commercial properties? At least a decade, which meant he was just the latest in ten years' worth of realtors who were saddled with the derelict.

There was something palpably eerie about driving through the big parking lot. Mostly it was the emptiness. The pavement and asphalt were pitted, and weeds grew through the cracks. As he got closer to the large storefront that had once housed a J.C. Penney's department store, he was struck by how dingy and rundown the place looked now. The paint had faded and peeled. The glass doors were boarded over and covered with graffiti, gang tags and what he guessed might be the names of heavy metal bands. A large concrete flower pot off to the side of the doors had been knocked over and lay in pieces on the trash-strewn sidewalk. He saw broken beer bottles and fast food wrappers in the now-barren flowerbeds. He guessed kids ignored the suggested social distancing due to the pandemic and came out here to party at night, with the cops rarely bothering to chase them away.

He needed to assess the condition of the mall's interior and determine what all would need doing in order to make it sellable. He had a feeling it would be a lot—probably worse than the exterior. Without regular maintenance, any such structure would succumb to blight. There were surely mold, rodents, rotten wood and burst pipes to contend with.

Before Michael, the Westgate Galleria had been assigned to a Boseman-Kline realtor who'd pulled a disappearing act six months earlier. One day Frank Hendrix went out to lunch and never returned. No one had any idea what had happened to him. There was an investigation, of course, but it turned up nothing. His car was never found. His credit cards showed no charges after the date of his disappearance. None of his relatives or friends reported having heard from him. Despite an extensive search, no remains were ever found. Everybody who knew him swore it wasn't like him to just up and leave without telling anybody. Which could only mean something bad had happened to him. What that might be, no one could say.

It was sad, but after six months, the firm had decided it was well past time to move on. His properties were divvied up among the other agents. There were some nice pieces to that portfolio. Even some downtown locations. But did Michael get a shot at any of those? Of course not.

He got the goddamned mall.

Off to one side of the boarded-up storefront, he spotted a service entrance—beige-painted metal doors with chains looped around the handles for extra security. He had a key with him that was supposed to open it, but Michael decided to take a full cruise around the mall before venturing inside.

The parking lots outside each of the mall's four major storefront entrances were separated by long concrete medians. He drove back out to the road encircling the area and then pulled into the lot outside the east-facing entrance. Unlike the previous one, this lot was not empty. A lone black Mustang was parked with its back end against the far median. The tinted windows were partly down, and puffs of smoke billowed from inside, accompanied by heavy metal music. Michael grinned. Just a bunch of young headbangers getting baked. Nevertheless, he had no intention of engaging with them. He wasn't a cop, and it wasn't his job to run off juvenile delinquents. Plus, he doubted they were wearing face masks, and he had no intention of catching the goddamned virus.

He did a faster pass outside the storefront entrance and then headed back out to the access road. In a few more moments, he pulled into the lot outside the mall's north-facing entrance. The layout here was different. There was no huge storefront entrance. The boarded-up glass doors had once granted entrance to the mall. Just inside was a small cineplex. This entry point was significantly farther back from the curb. Outside it was a small patio area with concrete tables. At one point it had been landscaped but now the topiary grew wild from years of neglect. Another solitary car sat in the approximate center of the lot, but in this case, it was a clearly abandoned vehicle. All four tires were flat, and the windows had been busted out. The car's lime-green paint job had faded from the sun, and the doors, hood and roof were covered in graffiti.

After making a mental note to have the car towed away as soon as possible, Michael parked his BMW at the curb at the edge of the patio, cut the engine, and got out. He put on his face mask and a pair of rubber surgical gloves. Though he'd not yet done a full circuit of the mall's exterior, he knew what the west-facing entrance would look like without having to see it—pretty much just like the first two he'd checked out, having also formerly housed a major chain department store.

In his research, he'd encountered little evidence of vacant or ailing indoor malls being successfully revived as shopping centers or anything remotely resembling what they'd been in better days. Most of the ones he read about were still sitting empty many years after the last of the big anchor tenants pulled up stakes or went bankrupt.

What was needed was some outside-the-box thinking.

He recalled one article about a shopping mall much like the Westgate Galleria. It was located in the south, and had been repurposed as the campus of a community college. A link in that article had led him to a similar story about another former mall that now housed a nursing school, also somewhere down south. If something like that could work in the south, why not here in Lancaster, Pennsylvania?

The situation wasn't as simple as that, though. He didn't yet know, for instance, whether there was sufficient demand for a community college or vocational school in the area. Off the top of his head, he could easily name several places already serving that need locally. The bottom line was that he had a lot of work and further research ahead of him if he hoped to transform this property into something capable of generating real interest.

Sighing, Michael stared at the mall, contemplating its forbidding exterior.

"Fuck me," he muttered.

One particular piece of spray-painted graffiti caught his eye: Scug wuz Here.

Michael grunted. What kind of dimwitted suburban troglodyte kid would call himself something like Scug? Well, if he had anything to say about it, the Scugs of the world wouldn't get to hang out here much longer.

He chuckled softly and started walking.

A short sidewalk branching off from the overgrown patio led Michael to the service entrance for the north-facing side of the mall. This time there were no heavy chains looped around the handles of the rusty beige-painted double doors. He was taken aback by this. All the service entrances were supposed to be chained and locked. After being vacant for so long, no one was paying for electronic security monitoring on the property, which made the chains a definite necessity.

His brow furrowed. Up until this moment, he'd assumed he would be entering a completely unoccupied building, but he was no longer sure about that. He thought about the black Mustang. That there were kids inside the car was another thing he'd just assumed. It was an assumption based primarily on the aggressive metal music pumping from the Mustang's speakers. But heavy metal had been around for generations now. The people in that car could be anywhere from sixteen to sixty, and maybe weren't as harmless as he'd assumed.

Michael chuckled. "Assumptions make an ass out of u and me."

He shook his head. A healthy level of caution was probably a good idea, but there was no logical reason to link the Mustang's occupants to the missing chains. The emptiness and desolation of this place was getting to him. He tested the service entrance doors and found them locked. His burgeoning paranoia faded at that revelation. The building was still secure.

He detached a ring of keys from his belt and sorted through them until he found the right one. It was labeled with a thin piece of yellow tape, upon which had been scrawled "WS" which stood for "West Service". He slid the key into the lock and turned it. Then, holding his breath, he grabbed the handle and tugged. The door opened easily, but with a groan. Michael exhaled.

After clipping the keyring back to his belt, he opened the door a little wider and peered inside. Dirt and dust pelted his hair. He was grateful for the face mask, as he didn't want to breathe that shit in. He stared into a dark and musty service corridor. Then Michael took out his phone and turned on the flashlight application. It took him several tries, as the rubber gloves didn't work well with his phone's touch screen. The beam wasn't as strong as that of the flashlight he kept in the trunk of his car. He could only see a dozen feet. He spotted nothing out of the ordinary—just an empty stretch of bland hallway. No homeless people. No detritus or debris indicating it had been used as a party site by kids. But beyond the emptiness was more darkness. He didn't want to rely on his phone as he went deeper into the derelict, and risk killing the battery. The flashlight was a must.

He hurried back to the BMW, popped the trunk open, and retrieved the heavy-duty flashlight. There was also a golf club in the trunk—a putter, left there from last week when he'd been out to the club for a quick nine. He'd been a little drunk when he got home that evening, and the putter had fallen out of his golf bag when he took it out of the trunk. On impulse, he grabbed the club, closed the trunk and started back to the mall.

He noticed that his gloves already had slight tears and holes in them, around the fingertips. He'd probably done it opening the car. Shrugging, he paused long enough to pull them off and drop them to the asphalt. He debated getting a new pair out of the car, but decided that he was overdoing it. He still had his face mask, after all. Michael continued on his way.

Back at the service entrance, he pulled the door open again, switched on the flashlight, and stepped into the dark corridor, aiming the beam ahead of him. The door clicked shut behind him, closing and locking automatically, as it was designed to do. Michael considered finding something to prop it open, but decided against it. The Mustang and its occupants were probably gone by now, but there was no point in granting them or anyone else easy access.

He moved down the hallway, aiming the bright beam ahead of him while resting the putter on his shoulder. The concrete floor was covered with an unbroken layer of undisturbed dust. Vacant cobwebs hung from the ceiling and light fixtures. His breathing sounded odd beneath the fabric of his mask. His footsteps echoed slightly.

Moments later, the echoes were answered by another sound.

Michael shuffled to a halt, cocked his head, and held his breath, listening. The echoes ceased. He extended his arm as far as he could, and squinted, peering into the shadows. The sound was not repeated. The flashlight beam suddenly seemed dimmer.

He breathed through his nose, trying to remain as silent as possible. He tried telling himself it was his imagination, but he didn't quite buy it. The sound had been very faint, almost inaudible, but higher in pitch, almost like the giggling of a mischievous child.

Michael shivered.

Then the sound came again, while he was still straining to maintain absolute silence. This time, it was accompanied by a second noise—an odd scratching sound. This was also difficult to hear distinctly at first, but it grew steadily louder over the next several seconds. Michael thought it sounded like someone was dragging something along one of the corridor walls.

His pulse raced. Sweat ran down his forehead and into his eyes. He felt dizzy.

The high-pitched tittering came again.

Much closer now.

Michael cleared his throat and raised his voice, trying hard to sound intimidating, despite his face mask's muffling effect. "This is a private property. I suggest you leave before I call the police."

This produced another round of laughter in response.

Michael slowly retreated a few backward steps before turning and fleeing. Maniacal laughter rang out behind him, loud and unrestrained. Michael screamed. He heard multiple sets of feet racing after him. In his panic, he dropped the golf club but managed to keep hold of the flashlight. The putter clattered on the concrete.

He gasped with relief as he saw a slanting beam of fading sunlight shining through the slightly open service door. Tears and sweat streamed down his face. His mask slipped from his face and dangled around his chin and neck. Salvation was a dozen feet away. Then a half-dozen.

Then he remembered that the door had shut behind him when he first entered the corridor.

As he neared it, the door snapped shut again. Shouting, he slammed into it with his shoulder, trying to batter it open with sheer brute strength.

The door did not budge.

The laughter was right behind him now.

Shrieking, Michael grabbed the door handle—and was instantly knocked off his feet by an unexpected jolt of electricity.

TWO

Celeste Sinclair stood outside of Kickers, a sports bar that had seen better days, just like the rest of this suburban Pennsylvania town. She stuffed her phone in her purse as a brown van pulled up beside her. A Billie Eilish song played on its stereo, audible from where she stood. The van was in better condition than any of the nearby buildings—a vintage 1978 Chevy, fully restored and customized. The only thing on the van from this era, other than the bass-heavy stereo, was a Bernie Sanders For President bumper sticker, and the mural emblazoned on the side, which was the logo for Lost Places, a popular YouTube channel dedicated to urban exploration of which Celeste was a member. The four people inside the van were all part of the Lost Places team, as well.

The portly twenty-three-year-old behind the steering wheel was Stuart Carlson. He scratched his long, bushy brown beard with one hand, and squinted to see over the smudges on his thick-lensed eyeglasses. Perched slightly askew atop his head was one of the team's branded Lost Places ballcaps. Affable Stuart frequently functioned on-camera as comic relief for the team. Everyone tried to be funny and engaging, of course, but it came a little more naturally to Stuart. Subscribers adored him.

Bradley Wilson rode shotgun. Lost Places was his creation, and while he acknowledged and appreciated the contributions of the rest of the team, he wasn't shy about occasionally reminding viewers that it was he who had originally come up with the idea. The viewers needed no such reminder, judging by his popularity among the commentators, one of whom had once described him as "serviceably handsome in the manner of a hand-me-down Matthew McConaughey". As such, Brad was the face of Lost Places. Blessed with the gift of gab, his personality was tailor-made for the front-and-center role.

Seated in the back were Audrey McAvoy and Chuck Clemons. They'd begun dating their senior year of high school, and were still together now, half a decade later. They'd never married or even seriously flirted with the idea of getting engaged. Whenever the other team members brought the subject up, Audrey insisted that marriage was an archaic, anti-feminist social construct she wanted no part of anyway. Celeste knew that Audrey did not believe this. She'd always been good at seeing through people, especially other women. Audrey was secretly eaten alive with desperation for something more, but she was too complacent to do anything about it. She was also only marginally cute and most likely doubtful of her ability to procure another man, much less one willing to make her secret desires reality.

And as for Chuck...well, there wasn't much to him. He was a fucking cipher, as far as Celeste could tell. Quiet. A gormlessly wasteful nothing. Celeste loathed him in a quiet, passive-aggressive sort of way. She hated his dull-eyed stupid face. Chuck was their camera guy. It was the perfect role for him. Having him on-screen would drive away viewers. It was one of those silent, understood things that everyone knew and never said anything about, though Celeste yearned to inform him fully of his utter lack of worth. The only reason she didn't was knowing that Bradley would be furious, and she didn't want that. He was her boyfriend, after all. No point in creating a strain on their relationship. Also, the rest of the team had known each other for years. They were tight knit, whereas she was a much more recent addition, tolerated primarily because their leader worshipped her. She strongly suspected the rest of the crew despised her, but Celeste didn't give a shit.

As for her own role in Lost Places, Celeste knew precisely what that was. She was there to provide sex appeal. A female counterpoint to Bradley's on-screen presence. She had a nice, busty figure and a gorgeous face with sculpted cheekbones, natural gifts she exploited with unabashed enthusiasm by utilizing a wardrobe consisting almost entirely of skimpy, too-tight clothes. Cold weather shoots required getting more creative in terms of wardrobe, but even bundled up for winter, she still came off as devastatingly attractive. She felt a little smug about that. Of course, Celeste's main gig was being an Instagram model, where she had close to a hundred-thousand followers. She'd done well enough at social influencing that she hadn't needed a day job in years. Starring with Bradley on his YouTube channel was something she'd started doing just for fun, as a favor to him, but Lost Places had turned surprisingly lucrative in its own right.

Bradley and the rest of the team had driven from their home base of Nashville. Celeste had flown from New York City to nearby Harrisburg International airport, and then caught an Uber. As she waited for the others to climb out of the van, Celeste glanced around. She missed New York already. There were a few glimmers of civilization here in the suburbs of Lancaster, Pennsylvania, including this place, Kickers. Dumb name, even for a sports bar, but she didn't care, as long as they were serving. She was famished. As Bradley and the others approached her, she caught a glimpse of a darkened shopping mall in the distance, barely visible and set far back across the highway. She assumed that it must be the Westgate Galleria.

"Hey." Bradley smiled, flashing whitened teeth as he embraced her, and kissed her cheek. "How was your trip?"

"Terrible." She pulled back a little. His breath smelled stale and sour. "They made me wear a mask the whole way. How was the drive?"

Bradley shrugged.

"Chuck whined about Covid all the way here," Stuart said.

"I didn't whine," Chuck said, shuffling up beside them. He sounded like he was panting behind his facemask. "I just think you should be more careful."

"I put my mask on every time we stopped, dude. And I used hand sanitizer after that shitty public restroom in Maryland."

"Yeah, but you didn't use it when you got gas. What if the person who used the fuel pump before you was infected?"

Stuart shrugged. "They said you can't get it that way."

"Who said?" Chuck asked. "Reddit?"

"Yeah."

"Can we not?" Celeste dismissed both of them with a wave of her hand. "I'm hungry."

Bradley nodded at Chuck. "Get your rig out."

Audrey frowned. "You want him to record us eating?"

"No, I want him to record us meeting up here. Then we'll eat."

While Chuck and Audrey returned to the van to retrieve their gear, Bradley had Celeste stand beneath an outdoor light at the edge of the parking lot.

"Pretend we're just now seeing each other," he said.

"Eat a mint first."

He grinned. "Do I have potty mouth?"

"Like something died in there."

Still grinning, he hustled over to the van and rummaged around inside the glove compartment. While he did, Audrey and Chuck returned, and Chuck began testing the camera. Audrey opened a plastic shopping bag and began handing out facemasks emblazoned with the Lost Places logo.

"Don't forget these," she said.

Celeste groaned. "I've had one on all day. The airport and then the plane ride, and then in the Uber. I hate these fucking things."

"We all hate them," Bradley said. "But we need to pimp that merchandise."

"And we don't need people like Chuck giving us a hard time in the comments," Stuart said.

Frowning, Celeste donned her mask, adjusting her hair so it would fall over the elastic bands.

"Ready?" Bradley asked.

Chuck gave him a thumbs up.

"Hey, what's up, guys?" Bradley looked directly into the camera and pretended he had just gotten out of the van. "This is Bradley. If this is your first time watching one of our videos, don't forget to subscribe below—and hit that Like button! You might also want to check out some of our other videos, like our exploration of the abandoned Higdon Hotel, Knoxville College, the Lake Shawnee Amusement Park, Centralia, and the former Tennessee State Prison."

"Creepy stuff," Stuart chimed in.

Bradley nodded. "We have just pulled up to this sports bar in Lancaster, Pennsylvania, where we'll be reunited with the lovely Celeste. In fact, I see her waiting for us over there!"

Celeste played along perfectly. Bradley's transition was remarkable. He seamlessly shifted from his off-camera sleepy slacker persona to a more excitable, high-energy demeanor. His ability to do this was uncanny even to Celeste, who was long-accustomed to feigning different moods and personality traits for cameras. It reminded her of Dr. Jekyll becoming Mr. Hyde.

After breaking off his embrace with Celeste, he turned directly to the camera again and lowered his mask. She did the same, reminding herself to stay six feet apart from him. Stuarts was right. They didn't need concern trolls leaving comments about them not social distancing.

"Our destination tonight is the Westgate Galleria shopping mall," Bradley said. "Located here in Lancaster, it was once a shiny monument to consumerism. Now, it's an empty, desolate husk functioning as a grim metaphor for the death of the American dream and an indictment of all the empty promises of Western capitalism."

"Sounds fun," Celeste chimed in, and then pouted at the camera with a duck face.

"Fun," Bradley agreed, "but also dangerous. Now…that's never stopped us before because that's just who we are. We're the Lost Places team. We are not afraid. We take risks. We do whatever we have to in order to deliver the content our fans know they won't find on any other channel. That's why you hit that Like button and subscribe. Like Wolverine, we're the absolute best at what we do."

"Damn right we are," Stuart said. "Is the pep talk nearly over, by the way? Because I have not yet had my daily quota of hot wings and that situation could become problematic for all of us if it isn't rectified soon, bro."

"Chill, bro. You'll get to resume your endless quest to achieve maximum girth soon enough." Bradley turned back to the camera. "First, let's be clear about something. Tonight's expedition may be the single riskiest thing we've tackled yet. We've hired a guide, who we'll meet in a little bit, but we don't know what we'll encounter inside the Westgate Galleria Mall, but we know it's been abandoned for years. There's a chance we'll encounter squatters, and what do we know about squatters, gang?"

Audrey raised a hand.

Bradley pointed at her. "Yes, Audrey?"

"They're unpredictable."

"Exactly! Most of the time they're harmless, although it's still best to stay out of their way. But once in a while, squatters can be dangerous. They might be mentally ill or addicted to drugs. Or both. Chances are good that they won't be wearing face masks or washing their hands."

Celeste nodded. "And everybody should wear a face mask, just like we are."

"I never leave home without one," Stuart said. "And if you visit our website, you can get one of these sweet Lost Places facemasks, too. Remember, heroes wear masks."

"In addition to the coronavirus," Bradley said, "there is always a potential risk for violence when encountering squatters. That's why we always stick together. The old cliché is true. There's safety in numbers. So…let's be careful and, like Celeste said, let's have fun!"

Chuck lowered the camera. "Looked good."

"Are you sure," Bradley asked. "Should we do another take? I don't want a repeat of what happened in Centralia."

"We're fine," Chuck assured him.

"Celeste," Ashley asked, "do you want us to get some pics for your Instagram?"

"While I'm looking like this?" Celeste rolled her eyes. "I've been flying all day and I'm a mess. No make-up, airplane hair, and these yoga pants have a hole in them."

"Sorry." Audrey's tone was cold.

"And besides," Celeste continued, "this dump makes a terrible background. Can you imagine? Hey everyone, here I am at some dive called Kickers in suburban Pennsyltucky."

"Speaking of which…" Stuart turned toward the sports bar. "Let's eat!"

Celeste handed her mask to Audrey. Stuart and Bradley did the same. Audrey quietly placed them back in the bag, along with her own. Chuck kept his on. Audrey returned the bag to the van and locked the vehicle. Then they all made their way across the parking lot.

Smiling as she took Bradley's arm, Celeste leaned close to him and whispered into his ear. "Way to rally the troops, chief."

Bradley laughed. "Couldn't do it without you, babe."

Celeste smiled again and squeezed his arm. "Damn right, you couldn't. And don't you ever forget it, or I'll cut your fucking balls off."

* * *

Michael blinked, unsure of what was happening. His mouth was dry, and his tongue felt like sandpaper. He smacked his lips together and tasted blood. Probing with the tip of his tongue, he discovered that he'd bitten the inside of his cheek. What had occurred? He remembered getting shocked when he'd touched the doorknob. Then he'd…

He didn't know. His mind was blank. Had he been knocked unconscious? Judging by the pain on the side of his head, he must have fallen and struck the concrete floor. He touched it gently, probing his scalp with his fingers. Then he winced. There was a big lump, but the skin didn't feel broken. When he pulled his fingers away, there was no blood. Slowly, he pulled his mask off and breathed deep.

He wondered what had broken the electrical current. Whatever had happened, he was damned lucky to be alive. He remembered his decision not to put on another pair of latex gloves before returning inside. Maybe he should have. They might have prevented him from getting shocked.

Michael spat on the floor and his mouth tasted less salty. He felt around in the darkness, looking for the flashlight. He eventually found it against the wall to his right. Groaning, he reached for it, but before his hand could close around the cylinder, he sensed movement from somewhere above him. It was quiet and stealthy, but it was there. Dust drifted down into his face.

What the fuck?

He squinted. Seconds passed. There was no repetition of that faint suggestion, so he dismissed it as a fault of perception. His senses were feeding him faulty data after that wicked knock to his head. The dust had been stirred up by his fall. There was nothing more to it.

Michael put his face mask back on, and then grabbed the flashlight. Just to confirm things, aimed the beam straight up.

And screamed.

The thing hanging from the ceiling screamed, too, mocking him.

It wasn't a bird or an insect or a homeless person or a rat. It was a monster. Several wispy, spider-thin legs protruded from a swollen, gray torso riddled with diseased, seeping pores. The thing's torso appeared more or less human, as did the head attached to an elongated, sweaty neck. It was also equipped with what took Michael a moment to recognize as a grotesquely oversized penis, which dangled from the opposite end of the pustulant torso like a stuffed tube sock. Something that looked sharp, metallic, and covered in black oil projected from the oozing opening at the end of the member. It was as if someone had surgically implanted the blade from a box-cutter inside the thing's massive dong. But as he gaped in horror, he realized it wasn't metal at all. It was a stinger.

The creature stopped screaming. So did Michael. Then it made an unnerving hissing sound and thrashed its head about as Michael hopped to his feet and made another crazed dash for the door.

He grabbed the doorknob and again went flying backward when another jolt of electricity blasted through him. This time, he landed on his left side, and his arm and shoulder broke his fall.

The abomination skittered across the ceiling, making an insectile chittering sound. Quite a bit more of the stinger protruded from the thing's penis now. More of that black, oily substance was visible. Droplets landed on Michael's forehead, burning slightly when it hit his bare flesh. Then the most disturbing thing of all happened.

The creature chittered at him. The sound was guttural and insectile. He got the impression that it was trying to communicate.

Michael shook his head. "Like fuck I'm standing around here and having a conversation with you."

He sprang to his feet and ran in the opposite direction, deeper into the black catacombs of the abandoned mall.

THREE

Church of Disgust's Veneration of Filth ended, and Logan Krebs stirred long enough to eject the compact disc, put it back into its jewel case, and reach for another.

The old Mustang's sound system was outdated in almost every conceivable way. Bluetooth connectivity was not a feature, so streaming music from a phone or other device was impossible. There was no auxiliary jack, nor a compact disc player. What the receiver deck did have, however, was AM/FM radio and a vintage cassette player. Totally old school.

This had been a problem when Logan inherited the Mustang after his father passed away. He wanted to listen to music in his new ride. Good music—not any of that commercial garbage on the radio. His father had left a handful of tapes in the glove compartment—Guns N' Roses, Anthrax, Sick Of It All, The Hellacopters, Body Count, King Diamond, AC/DC, Kix, Biohazard, and Social Distortion—and while they were all great, and brought back happy memories of his dad, listening to the same ten cassettes got old after a while.

Then Logan began buying old heavy metal cassettes off eBay, which was a weirdly difficult habit to maintain for very long, seeing as how he wasn't exactly made of fucking money. Some of those old tapes were relatively cheap, but a great number of them were shockingly expensive. He hadn't realized there was such a strong nostalgia market for them. It made no sense to him. The sound wasn't that great, and the cassettes were prone to getting devoured by the tape player. But he'd long since given up trying to figure out Boomers and Gen X'ers. They were weird about shit like that.

Logan was ultimately forced to get creative. He bought an old portable CD player at a pawn shop, with a cassette adapter that allowed him to listen to compact discs in the Mustang. This was an improvement, though the device was still prone to the occasional malfunction. There was a short in the adapter's wire and sometimes the music cut out. Annoying, but not a big deal. Wiggling the cord almost always solved the problem within a few seconds. And it allowed him to listen to newer stuff like the Bile Lords, Your Kid's On Fire, Broken Hope, Charred Walls of the Damned, and Church of Disgust, none of which were available on cassette.

A lot of people would find this haphazard music system intolerable, but to Logan, there was something almost endearing about it. A lot of the music he preferred was from decades ago, and the modern bands he liked were heavily rooted in those old sounds. Being just twenty years old, most of the good stuff had been recorded long before he was born. Listening to that kind of music via obsolete technology made him feel like he was plugged into a link between the past and the present, particularly when riding around in the Mustang, which was from the same era.

He replaced the Church of Disgust compact disc with De Mysteriis Dom Sathanas by Mayhem. Released in 1994, this album by the black metal pioneers was still one of the most evil-sounding pieces of recorded music Logan had ever heard, and he thought of the occasional bit of adapter wire crackle as an integral part of the listening experience. It made everything feel more authentic, somehow, especially when he was high.

Like he was right now.

The music was also currently performing another important function by masking the sounds of Cam Paulson and Tara Burke fucking in the backseat. Well…almost. The Mustang's old speakers had some serious kick to them, but were not quite loud enough to entirely blot out the gasps and grunts. Even if he hadn't been able to hear them, they were in such a state of frenzy that the car was rocking. Try as he might, Logan couldn't ignore it. He was getting kind of turned on, which bothered him more than a little, especially since Lizzie was passed out next to him in the front passenger seat.

He considered pulling out his phone and scrolling through the apps, but his service was currently disconnected due to non-payment.

Logan took another hit off his vape and glanced at Lizzie. She looked peaceful and almost angelic in her sleep, if one ignored the line of drool leaking from a corner of her mouth. A three quarters-empty fifth of bourbon rested between her splayed legs. She'd downed nearly all of that herself, but it was the pair of Oxys she'd taken that had sent her down into dreamland. Mixing alcohol and opioids like that was stupid, in Logan's opinion, but Lizzie had never been one to put much stock in anyone else's point of view, including his. Perhaps most frustrating was how smart she was. Lizzie had an intellect like no one else he'd ever known, and yet she continued to engage in stupid, reckless behavior.

She wasn't exactly his girlfriend, but she spent a good chunk of her free time with him and fucked him more often than she fucked anyone else. Given the pride she took in being polyamorous, she'd probably never think of him as her official boyfriend, but Logan figured he was the closest thing she had to one. That being the case, he couldn't help feeling kind of responsible for her. She would get pissed off at him for even thinking such a thing, so he'd never mentioned it. Lizzie saw herself as beholden to no one, responsible only to herself, a free spirit floating through the world in a perpetual drunken, druggy haze, entirely untethered to anyone or anything. And so, Logan watched with quiet desperation every time she recklessly overindulged. He constantly worried that she would overdo it one of these nights and accidentally kill herself. And he hated knowing that if it happened, he would be just another ineffectual bystander who had done nothing to help her. Even the slightest suggestion that she should maybe consider taking better care of herself earned nothing but her ire. It was useless to even try, which in turn made him feel hopeless. Sometimes he thought maybe he should just cut ties with her completely and wash his hands of the situation. Doing so would undoubtedly save him a lot of heartache somewhere down the line.

And yet...he just couldn't because he fucking loved her. Logan knew how Lizzie would react if he ever admitted his feelings for her. She'd be the one to instantly cut ties and never speak to him again.

Maybe that would be the easiest way. Maybe he should just get it over with—tell Lizzie that he was in love with her, so she'd quickly end it with him.

The thing that bothered him the most was that Lizzie didn't have to be this way. His thoughts returned to her impressive intellect. When she was sober, Lizzie was the smartest person he had ever met. She knew shit about art and history and science that amazed him. She could have had her pick of colleges, had she actually gone to one. But she never had. She'd been put on this path long ago in the past, by people in her past, and while it wasn't her fault that she'd ended up like this, she didn't seem inclined to break free either.

Logan took another drag on his vape and discovered that it was empty. He stowed it in the glove compartment, stretching to reach over Lizzie. Then he scrunched down in his seat a bit. His eyelids drooped. He felt himself sliding toward unconsciousness.

His increasingly fuzzy thoughts turned to the BMW they'd seen slowly cruise by a short while ago. The guy driving it looked like your typical business type. Logan figured he was probably harmless.

His eyelids drooped even lower. He heard someone snoring and dimly realized it was him. True sleep was just seconds away.

Then he sensed movement outside the car. He opened his eyes and saw something looming over the hood. Cam and Tara were oblivious, judging from the noise in the backseat. Yawning, Logan sat up straight and rubbed his eyes. Then he looked again, flipping on the headlights and wiping condensation from the steamy windshield.

"Holy shit!"

The figure standing in front of the car looked sort of like a person. It stood upright on two legs, but was unnaturally tall. Like, tall enough he could've been a superstar in the NBA, if not for the second head that sprouted from the middle of his torso. His skin was dry to the point of appearing pickled, and nearly all of it was exposed. A loincloth fashioned from a ratty old shirt was cinched tight around his waist, but otherwise, he stood naked. His arms were thin and unnaturally long, and his hands were grotesquely oversized by comparison, with each featuring noticeably more than the normal number of fingers. His jaw and brow each protruded slightly, while the face of the second, tinier head possessed a lipless mouth with tiny yellow teeth filed down to razor sharpness.

"Holy fucking shit!"

Logan heard Tara gasp in the backseat, and urge Cam to stop. Cam grunted in annoyance.

The thing bent forward at the waist, leaning almost all the way over the hood and grinned with both of its mouths. Whimpering, Logan pushed himself back against the seat. Then he reached for the keys dangling from the ignition. As he did, the thing outside turned its head and appeared to listen to something.

"What the fuck is that?" Cam finally piped up from the back, voice slurred from the Oxycontin.

Before Logan could reply, the creature stepped back and ran, moving in huge, loping strides. As Logan watched, it hopped over a grass median at the edge of the parking lot and disappeared from view.

Logan shuddered. "Tell me you guys saw that?"

"Fuck yes," Cam yelled. "I mean, shit, that wasn't a hallucination, right? We both saw the same fucking thing, right?"

"I don't know. Did you see a freakishly tall mutant-looking motherfucker with a tiny second head growing from his chest?"

Cam nodded, mouth agape. "Yeah…"

"I want to go home," Tara said, her voice edging toward hysteria. "Logan, let's go!"

"Good idea," Logan said, nodding. "Maybe the best idea of all damn time, in fact."

Logan turned the key in the ignition.

Then he frowned and tried it again.

Cam leaned forward and poked his head between the front seat headrests. "What's happening?"

Logan tried to start the car a third time. "Nothing. That's what's happening. The engine is dead."

"Fuck you, Logan," Tara shouted, getting dressed. "That shit isn't funny!"

"Do I look like I'm fucking kidding around? The car won't start! It's like some horror movie shit."

Tara began to cry.

"Pop the hood and check it," Cam urged.

"Fuck that," Logan replied. "You go out there and fucking check it."

"It's your car, dude!"

"And it's your fault we've been here so long."

"How about we do rock, paper, scissors?"

"Screw you," Logan said. "This isn't some game!"

As they glared at each other, both trembling, Lizzie stirred in the passenger seat. She opened her eyes, blinked, and then smacked her lips together.

"What's happening?" she mumbled. "Why is everyone yelling?"

Logan took a deep breath. "The engine is dead and there's some kind of monster outside."

She looked at him for a moment, blinked again, and then nestled back into the seat and closed her eyes. Her snores were drowned out only by Tara's sobs.

The flashlight's beam danced crazily over the cinder block walls and ceiling of the maintenance corridor as Michael ran. His pulse pounded in his throat and his chest burned. The tittering of the spider-freak faded behind him, but his ears began to ring.

I'm too young for a heart attack, he thought, panicked. What the hell have I been going to the gym three times a week for?

The light glanced across a closed metal door up ahead on his right. Hurrying over to it, he reached out with a shaking hand, stopping just before his fingertips could graze the surface. What if this one was electrified like the one back at the service entrance?

Michael decided that it didn't matter.

Gritting his teeth and trying hard to push back his trepidation, he grabbed the doorknob. When he realized he wouldn't be receiving another shock, he gasped in relief and turned the knob. It was unlocked. He hurriedly pushed it open and aimed the flashlight inside, revealing stainless steel shelves with an array of dust-covered cleaning supplies. A mop and bucket sat in the middle of the smallish space. It appeared he'd found a janitorial supply room. It smelled rank, but he couldn't identify the source.

Michael quickly ducked inside and closed the door behind him. It seemed strong and had a lock. He thought maybe he could brace it with some of that steel shelving for extra support. He turned the lock, and then moved over to the mop, deciding to use it as a weapon. The stench grew stronger. As he reached for the mop handle, Michael glanced down at the bucket.

A bloated human head floated in dank, filthy water.

Michael stumbled backward, hand to his mouth, struggling not to vomit. His throat burned from bile. He ripped his mask from his face and gasped for air, purposely aviding looking into the bucket again.

He ran the flashlight's beam over the shelves and saw other horrors among the cleaning supplies—several human skulls, various bones, and jars containing organs suspended in murky liquid. One of those jars held a pair of eyeballs with stalks trailing behind them. He swooned, nearly overwhelmed with the gruesome sensory input. For one moment, he was certain those disembodied eyes were staring at him with awareness.

Fumbling with the door lock, Michael staggered out of the supply closet, and fled further down the corridor, sobbing and gibbering. Repurposing this place as something new wasn't possible. It needed to be burned down, blown to fucking pieces and razed to the ground. Fuck his commission. Fuck the real estate business, too, for that matter. If by some miracle he made it out of the mall alive, he was going into some other line of work. Something safe and sane. Flipping burgers, or maybe becoming a professional dog-walker. Whatever. It didn't matter so long as he was never again called upon to explore the inside of some boarded-up portal to fucking Hell.

Sweat poured down his face as he ran. He felt a stitch in his chest. Michael spied another door up ahead. This one stood open, and he saw a flicker beyond it. It occurred to him that the spider thing could probably see his flashlight beam, so he turned it off and focused on that tiny light ahead. He dashed through the door, gasping for breath, and banged into a metal trash can.

"Shit..."

Even without the flashlight, Michael could tell that this room was significantly larger than the supply closet. He avoided peeking inside of the trash can, afraid that it might hold another grisly surprise. At first, he was confused about the light he'd glimpsed a moment before, as there seemed to be no obvious source for it. Cautiously, he closed the door behind him and waited for his eyes to adjust to the darkness. When they did, he noticed a second door on the far side of the room. The light was coming from beneath that. He was tempted to check it out, but he forced himself to stay where he was.

The space's function was difficult to discern in the dark. Maybe it had been a break room at one point? The walls appeared to be black. Michael was pretty sure that was their actual color, rather than just the gloom. He noticed a small section of scaffolding and some ladders leaning in a corner. Sidestepping the trashcan, he shuffled a few feet deeper into the room and soon perceived objects attached to the wall in three vertical columns, spaced evenly apart. Frowning, he crept closer. After a moment, Michael realized he was looking at the backs of three tall speaker stacks.

Speakers, he thought. That flickering light...

It dawned on Michael that he was in a room directly adjacent to the mall's six-screen cineplex, which sat at the far end of the property. He tried to remember the blueprints and floorplans he'd studied back at the office, and surmised that the door must open behind one of the movie screens—which meant that the flickering light could only be coming from something being projected on the screen. How the hell could there be electricity for running a film projector in a facility that had not been connected to the power grid or other utilities for years? Of course, how had there also been electricity to give him those shocks earlier, as well? Could someone be running a generator? If so, he didn't hear it. There was no stench of gas fumes. Maybe they had tapped into the grid outside and were pirating power?

He debated with himself for a moment about which way to go. If he went back out into the hallway, there was the possibility of contending with the monster. But the light from the movie theater scared him just as badly. Which way offered him the best chance at escape?

The door rattled behind him. Then something slammed into it. Michael dropped the flashlight and it rolled away from him.

Outside the door, the monster tittered and growled.

The door rattled again. The hinges groaned. Dust and dirt fell from the ceiling. The spider thing hissed.

Screaming, Michael ran toward the light.

FOUR

A gaggle of snickering, smirking fraternity brothers walked up to Kickers as Audrey stormed out into the parking lot, her phone in hand. None of the young men wore face masks. She jostled her way past all but one of them. Oblivious to her presence, the guy gestured with his arm, nearly smacking her across the face. She bumped into him pretty hard and kept walking.

"Watch it you stupid bitch!"

"Sorry," she said, turning around. "I couldn't see you from behind that cloud of fucking Axe body spray you're wearing."

Some of his friends laughed. Others among them jeered. The dude-bro looked stunned at first, and then angry. He balled one of his hands into a fist.

"What the fuck did you just say?"

Audrey shrugged. "Get the hell away from me before I light your fucking hair gel on fire. You've got enough product in there to—"

"Fuck you!"

The guy took a faltering step forward, but one of his friends grabbed his arm.

"Come on, dude," his friend said. "Let it go. She's not worth it. Somebody will film that shit with their phone, and you'll end up going viral."

Audrey nodded. "Your friend's right. Fuck with me and I'll put you on YouTube. I'll make you famous. Now go cry your privileged little white boy tears somewhere else."

"White boy…?" He frowned. "You're white too, you dumb bitch."

Ignoring the remark, Audrey continued down the sidewalk and further out into the parking lot. She didn't stop until she'd reached the van. She reached into her purse and dug out a half-empty pack of cigarettes and a cheap plastic lighter. Everybody else was vaping these days, but she had no patience for that pretentious bullshit. After wedging a cigarette in her mouth and lighting up, she dropped both items back in her purse and crossed her arms beneath her breasts. When she glanced back behind her, the group of young men were already gone.

"Assholes…"

She stared off into the distance, exhaling smoke through her nose without removing the cigarette from her mouth. Laughter echoed from the outdoor seating area. Lively music played over the speakers, echoing across the parking lot. Cars zipped by on the highway, headlights growing brighter and then dimming again. She envied all those people headed to points unknown, even without knowing anything about their lives. At least they weren't here, at this stupid sports bar in the middle of suburban Pennsylvania, forced to hold their tongue as they sat across the table from a woman whom Audrey loathed more than any other human being on the planet.

She heard gravel crunch to her left. Audrey turned and saw Chuck walking toward her. She sighed, exhaling smoke.

He indicated the cigarette with a tilt of his chin. "I thought you were trying to quit?"

"Trying, but obviously not quite succeeding. Not yet anyway." She dropped what was left of the cigarette on the pavement and ground it out with her shoe. "I feel the need more when I get stressed out. You know that."

Chuck nodded. "Yeah, I do."

They fell into an uncomfortable silence. Chuck scratched the back of his head and watched the passing traffic zip by on Route 30. She could tell by his body language that he was working up the nerve to say or ask something.

"What's on your mind, Chuck?"

"Same thing that's on yours. Same reason you left the table before the rest of us."

"Celeste."

"Yeah. Look, I don't like her, either, but there's not much we can do about it right now."

Audrey grunted. "Is that really true, though? I think we should talk with Stuart after we finish recording tonight. See what he thinks. Like, he pretends to get along with the bitch for Bradley's sake, but I'd bet anything he's disgusted with her, too."

"I wouldn't be so sure about that. You've seen the way she is with him."

Audrey rolled her eyes. "You mean that fake flirty crap? The cutesy comments and little touches on the hand? Okay, point. He does eat that shit up. He's single, so of course he does, but Stuart's not dumb. I'm sure he hears the condescension in her voice. I think he puts up with it because Bradley's his best friend. It's a solidarity thing."

"That's what I mean. They're too tight, and they go back too far. Stuart would never go against Bradley or risk upsetting him by criticizing his lady."

Audrey snorted. "Lady? That's one word I'd never use to describe Celeste Sinclair. Lady, my ass. That bitch is a straight-up ho if I've ever seen one. She's a fucking cunt."

Chuck was visibly startled. "I mean...that's a little harsh, no?"

"Fuck no! It's the fucking truth, and you know it. You've seen her Insta. A lot of that shit is borderline porn—just skirting the edge so she doesn't get reported and de-platformed. All the poses with barely anything on and god knows how many twerking and titty-shaking videos."

"Come on, Audrey. I don't like her either, but it's not right to judge her on that. Sex workers are people, too. It's 2020, right? We're supposed to be like sex-positive and supportive, right?"

"And we're also supposed to be wearing masks and social distancing, but do you see anybody else doing that? Fuck being sex-positive and supportive, at least in her case. I'm as enlightened as anybody, but not when it comes to that bitch. Celeste shits on us every chance she gets. Fuck her. I hope she gets the virus. I've had it with this shit."

"Yeah…"

"I fucking mean it, Chuck. I am so over it all."

"So, what are you saying? That we should we quit the team? Start our own channel?"

Audrey shrugged. "It might come to that if we can't make Bradley see the light. Like I said, next chance we get, we need to have a serious talk with Stuart. If I'm right and he feels like we do, we might be able to stage an intervention."

"I guess it's worth a try." Frowning, Chuck scratched the back of his head again. "But you better be prepared for the possibility that Stuart will tell Bradley."

"If that's what happens, then fuck it. Fuck all of it. We'll quit and get into something less toxic than this shit. Start our own channel, like you said. Maybe we move over to Twitch or something."

The pinched expression on Chuck's face indicated to her that he was doubtful, but he just shrugged and said, "Okay."

Audrey was not surprised. It was typical Chuck. Rocking the boat was something he avoided whenever possible, but he could be led in the right direction with a little reassurance and help.

She took him by the arm and started guiding him back toward Kickers. "Look, don't worry about it too much, okay? We'll talk about it later and figure out what to do when we're back home."

He sighed with obvious relief. "Sounds good to me."

They rejoined the others at their outside table. Audrey assured everyone that she was okay and feeling better after getting out into the fresh air for a few minutes.

Less than a half-hour later, they were piling into the van to head to the Westgate Galleria.

In the first few moments after Michael tumbled through the door into the movie theater, he had a sense of having been pitched backward in time by decades. Rows of moldering seats were bolted to a floor covered with a threadbare, maroon-colored carpet. The seats faced a blank screen framed by ragged, dirty curtains—also maroon. The seats were smaller and, as he knew from memory, significantly less comfortable than the type typically found in modern theaters, many of which now featured seats so large and plush that sitting in them was like relaxing in your recliner at home. Even after all these years, the space still faintly smelled of stale popcorn.

For a second, Michael forgot about his peril, and was overcome with a deep melancholy for something from his childhood—something long lost.

Then, the door slammed shut behind him. Squealing, he whirled around, fully expecting to see that the spider-freak had caught up to him. Instead, he saw nothing. Was it there, on the other side of the door, just playing with him like a cat with a toy? Was it possible the thing had given up its pursuit? Or was it a third possibility—that the monster was herding him to a certain location? And if so, why?

He turned away from the door and scanned the auditorium. At the back of the theater, high above the last row, was a window demarking the projection booth. A small point of light flickered somewhere behind it. It didn't seem to him that it was bright enough to account for the light he'd seen under the door earlier. He stared at the window and saw the light flicker again as something moved in front of it and then away.

Which meant that something was alive up there, and possibly looking down at him right now.

Michael wished he hadn't lost the flashlight. He felt his pockets, searching for anything he could use as a weapon, and then realized that somewhere along the way, he'd also lost his mask and his keys. Now he was locked inside this place, unless he went back to the original service entrance—which meant directly confronting the nightmare that had made its nest there.

He knew that the cineplex had glass exterior doors because he'd spent time looking at an online gallery of photos of the mall during its heyday. He could get out that way. The glass was undoubtedly thick and smashing through it might present a significant challenge, but he couldn't think of any other options.

He considered shouting to whoever was in the projection booth that he'd already called the police and that they were on the way, but given the horrors he'd so far encountered, he didn't think that whoever—or whatever—was lurking up there would be concerned with that lie.

It struck him that his visibility in the theater's interior was better than it should be. He looked around again and realized this was because the house lights were actually on, albeit at a very dim level. He realized now this was the source of the faint light he'd glimpsed in the corridor earlier. This was yet another indication that the mall was somehow connected to the power grid.

Michael drew in a steadying breath and hurried up the nearest aisle, peeking between the rows of seats as he went, in case someone was hiding there in the shadows. He also kept glancing up at the projection window, but there was no further movement from inside. When he reached the top of the sloping aisle without incident, he approached an exit door. He paused, wary of being electrocuted, then used the toe of his shoe to push it open. He peered out into a dark vestibule, seemingly empty save for another tall trash can. Like the previous receptacle, a rancid stench emanated from it.

Fuck that, he thought. I'm not making that same mistake again.

He gave the trash can a wide berth as he hurried through the vestibule, and spotted a pair of double doors that he assumed must lead to the lobby. Before pushing through them, Michael tried peeking through the little glass windows inset in the middle of the doors, but was unable to see anything. They were smeared with years of grime, and it was too dark on the other side. He wished again for a weapon.

Slowly, he pushed one of the double doors open and waited. The space beyond was silent and dark. He pushed it wider and slipped through. Instead of finding himself in the lobby, Michael stood in another wide hallway. To his left and right were entrances to more theaters. In front of him was a short ramp. The darkness here was almost palpable, and the silence felt unnerving. Michael's footsteps faltered as he slowly made his way down the ramp. He couldn't see more than a few feet in front of him, and even what he could discern lay cloaked in deep shadow.

He'd reached the lobby floor, and was able to make out the rough shape of the concession stand just ahead of him, when all of the lights in the place came on almost simultaneously. Michael yelped with alarm. There was a sudden flurry of movement behind the concession stand. Whatever it was hiding back there made no attempt at stealth. A dark form rose from the shadows and heaved itself over the counter, into the light. Michael gagged. This one was tall and—while visibly deformed—much more human-looking than the spider-freak. While the figure had physical characteristics that Michael associated with the male gender, he wore a leather dress. A top hat was perched crookedly on his head.

Michael glanced around, desperately seeking a weapon, and noticed that the floor was moving. Then he realized it wasn't the floor—it was an army of cockroaches, disturbed by the sudden burst of illumination.

The man in the leather dress doffed his hat to Michael and bowed slightly at the waist.

"Glad you could join us. Almost time for the show."

Screaming, Michael fled again, crushing scurrying cockroaches under his feet.

FIVE

Logan cautiously climbed out of the Mustang. He left the door open and took a few tentative steps away from the car. There was no sign of the deformed guy. Could he have just imagined it? Given the amount of booze and weed in his system, he would have said yes, but he wasn't the only one who had seen it. He turned back to the car and saw Cam crawling out of the backseat. He looked nervous and wired. The girls remained inside. Lizzie was still pretty much passed out. Tara stared, wide-eyed and panicked.

Cam stood beside him, shirtless and clad only in his ragged blue jeans and boots as he lit up a smoke and peered out at the abandoned mall's parking lot.

"Looks like that fucking mutant or whatever the fuck it was hightailed it out of here," he said.

Logan nodded, barely restraining a sigh of relief. "And thank fuck for that. I'm no pussy, but that guy would have torn my head off my shoulders."

"I saw this documentary on YouTube. You know a severed head is still aware for a few minutes after it's cut off? Like it's thinking and seeing and shit even though it no longer has a body?"

Logan shuddered. "That's fucked."

Cam shrugged. "Well, I won't give you an argument on that guy tearing your head off part, but you're definitely a pussy."

"Fuck you, Cam."

"Hey, I'm just telling you like it is." Cam flicked his half-smoked cigarette away and glanced meaningfully at Lizzie. Then he turned back to Logan again. "After all this time you're still letting that pill-popping ho walk all over you. That's the definition of a pussy, bro."

Logan's hands curled into fists at his side.

Cam flipped his long black locks of hair from his face. "The fuck you gonna do, Logan? Hit me? I'm only telling you this for your own good. I get that you've got it bad for the bitch, but all she does is use you and lead you on, while spreading her legs for practically anybody else. She's trash, dude, and you deserve better."

"Shut your mouth, asshole. She can fucking hear you."

"Are you serious? She's passed the fuck out. Lizzie can't hear shit right now."

Logan drew in a long, shuddering breath. He trembled with anger, and was embarrassed by it. He held the breath, willing himself to be calm. He unclenched his fists as he exhaled.

"You could at least have some respect for me, Cam. I'm supposed to be your friend."

"You are. Don't you get it, bro? I'm saying this because I'm your friend. I'm fucking sick of seeing you getting taken advantage of. I mean, you're not stupid. You must know she's only going to break your heart in the end, one way or another. She'll either stop fucking you for good or she'll overdose and wind up in an early grave."

"Seems kind of self-righteous coming from a guy who fucks around on his own girlfriend on a semi-regular basis and rarely goes more than one goddamned day without getting wasted."

"That's different," Cam said.

"Like hell it is, you fucking hypocrite. I'll bet that—"

The Mustang's suspension creaked. They both turned and saw Tara climbing out. She glanced around, frightened, eyes wide.

"Did you guys fix it yet?"

Logan shook his head. "Does it look like we fixed it?"

"No. It looks to me like you guys were having some kind of fucking pow-wow."

Logan glared at Cam for another moment. Then he sighed and shook his head, wiping his mouth with the back of a hand. "Something like that, I guess. We're just talking."

"About what?"

A tense moment elapsed as no one said anything.

Logan shrugged. "Nothing, really."

Tara frowned. "Doesn't feel like nothing. Your auras are both bright red…mixed with some orange. Like the color of fire."

Logan blinked. "What?"

Tara sidled up to Cam and put an arm around his back, leaning into him. "Every person has an aura, Logan. Most people don't see them because the way they perceive the world is so limited. But people such as myself, who are sensitive and tuned in to nature and the vibrations of the universe and shit can see them plain as day."

"Uh-huh."

"I'm serious. You know my cousin that lives over in Marietta?"

Logan nodded. "The one who works at the pizza place—Garganos?"

"Yeah, that's him, except he doesn't work at Garganos anymore. Now he's working night shift at target. Anyway, he was dating this Puerto Rican girl for a while, and she was mixed up in Brujeria."

"What's that?" Cam asked. "Like some kind of drug or something?"

"No, silly." She elbowed him in the side. "It's South American witchcraft. Anyway, one of my cousin's neighbors was this Amish guy who knew how to do pow-wow, and he helped her out, and then later, when we were hanging out one night, he taught me how to read auras."

Logan frowned. "An Amish guy taught you how to be psychic?"

"You don't believe me? Fine. It's okay. You're free to think what you want, just like anyone else. I'm comfortable enough with my truth to accept your doubt for what it is. Those who cannot see must be treated with compassion and understanding. That's what Levi said."

Logan glanced at Cam. The two of them snickered, and just like that, the bad energy between them dissipated.

"Assholes," Tara said. "One day you'll see how things really are, how we exist side-by-side with other realities and dimensions and creatures in perfect celestial harmony, and when that day comes, I'll expect an apology from both of you."

"Right." Logan's tone was patronizing. He couldn't help it. "Well...okay, then."

This elicited another burst of laughter from Cam. Logan snickered, too. The two friends clasped each other's shoulders and shook with mirth.

"Oh, fuck you both! And fuck you especially, Cam."

"You just did a little while ago, babe."

"Well, I hope you enjoyed it, because that'll be the last time for a long while. I deserve better than this kind of bullshit disrespect."

She leaned back into the Mustang for a moment, groping around for something in the backseat. Normally, Logan was good about not openly ogling his buddy's girlfriend, but this particular view was so enticing he couldn't help it. Seeing her long, bare legs extended like that through a pair of snug cutoff shorts that used to be skinny jeans…he couldn't resist. Other than the shorts, Tara wore only sandals and a tiny purple top, an ensemble that left virtually nothing to the imagination.

He realized Cam was staring at him.

"Sorry," he apologized.

Cam grinned. "Don't sweat it."

Tara backed out of the Mustang with her purse in hand. She slipped the strap over her shoulder and then began walking away.

Cam frowned. "Hey...where do you think you're going?"

"Away from you, asshole."

Cam hurried after her. “Tara, wait up. Just hold up, okay? I didn’t mean anything by it. We’re all just a little fucked up, and it struck me as funny. That’s all.”

He grabbed her arm, and she twisted free. “Don’t fucking touch me!”

“Okay! Jesus…”

“Just leave me the fuck alone. I mean it.”

Cam held his hands up in surrender. “You can’t walk home. You know how far that is?”

“I’m walking down to the Turkey Hill convenience store near the highway exit, and I’ll Uber it home from there.”

“That’s almost a mile away. It’s dark out. What about that thing we saw earlier?”

“I don’t give a shit.”

“Tara, use your fucking head. Call an Uber if you want, but at least wait here in the car where it’s warm.”

“The car’s not warm. It’s fucking broke. Just like you, loser.”

“Tara, it’s not safe!”

“Fuck off.”

She turned away and stalked off, heading across the parking lot, and passing under the shadow of a dead sodium light.

Cam threw up his hands. “Un-fucking-believable!”

“Dude, let her go,” Logan advised. “That fucking monster is long gone by now.”

Cam shook his head.

“She just needs to blow off steam,” Logan said. “You can make it right tomorrow.”

“Nah, bro, it’s all fucked up. She never gets that mad about anything. Like, ever. It’s over, I can feel it.”

“Sorry.”

Cam shrugged. “It’s okay. It’s not like it’s the end of the world, right?”

“Yeah, I guess that’s—”

He was interrupted by a scream.

* * *

Michael skidded to a halt as soon as he saw the grotesquely deformed human beings blocking his way out of the cineplex. Unlike the spider-freak, they did not look like the result of some deranged brand of scientific experimentation gone horribly wrong. They were clearly the product of a diseased bloodline and several generations of in-breeding. He didn't know how to reconcile the distinct otherness of the first freak with the degraded but undeniable humanity of these unfortunate souls. He wasn't sure it was possible. There wasn't much he was sure about at this point.

One thing did seem clear, however. The spider-freak and the deformed people had been working in tandem. For some unknown purpose, he'd been intentionally herded in this direction, lured through that open door by the low illumination.

It was a well-conceived trap.

Another realization was even more galling. The glass doors and surrounding plate windows were no longer in place. Fragments of glass gleamed on the tiled floor. The empty windows were covered in thick wood planks and blockaded by other junk.

The four adversaries blocking his way were all different shapes and sizes. One of the larger ones had a small conjoined twin growing out of his shoulder, and brandished a baseball bat with nails embedded in the barrel. The one next to him was a cyclops, with a single rheumy eye bulging from the center of its face. Wielding a rusted fire axe, the cyclops was the biggest of the group. The other two were more diminutive. One resembled an obscenely obese version of one of the little people from The Wizard of Oz. His face looked lopsided, as if someone had given one side of his head a dozen hard whacks with the blade of a shovel. His swollen stomach was leaking green ooze of some sort from several small holes in his skin. He wore a pair of hemmed-up orange-and-black parachute pants and a spiked leather collar around his massive, trunk-like neck. The other little one was the only female of the group. Fat, but only as rotund as the obese male. Her drooping, wart-covered breasts hung out of a ragged dress. More warts dotted her face and arms. She wore a necklace made of bones. Both of the mutant munchkins were armed with meat cleavers, and both weapons were stained with fresh, still-dripping blood.

Michael whimpered.

I am as fucked as fucked can be.

They stood several feet apart from each other. Michael supposed he could try catching them off-guard by sprinting through one of the gaps, but the fear of being quickly cut down kept him from doing so. But no way was he just going to give up and surrender, either. A last-ditch, desperate mad dash to possible freedom might be his only option.

"They won't hurt you," said a voice behind him, "long as you don't try to run. Turn around. Look at me."

Michael hesitated, not wanting to turn his back on the freaks, but also not wanting to keep his back to whoever was behind him. Finally, he let out a breath and turned around. The guy he'd encountered earlier—the one in the dress and top hat—grinned.

"Lucky you entered at this part, rather than Doctor Midnight's."

"I…what?"

"Most of the livestock ends up out there." The man waved his hand, gesturing at the walls facing the mall's interior. "You didn't. This will be a treat."

"What do you people want with me?"

"You see my hat?"

"Yeah…?"

"You know who wears a top hat? Show business people. And we have a show tonight."

The foursome tittered. One of them scraped their weapon along the floor tiles. Michael shuddered.

"What, uh...what kind of show?"

"A special show. Just for you."

"Look, mister…I don't think I got your name?"

The man in the dress doffed his top hat in a mockery of formality. "I'm Scug."

Something about that name…Michael was sure he'd heard it before. A deep line formed in the middle of his forehead as he struggled to remember. Then it came to him. He'd seen it scrawled across the outside of the mall in spray paint.

Scug wuz Here.

The use of the past tense now struck Michael as a cruel joke, because it implied the subject of the graffito had come and gone, departing forever after leaving behind the testament to his passage through this territory. In fact, Scug was still here, holed up in the abandoned shopping center with an unknown number of others of his kind. He guessed they'd been here for years by now, if the fading spray paint was any kind of accurate indication. The mall had been neglected and forgotten for so long that it had become host to possibly the strangest brood of squatters the world had ever known. This place didn't need a commercial real estate agent. It needed a fucking tactical team armed with flamethrowers.

Michael cleared his throat. "Well...Mr. Scug, my name is Michael. Michael McCafferty."

"Hi, Mike."

"H-hello. I'm from Boseman-Kline Commercial Realty."

Scug frowned. "Am I supposed to know what that means?"

"Well…we own this property. This mall. We—"

"You don't. Not Boseman Kline. Not you, Mike. And I tease. I know Boseman-Kline." He turned his head and spat on the floor. "I know it well."

"Oh." Michael held up his hands in placation. "Look, I empathize with your perspective. And a legal case for squatters rights could certainly be made. In truth, now that I've seen how you and your…friends…have built a home here, I'd be willing to testify to that on your behalf. You'd just have to…let me leave, of course. I could put you in touch with several reputable attorneys tomorrow."

Scug shook his head. "You can't leave. Like I said, we have a show for you."

"How did you create a show just for me when you, uh… people had no idea I existed until today? Because I just don't see how that's possible."

"Well, not for you specifically. For the powers you represent."

"Boseman Kline?"

Scug waved his hand dismissively. "We knew one of his friends would come again. We wanted to be ready. Been practicing filmmaking."

"Whose friends?"

Scug didn't answer. Michael decided to try a different tact.

"Listen, I can assure you that I don't mean you any harm. Honest. I didn't even know you were here."

"Follow me," Scug ordered. "If you don't, they'll drag you."

He turned away from Michael and waved an arm in the direction of the ramp leading to the screening theaters.

"This way."

Michael felt the blunt end of something hard poke him in the back. He guessed it was probably the head of that nail-studded baseball bat. He shuffled forward, following Scug. The others loped along behind him, giggling and snuffling. Michael did his best to ignore them. Scug was nominally the boss here, but his minions didn't seem too mentally stable. He had to assume anything even resembling a gesture of defiance came with a risk of getting his guts perforated or his head chopped off and put in a trashcan.

They went up the ramp and then down a hallway toward the theaters. Michael noted glumly how he'd traversed this passage only a few minutes earlier, but now that he wasn't fleeing, he had time to note details about the décor. The display cases along the walls that had once housed posters for upcoming movies were mostly empty now, but the few yellowed posters that remained had all been marred with garish, obscene doodles and graffiti—bizarre sexual organs and cartoonish-yet-depraved brutality and violence. Much of it appeared to have been drawn by a child, or perhaps multiple children. Several times he saw a bizarre phrase repeated—OB RULZ—etched, carved or spray painted on various walls. The carpet had splotchy brown stains, and was littered with dead insects and debris. Mildew dotted the dingy walls, and a jungle of spiderwebs dangled from the ceiling and light fixtures.

Then he caught sight of something else—a yellowed poster tacked to the wall. The artwork on it had faded to indistinguishable blobs, but the lettering remained partially legible. It read The Flaherty Brothers Traveling Carniv. The rest was obscured by grime. He was sure the partial word was probably Carnival. Was that where these freaks had come from? Some kind of old school traveling carnival? Did they even have those anymore?

"Come on," Scug insisted. "Forget that poster. Jax, tell the kids I don't want to see this in our space. That's Midnight's shit. Not ours."

One of the mutants behind Michael mumbled a deep, sonorous affirmation. Michael jumped. Until now, the only one he'd heard speak was Scug. And, he supposed, the spider-thing—although the sounds it had made weren't anything like human speech.

"The theater is our space," Scug continued. "That was the deal. Our clan's area. Not theirs. This shit doesn't belong here."

Scug pulled open one of the double doors and waved him through. Michael immediately smelled a familiar foul stench coming from a large trashcan in the corner, and deduced they were back in the same theater he'd just fled from minutes before. It was lighter inside now, however, and he could see better. The room was in the same horrid shape as the rest of the building.

He was poked and prodded from behind multiple times as he walked down the aisle. When they were about halfway to the screen, Scug ordered him to stop and move into one of the rows of seats. Michael did as instructed, trying to stay calm, but his hands began to tremble, and his lips felt numb and swollen. He was cold, yet sweating profusely.

Shock, he thought. I'm going into shock. Panicked. Got to keep it together. Talk my way out of whatever this is.

He breathed deep through his nose, and immediately regretted it. His captors smelled like walking sewers. Coughing, Michael shuffled between the rows and kept going until Scug told him to stop. He took another breath through his mouth and could almost taste the stench.

Scug settled into a seat. The hinges creaked and groaned. He patted the seat next to him.

"Sit."

Michael struggled to keep his tone calm. "What are you planning to do to me?"

"Well…" Scug paused, and turned to look at him. "If you don't do as I say, I'm going to cut your dick off, hang it up to dry, and make some man-chew."

Michael gaped. "M-man chew?"

"What your people call beef jerky. Now sit."

"But…social distancing…"

Scug frowned. "What?"

Michael hesitated. Was it possible these people didn't know about COVID-19? He supposed so. Given their diseased appearances, he doubted they had access to regular healthcare.

"Social distancing," he repeated. "We're supposed to stay apart?"

"We do. Our people stay here. Midnight's people stay in the rest of the mall."

"I don't know what that means," Michael said.

"I don't know what you mean, either."

"There's a pandemic," Michael explained. "The coronavirus. A lot of people are dying from it. We're not supposed to sit next to each other. Particularly in venues like this one. We need to stay at least six feet apart."

"Ah!" Scug nodded and then shrugged. "I heard about that. Doesn't bother us. Our people survived it the last time. We'll survive it this time. Now…sit. I won't tell you again."

Michael pushed down the seat and sunk into it. He felt springs poking his back and smelled a waft of mildew. The guy with the conjoined twin growing out of him dropped into the seat on his right, spreading his legs wide as he braced the handle of the baseball bat against the row in front of them. Michael shifted, turning his knees away from the hideous twins in order to avoid touching him. The tiny second head turned toward him and smiled. After a moment, its bigger brother did the same.

"Gax likes you." His voice was surprisingly deep and melodic.

Michael stammered, "W-who's Gax?"

Still grinning, he tapped the second head growing out of him. "This is Gax. And I am Jax. Nice to eat you."

"Uh…eat?"

"Enough," Scug shushed them. "It's bad manners to talk at the movies. We'd never been to the movies before we came here, but that's what it says before each one."

Michael nodded, struggling not to scream for help. He knew logically that no one would hear him. No help was forthcoming. He had to get out of this on his own. But between the stench roiling off his captors, the bizarre setting, and his own panicked terror, his senses were so overwhelmed that he could only sit there and try to comprehend the conversation.

His gaze lingered over Scug's dress. The leather was strange, varying in shades and patterns. There was a single rose over the left breast and some sort of tribal symbol across the hem. Michael blinked twice, and then realized with dawning horror that they weren't patterns at all. They were tattoos—and the leather was human skin, sewn together from multiple victims, judging by the color variations. He reeled in revulsion, yet couldn't look away. Then he realized that the dress was looking back at him. A tormented, stretched face had been sewn into the side.

"You like it?" Scug grinned. "Make them all myself."

"I…"

Scug suddenly leaned forward and poked his head around Michael, addressing the conjoined twins. "We need the camera. Where's Klavo?"

Jax stood up and shouted, "Klavo! It's time."

Michael saw a diminutive figure appear down by the movie screen. He moved to the center of the front row, facing them, and raised an old camcorder. A small light on the device glinted, indicating that he was recording.

"Good." Scug turned and waved at the projection booth.

A moment later the house lights dimmed and the screen in front lit up.

Michael had no idea what to expect and was slightly surprised when a vintage ad ostensibly from theater management began to play. Cartoon characters out for a night at the cinema appeared on the screen as a narrator urged patrons to be respectful of other theatergoers by not talking during the movie.

Scug turned to Michael, Jax and Gax. "See? You be quiet at the movies. Those are the rules."

Jax nodded. "Sorry."

Gax gibbered unintelligibly.

The narrator further advised use of the proper receptacles when getting rid of trash. This was followed by another vintage spot, this one for Chesterfield cigarettes. It was in black and white and heavily pocked with grain. Michael frowned. These clips were from the Fifties, rather than the early twenty-first century. Where had these freaks procured them? The mystery of it was bizarre enough to temporarily distract him from his overriding fear.

That lasted until the two diminutive mutants moved into the row in front of them from opposite sides and kept coming until they met in the middle. Their blood-stained meat cleavers dangled from leather loops at their waists. Their chubby fingers clutched multiple popcorn bags and soda cups. Scug and Jax took theirs eagerly. Michael stared at the ones offered to him.

"Go on," Scug told him, "take them. They're free. Don't be rude. It's not a movie without some popgore and a drink."

Michael did as he was told. His stomach twisted up in knots. The last thing he wanted was a bag of greasy popcorn leftover from decades ago. He tentatively stuck his hand in the bag. Only then did that one word that wasn't quite right truly register in the forefront of his mind.

Popgore?

He yanked his hand out of the bag. There was something wet and slimy clutched in his palm. He opened his fingers and gagged when he saw the bite-sized bits of bloody flesh. The mutants cackled as he screeched in revulsion and flicked the flesh pieces away from him. A peek inside the bag showed it was filled almost to the top with more of the same. He dropped the bag on the dirty floor and kicked it under the seat in front of him. He bolted upright, intent on making a run for it, but was immediately shoved back down from behind. Twisting his head around, Michael saw the Cyclops. Unlike the others, this mutant did not smile.

Scug leaned close. "So…you decided on man-chew then?"

"N-no!"

"Then watch the show. I won't tell you again."

Michael managed a terse nod. "Okay."

The old advertisements ended, and the screen went blank for a second. Then, a new scene appeared. There was no production company title page or opening credits, and the transition was jarring. The view was of a poorly lit room with no furniture and no one in it aside from, presumably, the camera operator. The scene remained unchanging for several moments—the camera absolutely still—until the camera operator abruptly began to move deeper into the room, not stopping until they reached the rear. At that point, the camera slowly panned around and showed the open door of the room. The view again remained unchanged a few moments longer.

Then someone outside the room threw a man dressed in business attire through the door. The man cried out and fell to the floor, whimpering. After a minute, the man rose shakily to his feet.

The camera then zoomed in for a closeup of the man's tear-streaked face.

Michael gasped.

It was Frank Hendrix, the real estate agent who'd had the mall in his portfolio before Michael. The one who had disappeared. This wasn't some pretentious piece of forgotten Hollywood cinema verité. This was actual footage of the missing Boseman-Kline employee, likely filmed somewhere here inside the mall.

The camera zoomed out again for a wider view as another form entered the room. This person was huge and hulking, with a head the size and texture of a rotten Halloween pumpkin covered with thick knots of diseased-looking brown tissue. Despite the figure's horrific appearance, there was something almost innocent in his expression. His face was infantile. He carried a huge club that looked like it was fashioned from the trunk of some massive old tree. Frank turned away from the camera as the hulk swung the weapon.

On screen, he shouted, "No!"

Then his head was obliterated by the crushing might of the club, bursting as blood and brain matter splattered the camera lens.

The screen went black and the house lights came on again.

Michael sobbed.

"Did you like it?" Scug asked. "Took us a while to learn how to make movies. But we've had some help, and we're getting better. Frank was one of our first attempts. Figured someone he knew would show up sooner or later. Took you long enough."

"Why?" Michael shuddered. "Why would you do that?"

"He was an intruder. This is our home. Right now, we're just paying rent. But it's still a home. I won't let anyone take that away from us again. Not after last time."

"But why kill him? Frank wouldn't have hurt you."

Scug shrugged. "We love to make heads explode. Especially Lorok. It's a tribute to Noigel."

The other mutants stirred and whispered in what sounded like awe or reverence.

Michael leaned forward and wretched, vomiting on his shoes. Steam rose from the mess. Gax sniffed the air with his tiny nose and drooled. Michael wiped his mouth with the back of his hand, and tried to catch his breath.

Then Scug said something that struck him as odd, even under such bizarre circumstances. "Is your seat comfortable?"

Michael sniffled. "What?"

"The chair. Is it comfortable?"

Michael shrugged.

"Answer me."

"Yes." Michael nodded. "It's comfortable."

"Good. See, we rigged it special. Haven't had a chance to test it until now."

"What?"

Michael felt the Cyclops grip his shoulders and push him down into the seat hard. Much harder than before. The force activated a trigger mechanism planted beneath and a grid of rusty steel spikes shot upward through the padding. Michael shrieked as they punctured his thighs and ass. The mutants laughed and pointed as he struggled in vain to lift himself off the spikes.

"It works!" Scug nodded with approval. "Klavo! Did you get that?"

The dwarf in the front row lowered the camcorder and flashed a thumbs up gesture.

Michael stared down at his blood, and felt the seat grow warm and wet. Then he glanced back up at Scug.

"You…you said you wouldn't kill me…"

"No, I said I wouldn't cut your dick off and turn it into a man-chew. And I won't. Instead, I'll turn you into a new dress. Won't need your legs or ass for that. Or your head."

"My…what?"

Scug and the others rose from their seat and hurriedly moved out of the way as the heavy footsteps of a new arrival clomped down the aisle. Michael wailed, thrashing, as the giant from the movie appeared, carrying the same club he'd used to kill Frank. The weapon was propped casually on the behemoth's shoulder. The hulk smiled happily. Drool dribbled down his chin.

"This is Lorok," Scug said. "He was just a baby when we came here. Look at him now. Only eleven years old, but big already. He grew fast. So much like his Daddy."

"Noigel," Jax murmured.

Michael shook his head. "No…no…no…"

Lorok lifted the club off his shoulder and reared back to take a swing. He squealed with obvious delight.

"Nonononononono…"

Michael continued shaking his head until it was smashed apart. On the last shake, his brains dribbled out over his shoulder. Only then did he stop.

But Lorok didn't.

SIX

At first, Logan thought it was Tara screaming. Then he realized that the shrieks were coming from the Mustang.

Cam glanced back at the car, and then in the direction Tara had gone.

"Come on!"

Not waiting for him, Logan ran, positive that the creature had returned and was menacing Lizzie. He'd heard her scream like this only once before, after being jolted out of sleep by a particularly terrifying nightmare featuring her horribly abusive father. But as he neared the car, he discovered that only part of his assumption was true. Lizzie was screaming, yes, but the creature was nowhere in sight. Instead, two other creatures stood outside the Mustang, reaching into the open passenger window and trying to drag Lizzie out of it—a task made more difficult by how fiercely she fought and kicked, despite the booze and pills in her system.

"Hey," he yelled. "Leave her alone!"

The attackers paused and shuffled backward in surprise, giving Logan a better look at them. They were not inexplicable monsters or creatures from another planet. They were, instead, grotesquely deformed human beings. They were shorter than the freakishly tall one they'd encountered earlier, but stockier and thickly muscled. One feature they did share in common with their presumed cousin was the sickly gray flesh, much of which was covered with pustulating sores. Then Logan realized that one of them was more deformed than the other. It's left arm was normal-sized but equipped with a tiny hand, and its right arm was a flipper. A circus sideshow somewhere was missing its freaks.

Logan heard Cam's footfalls behind him as he rounded the car. He lowered his shoulder and plowed into the attacker closest to the car. His opponent grunted as Logan drove him to the ground, pinning him. The inbred struggled, squirming beneath him as he punched it in the face, right in the center of the guy's warped features. There was no snap of bone as the purplish nose imploded, squirting blood and some kind of green goo all over Logan. His knuckles tingled. Grimacing in disgust, he raised his fist again. The tingling increased. It wasn't a burning sensation. Not exactly. Logan hesitated, imagining that he could feel infection or disease sliding into the pores of his skin.

"Whoa," Logan muttered. "The fuck is this shit?"

What if these fuckers had the coronavirus? He hadn't given the pandemic much thought until now, other than to complain about things being shut down. He wished too late that he was wearing gloves and a mask.

Lizzie tumbled out of the Mustang and landed hard on the asphalt, shrieking as she banged her knees and scraped her palms on the abrasive surface. She rolled onto her back, moaning in pain.

Logan's opponent managed to get an arm loose and punched him back, connecting with his jaw. The force of the blow snapped his head back, and for a second, he felt woozy. Stunned, he couldn't move as the other attacker smacked him in the face with its flipper. Logan's ears rang so loudly that he could no longer hear Lizzie or Cam. Breathless, Logan flopped over onto his back. Grimacing in pain, he tried sitting up. When he gritted his teeth, he tasted blood.

The inbred with the normal arms grabbed Lizzie by the feet and dragged her away from the Mustang, toward the boarded-over entrance to the mall. She wriggled and screamed, swatting at him with her fists as her long blonde hair spread out behind her. Her struggles ceased when his companion backhanded her with his flipper. Lizzie went limp.

Logan shouted, enraged, and made another attempt to get to his feet. Instead, he staggered sideways and dropped to the pavement again.

"Yo, Flipper," Cam yelled. "Try that shit with me, you motherfucker!"

As Logan watched, Cam charged the abductors and tried wrestling Lizzie away from them. The one with the flipper quickly intervened, wrapping both of its weird appendages around Cam's waist and yanking him off-balance. Cam drove an elbow backward into his assailant's face. Flipper screeched with what sounded like equal parts pain and outrage, but didn't turn loose. Cam was dragged farther away from Lizzie and the other inbred.

Logan finally regained his footing. He spat blood and took a deep breath.

Flipper abruptly relinquished his grip on Cam, who immediately spun around and started swinging his fists. Logan marveled at how fearless his friend appeared to be. As Logan shuffled toward Lizzie's captor, he grinned.

Flipper was about to get fucked up.

"Kick his ass, Cam," Logan cheered. "Stomp that motherfucker into the pavement!"

Flipper's namesake appendage opened in the middle, revealing itself as more of a pincer than a flipper. The inside was lined with sharp teeth. It caught Cam's arm in mid-swing and sliced through his forearm with stunning ease. Cam shrieked as his hand and part of his arm dropped to the asphalt. Blood pulsed from the stump.

Logan screamed. Another scream rang out from somewhere nearby. Logan glanced in that direction and saw Tara. Apparently, she'd decided to return to the car.

He turned back in time to see Flipper thrust his pincer into

Cam's abdomen, driving it deep like a spear, and then yanking it back out. Cam's intestines came with it, glistening white and purple in the dark. Logan and Tara screamed in unison. Cam turned to them both, staring wide-eyed, mouth working silently, as Flipper reached into the cavity again and extracted another helping of viscera and shredded organs, all of which fell in a wet pile on the pavement. Cam raised a faltering hand and waved at Logan. Then he toppled over, face first into his own innards. He twitched for a moment, and then lay still.

"Cam," Logan yelled. "Oh, Jesus fucking Christ! Cam?"

Sobbing, Logan hurried back to the Mustang and reached inside to yank the keys from the ignition slot. Unfortunately, the old car didn't have a latch to easily pop the trunk open. He hurriedly unlocked the trunk with the key, flipped up the trunk lid, reached in, and hauled out the tire iron that lay next to the jack. Turning, he raised the weapon.

"Okay, you—"

Flipper, his partner, and Lizzie were gone. All three of them had vanished, as if by fucking magic. It had happened inexplicably fast, while he was busy getting the trunk open and retrieving the tire iron. Panic gripped him. He raised his face to the sky and wailed.

"Logan?" Tara sniffled behind him. "I saw where they went."

He stared at Cam's body for a moment, watching the steam rise from his corpse. Then he turned to her.

"Show me."

Together, they walked towards the abandoned shopping mall.

Stuart turned down the stereo and turned on the high beams as he drove the van into the parking lot near the shopping mall's north-facing entrance. The bulbs in the overhead lamps were burned out or broken, and apparently, no one had ever bothered replacing them. The darkness was disconcerting.

"Hey," Bradley protested. "Why'd you turn it down?"

"I thought I heard something."

"I heard something, too," Bradley said. "The new Dot Com Intelligence song featuring MJ Withers. I've been waiting for months for them to drop that track. And then you turned it off."

Stuart took one hand off the steering wheel and pointed at a black BMW and a bright red Chevy Malibu, both of which were parked curbside.

"That our guy?"

"Let's see." Bradley checked his phone, quickly scrolling through a text message. "Yeah. Red Chevy Malibu. That's him."

Stuart parked the van and cut the engine. He then twisted in his seat and peered into the back. Verifying that Chuck was filming, he stared straight into the camera. "We have arrived. My name is Stuart, and I've been your captain today. I hope you enjoy your stay in Shithole, Pennsylvania."

The Chevy's door opened and closed as a man got out.

"All right," Bradley said, his voice again infused with its familiar upbeat cheer. "We are about to meet Mark Hereford, our local contact. If you remember our four-part series about Mammoth Caves, Mark left a comment on one of those videos and suggested that we come north to check this place out. After researching the mall and talking more with Mark via email, we agreed that it was perfect for a video. So, everybody gear up! It's time to roll."

They piled out of the van and Stuart moved around to the rear and began handing each of them a lightweight backpack—except for Celeste. As usual, she carried only a small designer handbag, the thin strap of which was draped over her bare shoulder. Inside each backpack was a first aid kit, a bottle of water, and bags of jerky and trail mix.

"Sure you don't want one?" Stuart asked Celeste.

She rolled her eyes, and then turned to verify that Chuck was filming something else. Then she turned back to him.

"It's ridiculous overkill. We're just going to poke around inside a decrepit old building for a few hours—not venture deep into the heart of some dense and treacherous wilderness.

Stuart shrugged. “Whatever. You get hungry, you can’t have any of my trail mix.”

He closed the van doors, locked it up, and joined the others on camera, as they greeted Mark Hereford.

Celeste glowered at Stuart as he walked away. Let them play intrepid explorers all they wanted. Her role here was to look cute for the camera and help pull in a bigger audience. She was the only one here with genuine sex appeal, aside from maybe Bradley to a much lesser degree. These other ordinary losers could all be easily replaced.

I’m the only one that’s indispensable, she thought with a smile.

She was still smiling when she moved into the space between the parked vehicles with the rest of them and got her first look at Mark Hereford. He was completely unlike what she had expected. She’d met Lost Places fans before. He did not look like any of them. Hereford was extraordinarily handsome. She guessed him to be somewhere in his mid-to-late twenties. He was tall and built like a dedicated weightlifter, but not the gross steroid junkie kind. His wavy blond hair, blue eyes, and chiseled jaw made him look like a movie star. He also had a palpable rugged toughness to him that marked him as far more than just a pretty boy. Equipped with an Old West-looking gun belt and dressed head-to-toe in khaki attire, he looked like he was about to head out on fucking safari. He wore no facemask.

Excited and intrigued, Celeste decided she would have to find some way to get with him before the night was over. The mall was a big place. At some point while the rest of them were occupied with their explorations, she would lure the man to a private spot away from the cameras and fuck the shit out of him. She felt no sense of shame or disloyalty to Bradley in thinking this. There were times when life presented you with temptations so powerfully delectable and alluring that passing them up wasn’t an option. This was one of those times. And so what? It wasn't like she was planning to marry Bradley. If things worked out the way they should, he would never even know about it. If Hereford got clingy later, or tried to make the tryst public, she'd just Me Too him—claim he assaulted her, and that he was a creeper.

She watched the grinning Hereford exclaim to Bradley and the others what a big fan he was. There was no hand shaking. Not in the year of the pandemic. But his excitement was palpable, and his grin grew broader as Bradley formally introduced him to each member of the team. Celeste was already aroused, but the intensity of her desire magnified when Hereford greeted her. They did not touch, yet something electric and magnetic passed between them during a moment of prolonged eye contact. When he complimented her on her beauty, she giggled, not bothering to hide how much the moment of flirtation pleased her. She was delighted to note that Audrey looked annoyed by the apparent slight.

Bradley shot her a look of possessive concern, but Celeste ignored it. Let him feel threatened. Let him get mad. Despite his on-camera bravado, he was a pussy. There was nothing she might do that he wouldn't forgive in the long run.

Bradley cleared his throat. "Can you tell us a little bit about the history of the mall, Mark?"

Hereford looked at Celeste, rather than Chuck's camera. "Well, the Westgate Galleria opened in 1976. Back then this was a booming area. You had the Harley Davidson plant and the paper mill across the river in York County. Here in Lancaster, there were tons of manufacturing jobs and farming was still big. And of course, folks commuted to Philadelphia and Baltimore back then, as well. If you could go back in time, you'd scarcely recognize the landscape compared to today."

He made a sweeping gesture with his hand to indicate the general environs, while Chuck fiddled with the camera's lighting attachment.

He's good, Celeste thought. He's really fucking good.

She knew little of Hereford's background, except that he was a local with a deep knowledge of the area and its history. She had no idea if he had any on-camera or other performance experience, but she had a hunch he wasn't exactly green at this sort of thing. He was too much of a natural.

So far, however, he was only telling them things they already knew from their research. Celeste wasn't much of a details person, especially not when it came to planning episodes of Lost Places, but she understood the reasoning. The background Hereford was providing was for the benefit of the average YouTube viewer, not for them. From what Bradley had told her prior to embarking on the trip, Hereford's expertise would primarily be of use to them once they were inside the mall—something he himself had apparently done numerous times before. He supposedly knew his way around, and had assured Bradley that the location was perfectly safe so long as they paid attention to what they were doing and followed his instructions.

Celeste smiled, thinking how that shouldn't be much of a problem. She intended to stick close to Mr. Hereford. Very close, indeed.

Bradley took over, addressing the camera as he slid a headband lamp into place over his head. As he explained for those who would eventually be watching on YouTube, all members of the team would be wearing similar units as they made their way through the mall. Celeste detested the necessity of wearing so ugly an accessory, but she didn't want to go stumbling around in the dark either.

He also explained to viewers that they would not be wearing facemasks while filming, and had Hereford verify on camera that he had been practicing social distancing. Hereford assured them that he had been doing so since the start of the pandemic, following the governor's orders.

"As we've already seen," Bradley said, "the Westgate Galleria is a husk of its former self. Abandoned for many years, it is a relic of a different time, what many in this town would say was a better time. The boarded-over doors and gang tags make it look like a pretty forbidding place now. Mark, you've said this is an essentially safe place as long as the proper precautions are followed, but are there any particular potential dangers we should be aware of before heading in?"

"Not at all." Hereford shook his head, seeming to radiate reassurance. "Just follow my lead and everything will be copacetic."

"You gonna use that small-town charm to get us out of trouble?" Stuart asked.

"Don't need to." Hereford patted the pistol holstered at his side. "In the unlikely event we encounter hostiles, I'm ready for them."

Bradley frowned. "Hostiles?"

Hereford shrugged. "Yeah, you know, the usual kind of people who get into places like this, places that have sat empty for a long time. Squatters and junkies. Street people. Mostly they're harmless, but now and then they can be troublesome."

"You got a permit for that thing?" Stuart asked.

Hereford nodded. "I've got a concealed carry permit. But I'm not one of those guys that carries an AR-15 into Walmart. Like I told Bradley over email, I'm a big fan. I've done my share of urban exploring, too. This is just some extra insurance that I always bring along."

Frowning, Celeste spoke up before Bradley could utter his next innocuous question. "Do you really think we'll run into any mangy-ass bums in this goddamn place?"

Stuart chortled loudly and shook his head in phony dismay.

Hereford chuckled, too, eyeing her in a way that made her tingle.

"Hold up." Bradley raised a hand. "Audrey, make a note to have Chuck edit here."

"Roger that."

Bradley turned to Celeste. The look of dismay on his face was much more genuine than Stuart's.

"What?" she asked.

"Baby, come on now. You know you can't call them bums

anymore, at least not on camera. It's 2020. They'll roast us in the comments and on Twitter. We've got to be conscious of social justice. We've talked about this kind of thing before, remember? Back when we toured those abandoned tenements in Atlanta?"

Celeste rolled her eyes. "Whatever."

"No, not whatever. We always have to be mindful of our optics. You can't say anything problematic like that on camera. Our sponsors don't like it, and our subscribers will lose their shit."

"Oh, so it's okay for Stuart to be problematic but not me?"

"Hey." Stuart held up his hands. "Leave me out of it."

"Seriously, Celeste," Bradley said, "you've got to watch that."

"Fine," Celeste snapped. "I heard you the first fucking time."

Audrey breathed a muffled hiss, but Celeste ignored her, focusing instead on Bradley's wounded expression. She almost laughed.

"Okay." Bradley nodded at Chuck. "Go."

Chuck nodded, and swung the camera back to their guide.

"Always a chance we might run into a bum or two," Hereford said, responding as if nothing had happened, "but I promise it's nothing to worry about, not with me there to clear the way. And anyway, I didn't encounter a soul last time I did a tour of the mall and that was just last week. So take my word for it. We'll be fine."

Celeste smiled, noting that he had purposely used the same word that had so offended Bradley. "Thank you, Mark. That's so reassuring."

Bradley glared at her a moment, clearly upset by the ongoing flirtation. Celeste kept smiling as she looked her boyfriend in the eye with an air of unspoken challenge.

Go on, she thought. Say something about it. I fucking dare you.

But, as she suspected, he didn't.

"We can get some more background stuff later." The wounded expression abruptly vanished, replaced by his upbeat host persona. "Let's get going, shall we? Mark, can you lead the way?"

"I'd be honored."

A silent beat elapsed.

"That your Beemer, by the way?" Bradley asked, indicating the car parked near the red Malibu.

Hereford frowned. "No. Not mine. I have no idea who that belongs to. It was here when I arrived."

Now everybody was looking at the unoccupied luxury car. Chuck walked over to it, slowly panning with the camera. Celeste noted that he took care not to film the license plate, lest their video get pulled for a privacy violation complaint.

Stuart scratched his beard. "Doesn't look abandoned. Too clean. Too new. And I don't see any rich people loitering around. Could they be inside the building?"

"I don't see how," Hereford responded. "The mall's still closed up tight…except for the place I use to get inside, and nobody knows about that."

"Then where's the driver?" Audrey asked. "I mean, they've got to be around here somewhere."

"Maybe they're taking a leak over in the bushes," Stuart said.

Audrey nodded. "Maybe we should wait."

"I don't think we need to worry about it." Bradley shrugged. "The car could have been stolen and dropped. Who the hell knows?"

"You don't want to wait?" Audrey frowned.

Bradley shook his head. "I don't see the need. Let's move out."

He started moving toward the mall's boarded-up entrance. The others glanced around at each other a moment before shrugging and following.

"Not that way," Hereford called.

They all turned to look at him.

He smiled again, his eyes pausing on Celeste. Then he gestured. "This way. Follow me."

SEVEN

What Lizzie saw of the mall's interior as she was borne through it over the shoulder of her abductor was like glimpses of the ramshackle back alleys of a major city in the nineteenth century—grimy, sprawling, and characterized primarily by decay and squalor. She still didn't understand what was happening, but she knew she was inside the mall. The fog in her brain had cleared enough for that realization. Fire flickered inside a metal trashcan, providing meager light. In addition, lanterns hung from drooping wires and strands of unlit Christmas bulbs were strung up everywhere.

The air stank of mildew and smoke and piss. Those who'd frequented the place during its glory days would see little they recognized among the maze-like guts of the place. A wrought iron bench where bored husbands had once waited outside a store while their wives tried on an endless succession of outfits. The shaft of an elevator that had once carried customers from the first floor to the second. A flipped-over golf cart once used by mall security. But that was all.

Something lived under that golf cart now—a hunched little thing with eyes that glowed yellow in the dim light. The cart was braced by several uneven pieces of rotting lumber to keep it from tipping onto its side. The small creature gnawed on a bone, slurping strips of raw, pink meat and gristle as it watched Lizzie go by. The look it gave her was not a friendly one. It hissed and shifted in an apparent effort to guard a meager pile of trash. She was reminded strongly of Gollum in the Lord of the Rings movies. Or maybe Sesame Street's Oscar the Grouch.

She wondered how much of what she was seeing was her drugged state, and how much was real. But she decided all of it must be real. She'd been this messed up many times before—even more than she was now—and she had never hallucinated.

The little beast was but one of many of the mall's strange inhabitants. She was carried past more fires, and saw more horrors. A lot of them were deformed in ways that made her stomach knot with revulsion. They were missing limbs or had heads that looked too big for their bodies. Others had abnormal appendages that didn't look human—flippers, claws, and tentacles. She saw bodies that resembled stretched-out lengths of oozing gray putty and others that looked two squat or too wide. Bugged-out red eyes peered at her. One of the deformed people had only one too-large eye. Another had no eyes at all, just a smooth blank slate above the nose. She had a sense there were even more oddities in the many side passages she glimpsed, but they were concealed in total darkness.

Lizzie also spotted people who did not appear deformed in any noticeable way. Broken and sickly, for sure, but not deformed. They wore filthy, rotten clothes that revealed glimpses of spindly legs and pale, sunken chests. Some of these people wandered about freely with dazed or drugged expressions, while others were locked in large dog crates on the floor.

Her captor cleared his throat and spat a massive wad of red and green phlegm on the dirty floor. Several smaller creatures scrabbled forward, fighting over the disgusting mass. One of them slurped it up off the floor while the others tussled. Cringing, Lizzie closed her eyes.

When she opened them again, she saw some of the people in the dog crates reach their fingers through the slats. A few begged for help in weak, pitiful voices. She closed her eyes again until the voices ceased. When she opened them a second time, the crates were behind them and out of sight.

Over the years during which the mall had stood derelict, its interior had undergone a radical transformation. Gone were the wide-open spaces once strolled by legions of consumers. The mall's new inhabitants had filled those spaces with a maze of poorly built and tightly packed-in structures, many of which leaned precariously. She spotted multiple rickety wooden ramps constructed from old pallets that connected the first floor to the second. There were also several canvas chutes that apparently allowed rapid descent to the first floor. Why anyone would utilize these improvised means of floor-to-floor movement rather than original and much sturdier sets of stairs in place at multiple points throughout the mall, Lizzie could not imagine.

Children with dirty faces and cunning, darting eyes wandered about. She saw some of them fight each other in a shockingly vicious manner, rolling about on the floor, biting and clawing at each other as they screeched and howled like feral savages. She didn't know what the conflict was about. Maybe they didn't either. They were like a nightmare version of the street urchins from the tales of Charles Dickens. The combatants seemed entirely oblivious to Lizzie and her abductors as they quickly skirted the skirmish and continued making their way through the strange maze.

They soon entered a slightly more open area, this one also lit primarily by lanterns and trashcan fires. The walls of this space were painted with vividly rendered scenes out of some horrendous hellscape, depicting a multitude of bodies twisting in flames as their melting flesh dripped from their bones. Also depicted were numerous obscene sexual violations of human beings by demonic-looking creatures. Decaying yet animated corpses were shown writhing on crucifixes. In one corner, a naked woman with a joyful smile and snakes growing out of her head dangled a crying baby above a bubbling cauldron of molten liquid.

Lizzie shuddered, longing for a return to the comfort and oblivion of Oxycontin and whiskey. What made it all so much worse was the obvious immense level of artistic talent behind the painted murals. A more cartoonish or amateurish effort would have allowed for a greater level of psychological distance, but that was not possible here. During her fleeting time inside that space, Lizzie could almost believe she actually was in Hell itself, the real fucking thing.

Maybe I am, she thought. Maybe I died back there in the car, and this shit is really Hell.

Lizzie and her abductors entered a narrower, darker space—a passage leading from the mural room to some other space. Within a few seconds, she realized they were moving subtly downward. The slope abruptly steepened and they proceeded much faster for a short time. Then they were suddenly on level ground again and enveloped in total darkness. There were no hanging lanterns here. No candles or fires or ambient light from the outside. She trembled as tears leaked down her face.

Belatedly, she realized they'd come to a complete stop. Some silent moments passed. Then came a loud clanking sound as a set of tall double doors began to swing inward, flooding the passageway with light, and revealing the largest chamber they'd encountered yet.

Lizzie began hyperventilating at the horrors on display. She wished that she could pass into unconsciousness again.

This was it. The real goddamn thing.

Hell itself.

Lizzie began to scream.

* * *

Tara raised a slender arm and pointed. Logan squinted. As best he could tell, she wasn't directing his attention to anything other than the boarded-up mall entrance.

"I don't get it, Tara. Where did they go?"

Tara's tear-streaked features twisted, showing her frustration. She jabbed her finger in the same direction in a more emphatic way.

"Right fucking there, Logan. That's where they went. Through the front entrance"

"But it's all boarded up. How did they get through?"

"Some of the boards are fake. It opened in the middle and swung outward. It closed again as soon as they carried Lizzie through it. You were poking around in the trunk."

Logan closely scrutinized the boarded-up entrance. He hadn't noticed it at first because he hadn't been looking for it, but right down the middle—between sections of weather stained plywood—was a narrow vertical space, probably no more than a half-inch wide, if that. A small crack in the facade. Insignificant to any casual observer.

His thoughts returned to Lizzie and he felt overwhelmed with helplessness and frustration. Her fate was hanging in the balance while he just stood here doing nothing.

"I'm going after them."

She glanced back at Cam's still steaming corpse. "Don't leave me out here…"

"I'm not. You're gonna go to the Turkey Hill convenience store, like you'd planned on in the first place. When you're there, and you're safe, call the cops. Tell them to send a fucking S.W.A.T. team."

"I'll call them now." She pulled out her phone.

"No, don't."

"Why not?"

"Because the longer you stand here, the bigger the chance you'll get hurt. We already lost Cam and Lizzie. You've got to stay alive. Get to the store, where there's lights and people. Then call."

He walked up to the door with the tire iron clenched in his fists. It was a solid piece of steel, long and hefty. He thrust the claw end into the crack between the sections of plywood. Before he could apply his weight and muscle to it, however, Tara gripped him by the arm with a firmness that surprised him, forcing him to look at her.

"Logan, you can't do this on your own. Who knows how many more of those things are in there? We've seen three. There might be more. You can't fight them with a fucking tire iron."

Logan scowled. "Or it might just be the ones we've already seen. I can't wait for help, Tara. I've got to get Lizzie out of there while there's still a chance she's alive. You saw what they did to Cam. I'm not going to let that happen to her."

"There's too many unknowns here, Logan. That's the point. And you're no action hero. Come on, dude, you know that. This is a job best left to the police. I'm calling them now."

She took her phone out of sleep mode. The screen illuminated her face in the dark.

"Go ahead." He turned his attention back to prying open the door. "Just tell them not to fucking shoot me when they storm the place."

"Wait," Tara insisted. "Don't do anything else until they get here!"

She grabbed at his arm again, but this time Logan pushed her away. Not forcefully or maliciously, but it was enough that it jostled Tara. The phone slipped from her hand and clattered across the pavement. They stared at each other, mouths agape.

"You…asshole."

"I'm sorry!" Logan bent and scrabbled for the phone. He turned it over in his hand. The screen was shattered, and the light was no longer on. He held it up sheepishly. "I guess you didn't have a protector on it."

"You think so, genius? Does it even fucking work at all now?"

He investigated, pushing buttons and tapping the screen. "No. It's dead."

"Well, that's just fucking wonderful, Logan."

"I'm sorry," he repeated. "I'll buy you a new one."

"Fuck that. Get yours out and call the cops."

"I can't. I didn't have the money to pay my bill this month. It's shut off."

He turned away as she laughed scornfully, and refocused his attention on the door. "Somebody will come."

"Nobody is fucking coming. Take a look around you. This is the bad part of town. Didn't used to be, but it is now. This place isn't anything close to a priority for anybody, let alone the fucking cops. Think about it, dude. This is actually the ideal spot for getting away with murder over and fucking over again."

Logan grunted, throwing his weight against the tire iron. The plywood groaned. He thought of the several other times he and Cam and other friends had camped out here in the parking lot at night. It was a perfect place to get high and party without fear of getting caught precisely because the police virtually never patrolled the area. He'd never worried much about the shady night dwellers who loitered around the mall after dark because they were shady in a normal way. Junkies, prostitutes, and homeless people. As long as you kept your distance and didn't meddle in their affairs, they weren't a real danger. Or at least that had been their general perception until now. What if they'd been wrong about all of it? What if the night dwellers were colluding with the inbred freaks in some way?

"Logan, come on. Let's go call the police."

"Fuck the police."

Frowning, he gripped the tire iron harder and gave it a single, half-hearted crank. The plywood groaned again, but didn't budge. He tried one more time, putting significantly more strength into it, but the end result was the same. He wouldn't be getting into the mall this way. Logan sighed, cringing at the sound of surrender and hopelessness he was making. He took the tire iron out of the crack and pointed the claw end at a spot down at the far end of the sidewalk.

"What about that other way in, the door along the side? I think it's some kind of service entrance."

"It's chained up, isn't it? Probably locked, too. You're not getting in through there, either. Not without keys or dynamite to blow it the fuck open. Accept it, Logan."

"They took Lizzie, goddamn it!"

"And they killed Cam! There's nothing we can do. The sooner we bring in the cops, the better Lizzie's chances are of living through this."

He nodded, shoulders slumping in resignation. "Okay. You're right. Let's get down to Turkey Hill."

They moved away from the boarded-up mall entrance and stepped down from the curb to the parking lot asphalt. Tara took him by an arm and leaned in close, shivering in barely suppressed revulsion as they skirted Cam's corpse and the wide pool of blood surrounding it.

She sniffled. "I can't believe he's dead."

Suddenly there was little trace of Tara's characterizing confident belligerence. Now she only sounded scared and vulnerable. "I guess you guys didn't get the car running?"

He shook his head. "Didn't get a chance."

She stopped, staring at Cam.

Logan cleared his throat and tugged at her arm a little more firmly. "Come on. Don't look at him. These motherfuckers will pay for what they've done, I promise you that."

"Well, first we have to get to the store."

"Maybe we should run."

She nodded, unhooking her hand from his arm. "I think you're right."

At that moment, the headlights of a large vehicle swooped around a bend in the road encircling the mall. Logan thought it might be a cargo van of some kind. The headlights abruptly turned toward them as the vehicle roared into the parking lot with a squeal of tire rubber. The headlights filled their field of vision, making them squint and take a few instinctive steps backward.

"Okay," Tara gasped. "I guess I was wrong. Maybe help arrived after all."

The van squealed to a halt. A side door slammed open and several dark forms bearing weapons leaped out and charged toward them.

Logan tugged at Tara's arm. "Run!"

She needed no additional prompting.

They ran.

EIGHT

According to Hereford, the east-facing side of the mall provided direct access to the structure's upper level. Back in the day, patrons interested only in visiting a particular shop or set of shops on the second floor without having to climb a set of steps, ride the escalator, or wait for an elevator would enter the mall here. After passing through the Macy's department store, they would have had access to Waldenbooks, Orange Julius, Chess King, Victoria's Secret, Gadzooks, Spencer's, Suncoast Video, Listening Booth and many others.

Listening to this description, Audrey realized she'd never even heard of half those retailers. Listening Booth? She assumed that was a music store. But what the hell was Chess King? And Waldenbooks? Was that like Barnes and Noble? Being in her mid-twenties, she was far too young to have truly lived the mall shopping experience. She thought about the old movies she'd watched on cable as a kid—Mallrats, Fast Times at Ridgemont High, Valley Girl, Chopping Mall and Dawn of the Dead. That was the sum total of her knowledge as far as shopping malls were concerned.

Memories of the latter were particularly prominent in her mind as they followed Mark Hereford through the wide service corridor, their headband lights bobbing in the darkness. A putrid stench hung in the air as they carefully made their way through the debris-strewn passageway. The smell was one she recognized from childhood summers spent on her grandfather's farm, where Audrey had occasionally stumbled upon dead animals out in the fields. Something had died in here not long ago, and its corpse was somewhere nearby. She only hoped it was a dead animal and not the bloated body of some alcoholic derelict.

Despite her loathing of Celeste, she was in no more of a hurry to encounter squatters than Bradley's trophy girlfriend was. In fact, the possibility of such a thing happening was something she'd considered early on during the planning phase of this expedition. The rest of them didn't know it yet, but Mark Hereford wasn't the only one packing heat tonight. She was carrying a Sig Sauer P226 and two full magazines of ammo in her backpack. Even Chuck didn't know she'd brought the gun along on the trip, mostly because he was so anti-gun, just like many of their other friends. Audrey pretended she was, as well, at least on social media, because that was better than hearing their incessant recriminations. And in truth, she supported things like assault weapons bans and strict licensing. A person didn't need an AR-15 to hunt deer or squirrels. You needed a license to fish or drive a car or own a dog. You should need one to own a gun, as well. But she wasn't for completely banning firearms. There were times when you needed one. And so, she lived a double life when it came to America's Second Amendment. Every time there was another mass shooting, she joined the online calls for stricter gun control, while inwardly hoping cooler heads would prevail and simply pass some common sense laws, instead.

She heard someone cough up ahead, but wasn't sure who it was in the dark. Audrey was at the rear of the procession, while Hereford and Bradley lead the way, walking side-by-side as the star YouTuber asked questions and the guide answered his queries. Chuck was right behind them. He stayed silent the whole time, focusing on his job while Celeste was her usual chatterbox self, walking directly behind him and interjecting questions and comments of her own whenever she felt like it, completely heedless of whether she was interrupting anything interesting Bradley or Hereford might be saying.

This was typical Celeste behavior, irritating and relentlessly self-centered. The shameless way she was flirting with Hereford made Audrey sick to her stomach. She also didn't much enjoy the way the men endured her insufferable behavior without complaint, though she did have to grudgingly hand it to Bradley for his rare criticism of his girlfriend's on-camera insensitivity earlier. As reprimands went, it was pretty mild, but Audrey believed it represented a significant shift in team dynamics.

She fumed silently, making sure not to bump into Stuart, who was in front of her. What made her even angrier was how she understood the way the guys were around Celeste on the most basic level. The woman was not just attractive. She was gorgeous in a way that would make her stand out in virtually any crowd, even in a group of real celebrities instead of just a team of moderately popular YouTubers.

In private conversation with Chuck, Audrey often made fun of Celeste's prissy mannerisms and speech, performances that left him howling with laughter. What she had never shared with Chuck was how even she sometimes entertained the occasional lustful thought about the team's resident sex symbol. This was especially true in warmer weather, when Celeste was inclined to dress as skimpily as possible, showing as much bare skin as she could without getting flagged. On days like that, Audrey wasn't immune from allowing her eyes to linger, though she'd never admit it to anyone. Not because she feared judgment from anyone in her social circle regarding her bisexuality. No, what she really feared was the power the admission would give Celeste over her. It only made her resent the bitch even more.

Everybody wanted Celeste, whether they were willing to say it out loud or not. It gave her power she didn't deserve. Celeste was fully aware of it, too.

A strange thought intruded as she stewed in her resentment. The old mall was potentially dangerous, particularly at night with the lack of extra ambient light. It wouldn't be all that difficult for a sufficiently motivated person to stage another person's fatal accident.

She flinched. Despite the presence of the gun in her backpack, she'd never considered herself a person with anything other than an ordinary capacity for violence. Yes, she believed she could defend herself in an aggressive way should the need ever arise. She'd done so against a MAGA idiot at a Black Lives Matter protest several months ago, kicking the guy in the balls and dropping him to the pavement after he'd gotten in her face while not wearing a mask. But murder was something she'd never seriously entertained. She was even against the death penalty, for goddess's sake.

And yet…

Despite that first flinch, Audrey did not experience the instinctive revulsion she would've expected upon entertaining such a thought in even the most fleeting way. As mere imagination, it could perhaps be forgiven. A simple recognition of what was possible in a setting like this. But what she was thinking was more than that. She recognized that truth for what it was within seconds of the idea solidifying in her head.

If Hereford was correct, upon exiting this corridor and entering the main part of the mall, they would be on the second floor. She pictured Celeste leaning over the glass barrier lining the walkways there—if one still remained—for a look at the mall's bottom floor. The scenario expanded in her mind as she imagined approaching Celeste from behind while everyone else was distracted in some way. She would act fast, her hands going to Celeste's exquisite ass and the back of her head at the same time, lifting her up and over the rail in just a couple of seconds. She could then quickly retreat back into obscuring darkness before the rest of them heard Celeste's screams and the wet splat of her body hitting the floor far below.

Audrey smiled in the darkness.

The team would be rid of its single biggest source of internal strife, but, perhaps more importantly, Celeste's death would be a potential boon to the popularity of their YouTube channel. Bradley would, of course, be distraught, but Audrey believed his pragmatic side would soon reassert itself and view the tragedy through the lens of how it could benefit all of them.

It would be a big story. Maybe not on the Boomer cable news stations, but it would certainly be trending on social media. Millions of people would rush to check out their exclusive videos of the dead model's final night on earth. Each of them—Bradley, Stuart, Chuck and Audrey—would record and post their own remembrance or testimonial, which in turn would generate even more clicks and impressions.

Audrey liked the idea of being the center of attention for a change.

Her smile grew wider, and when the rotten stench grew stronger, she barely noticed.

Hell, as it turned out, wasn't another dimension. Hell was what had once been a massive underground parking garage beneath the shopping mall.

Lizzie gaped, wide-eyed and sweating. There was no lake of fire, nor any cavorting horned demons, but there were bodies and souls in torment aplenty, the most prominent of which was the Pillar of Souls. It was different than the other concrete pillars in place throughout the underground level to support the roof. In fact, a massive hole had been smashed through the center of that roof. The Pillar of Souls extended from the floor of the garage, continued up through that hole in the roof, and extended up into the mall itself. The Pillar was comprised primarily of flesh and blood. Beneath the exterior of human skin was a towering column of scrap metal and wood. This was the Pillar's skeleton. The metal was visible in places where the corpses had rotted away to almost nothing. The living bodies which formed most of the Pillar's outer layer of soft tissue were tied to the metal and sewn to each other, a cloak of stitched-together nude flesh encircling the wide column all the way up as far as Lizzie could see. There were more living prisoners affixed to the Pillar than dead, kept alive through a complex system of intravenous tubing connected to a huge vat located at ground level. The vat was filled with some vile form of organic nutrient. The stench wafting from it made Lizzie's eyes water and triggered her gag reflex.

She vomited on the concrete floor as her captor lifted her off his shoulder and dropped her onto a metal table with leather straps attached at the corners. Her abductors pawed at her, tearing and removing her clothing. Lizzie tried to fight back, but was still nauseous and her strength seemed to ebb. They easily overpowered her. Within seconds, she was nude. They stretched out her limbs and secured her to the table with the straps. She screamed at them to let her go and leave her alone, but they just laughed and leered at her through their misshapen features. The one with the flipper-claw thing in place of a normal arm licked his lips and pawed at her breasts with the strange appendage, eliciting more screams and cries of protest. She bucked against the straps holding her in place when the appendage lingered between her legs

Then a stentorian shout echoed from somewhere in the shadows. Lizzie's tormentor jerked the flipper away from her with terrified immediacy, bowing and scraping along with his equally repulsive compatriot as they retreated from the table.

In the moment of silence that followed, Lizzie heard the Pillar moaning in a multitude of voices.

She choked back a sob and tried to yank free of the straps, but to no avail.

High-heeled footsteps clacked across the concrete floor. She lifted her head and saw a masked man in a blood-spattered white lab coat open over green scrubs. His gender was evident from the bulge in the crotch of his pants. He was tall but tottered around on a pair of black stiletto heels that were at least one size too small and made him appear several inches taller than he actually was. As he walked, he leaned forward at all times in an apparent effort to keep from toppling over. The mask obscuring his face was of President Richard Nixon.

Despite her terror, Lizzie frowned, incredulous. "What the fuck are you supposed to be?"

His guttural chuckle was distorted by the plastic mask. "I am Dr. Midnight."

Lizzie didn't scream. She didn't whimper or beg or cry.

Instead she laughed.

"Come on," she gasped, breathless. "That's the stupidest thing I've ever heard. What's your real fucking name?"

"The name bestowed upon me at birth is none of your concern. As lord of this realm, I reject all that came before my time here."

She opened her mouth to respond but he interrupted.

"Here, in this place of my creation, my identity is what I say it is. Thus I am Dr. Midnight, architect of nightmares and dark destinies. Your fate lies in my hands—hands capable of perpetrating acts of cruelty so vile and unspeakable as to make history's worst fiends tremble at their mere contemplation."

Lizzie's courage evaporated. He leaned over her and peered directly down through slits in the plastic mask.

"Yet," he continued, "on exceedingly rare occasions, they are also capable of mercy. The latter is more likely by a nearly infinitesimal degree when my subjects treat me with the respect and deference I demand. Do you understand?"

Lizzie trembled as his gloved fingers seized her wrist and rubbed it gently. "Yes. I... understand. Please don't hurt me."

Somewhere in the shadows, the two who had brought her here tittered at this remark.

"Silence!" Dr. Midnight's voice was whiplash-loud, reverberating throughout the subterranean garage, compelling instant obedience from his assistants. Even the suffering souls tied to the Pillar of Souls fell quiet.

Belatedly, and with dawning panic, Lizzie realized there were more prisoners than just the unfortunates sewn onto the Pillar. At least a half-dozen more metal tables surrounded the Pillar, and all but one had another nude person strapped to it. Next to each table was an array of equipment, some of which looked to have legitimate medical uses while others looked like instruments of torture pilfered from a medieval dungeon. She hadn't noticed them before, either due to shock or lighting or the fact that the Pillar dominated so much of her initial view. Now that she was aware of them, her resolve shattered. Lizzie began to cry.

"Please let me go. I won't tell anyone about any of this, I swear. I… I'll do anything you want. Anything at all. I don't care how depraved or fucked-up it is, just as long as you don't hurt me."

Now it was Dr. Midnight who laughed. "Your offer is meaningless. I can already take anything I wish from you. I can already compel you to do anything I desire. Do you not believe me?"

"I believe you. But I can be of use to you." She lifted her head again and turned it side to side, looking at the other captives. Several of them lifted their own heads and looked back at her. Others appeared unconscious or just not moving, possibly even dead. "Let me be your assistant. You need one smarter than those freaks who took me. I'll prove my worth by operating on one of your other subjects. Under your guidance, of course."

Dr. Midnight stared down at her in contemplative silence a moment.

"Intriguing," he murmured.

Then came another of those creepy chuckles as he undid the strap around her right wrist.

Lizzie bit her bottom lip. She was afraid it was a trick.

Dr. Midnight raised one finger. "You will be monitored every moment, of course. There will be no hope of escape, nor any hope of overpowering either myself or the others who assist me in my endeavors here. Any attempt to do so will result in your immediate addition to my masterwork."

He nodded at the Pillar.

"I won't let you down, Dr. Midnight."

He finished unbuckling the other straps.

Holy shit, Lizzie thought. This is actually working. He's even crazier than I thought.

She sat up and rubbed at her sore wrists. "Thank you."

"This way, new disciple."

"Can I…get a drink of water first?"

He shook his head. "After we are finished. There is work to be done first. Great work."

He turned away from her and approached another of the gleaming tables.

Lizzie considered grabbing a scalpel off the table and stabbing him in the back, but then thought better of it. After the briefest of hesitations, she got up and followed him.

NINE

"Who the fuck are these guys?"

The people from the van fanned out as they chased after Logan and Tara, choking off all obvious escape routes. As a result, the two now ran back toward the boarded-up mall entrance. Logan had a sense that their pursuers were forcing them in that direction purposely, like hunters herding wild animals. A panicked glance over his shoulder seemed to confirm this.

Logan didn't want to die. It had taken an evening of mortal terror to clarify that for him. There were so many things he still wanted to do with his life. The directionless path he'd been on—the drinking and getting stoned all the time—it was all something he'd fallen into after his father died—a flailing and predictably ineffective way of dealing with his grief by trying to numb it out of existence. It was only now, with his life imperiled, that he realized he still harbored a desire to get his shit together—to go back to school, to vote in the election, get a new job, get married and start a family. All the things he'd spent so much time trying to convince himself he didn't want because they were so lame.

Only those things weren't lame.

Those things were life.

People desired those things because of the sense of comfort, safety, and belonging they provided. Logan wanted all of that. He'd had it with his father, but then it had been ripped away. He wanted it again. But this time, he would be the architect rather than just a mostly unappreciative beneficiary.

He glanced at Tara as they scrambled over the curb and neared the sealed entrance. She was so beautiful. And smart, despite her flaky affectations. Possibly as smart as Lizzie. Tara deserved to have the suburban existence he was picturing in his head. Lizzie deserved it, too, but Lizzie was probably dead by now. Even if she wasn't dead, people like Lizzie often ended up making life miserable for anyone who tried to love them. Lizzie had years of therapy and numerous trips to rehab in her future. No matter how much comfort, safety or sense of belonging he tried to provide her, it would be a life filled with grief and addiction-fueled drama. None of that was Lizzie's fault. The blame lay with her monster of a father. But that didn't change the reality of what kind of person Lizzie was.

But Tara…

They reached the entrance and turned around, putting their backs to the plywood.

They were out of room to run.

Logan glanced quickly at Tara. Her cheeks were wet with tears. Her expression was overwhelmingly defeated. He gripped the tire iron. They were outnumbered, but they weren't defenseless. Fuck it. He was going to live. So was Tara. He was setting off on that new path starting now.

He leaned in close to Tara. "Get ready to run when I tell you."

Then he did an impulsive thing, something he never would've dreamed of attempting while Cam was still alive. Or even right up until this moment, with his heart hammering. He leaned in even closer and kissed her full on the mouth. The moment of eye contact that followed as they broke the kiss was perhaps the most intense moment of his life.

Turning away from her then was the hardest thing he had ever done.

He raised the tire iron. "Okay, you motherfu—"

One of their pursuers threw an axe at him. Time seemed to slow. Logan saw it flying toward him through the chilly night air. It was a double-bladed weapon that looked like something out of medieval times.

Then the axe passed from sight and, curiously, his point of view changed. He saw the sky and the dirty sidewalk both go spinning by in a blur. He tried to yell, but found that he had no voice. Nor could he feel the tire iron in his hand anymore.

The world stopped spinning and Logan realized he was looking up at Tara. Had he fallen down? Was that why she was so tall and seemingly askew?

She stared down at him, screaming, clawing at her own face with her fingers. He tried to tell her that he was okay, but again, he had no voice.

Frowning, Logan flicked his eyes to the right, and saw something he didn't understand.

It was a body—a headless body—standing next to Tara and pumping blood out of its stump of a neck.

Slowly, the body teetered back and forth. Then it collapsed next to him.

He spotted the tire iron still clutched in its hand, and understood what had happened.

Logan's last conscious thought was that he wished he could still scream.

Shrieking, Tara lunged forward and snatched the tire iron from Logan's dead hand. The tool was warm and slick with blood, and she had difficulty keeping a grip on it. She felt hot and flushed all of the sudden, and her ears rang. Swooning, she pressed her back against the plywood and readjusted her handhold on the weapon. She glanced about, searching for an escape, but saw none.

Some of the people who'd chased them pointed and laughed as Logan's decapitated head blinked. A flash of anger cut through Tara's shock and horror. This was entertainment for them—a piece of macabre live theater. Logan was more like a puppet to them than a human being.

She screamed again, and they turned their laughter on her. Now she was their entertainment—their vulnerable plaything to swat around like a rat in a fucking cage. Tara gritted her teeth as the ringing in her ears began to subside.

Slowly, they closed in around her. Some of them were deformed like Cam's killers. Others looked like normal human beings, albeit grimy and dressed in rags. She counted eight of them in all.

Tara raised the tire iron with both hands. "Stay the fuck away from me!"

Ignoring her, they shuffled closer.

Tara shoved away from the entrance, and tossed the tire iron at one of the people on her left. Before they could react, she dropped to her hands and knees, and quickly scuttled forward, slipping between the spindly bare legs of two menacing mutants. She yelped in victory, realizing that she'd caught them off guard. She sprang to her feet and ran. Adrenaline propelled her forward. Her pulse pounded like a drum in her chest and throat. Her shoes slapped loudly against the pavement.

Then her footfalls were joined by others. She heard them giving chase again, but didn't risk turning around. Some of the pursuers hooted and made wild cries.

Tara wished she hadn't tossed the tire iron.

Then, for the first time in her life, she wished she had a gun. She loathed guns and the people who fetishized them, believing that private ownership of all firearms should be illegal. It had long been her stance this was the nation's only hope of ever beginning to heal itself and erasing its long legacy of violence and oppression. But now she wanted one more than she'd ever wanted anything. A gun like the ones in the movies.

If she had a gun like that, she would turn around right now and blow away every last one of these subhuman pieces of shit.

The thought seemed like a betrayal of self, a violation of the very core of her identity. It made her feel sick—sicker than she already felt. Killing another human being was never justified, even in self-defense. Hers was a radical strain of pacifism, one she'd never feared proclaiming to anyone online. But her desire for the gun—and the desire to kill—was real and undeniable.

The sounds of pursuit grew dim as a new noise joined the din. The cargo van, which Tara had completely forgotten about, raced alongside her, engine revving. She glimpsed the driver through the open window. He had a gaunt face, with eyes sunk deep in their sockets and a long, pointed chin. His complexion was that of a fish's belly. Long, stringy gray hair ringed a bald scalp with a huge red birthmark in the middle of it. He grinned when he saw her looking at him. She couldn't be sure from this distance, but it looked like his teeth were filed and pointed.

The driver hit the gas and the vehicle surged ahead of her. Braking hard, he then cut the wheel to the left, blocking Tara's way. She dodged right, trying to go around the back end of the van, but the driver put it in reverse, blocking her again. Tara screeched in frustration. The driver laughed. It was a hauntingly hollow sound, barely audible over the engine.

Tara cast a terrified glance behind her and saw that the pursuers on foot had almost caught up. There was only one thing to do. She cut to the left and started running sideways across the parking lot, away from the exits and the relative safety of the highway and the convenience store. The van turned and quickly sped up again, keeping pace with her. The wheelman swerved close and thrust an arm out the window, trying to grab her. Tara barely slipped his grasp. She caught a glimpse of long, yellow fingernails. Like his teeth, they appeared to have been sharpened.

Up ahead was a weed-covered hillside median surrounded by a concrete boundary. Dead shrubs were spaced at regular intervals along the median's length. If she could reach it, Tara reasoned, it would give her a temporary respite from the van. She'd still have to contend with the others, however.

She raced toward the area, running at an angle that allowed her to glimpse her pursuers. One of them lost their footing and stumbled awkwardly in the direction of the van. There was a loud slam as vehicle and flesh collided, followed by several sickening crunches as the victim fell beneath the van's tires. The driver never braked.

Tara reached the median ahead of her pursuers and charged up the side. She made it halfway to the top before her sandals began to slide on a barren patch of ground. Sharp fingernails clawed at the backs of her calves, breaking the skin. Screaming, Tara jerked her foot loose from the attacker's grip and then kicked. Her heel hit something solid, and she heard a crunch and a squeal of pain. Tara smiled at the sound.

She got her feet braced and scrambled upward. At the top of the median, Tara stood upright and pushed her way through some of the dead shrubs. Withered, brittle branches pricked at the bare skin between the waist of her denim shorts and the bottom of her tiny top. She started down the slope on the other side, but began to slide again. This time she just leaned into it, gliding down the slope with her arms outstretched like a surfer riding a particularly gnarly wave.

On the other side of the median, the others were having difficulty reaching the summit. Like her, they slipped and stumbled. It gave Tara enough time to reach the bottom of the hill and clamber over the concrete boundary to the other parking lot.

Gasping for breath, she was about to start running again when she spied an abandoned skateboard tipped over on its side over by the concrete base of a lamp pole. Like all the other sodium lights, this one was non-functioning. On impulse, she kicked the skateboard in a practiced way that she remembered from her youth. It flipped into the air and landed upright on its wheels. Then Tara hopped on with one foot and shoved away with the other.

There was no immediate issue with the board as it began to glide rapidly across the pavement, allowing her to quickly outdistance her pursuers. She was halfway across the lot, approaching another of those tall medians when she heard a whickering sound behind and above her. Tara reflexively hunched her shoulders in anticipation of being hit by some object, but it sailed harmlessly through the air in front of her and landed on the pavement.

She grimaced. Jesus fucking Christ.

Someone had hurled an actual spear at her, one that looked as primitively fashioned as anything she'd seen in a museum.

This, she thought, is fucked.

Tara hopped off the skateboard as she reached the next median, picking it up and cradling it in the crook of an elbow as she began to scale the slope. Near the top, she risked a glance back and saw she'd left her pursuers far behind. In fact, it appeared as if they'd stopped chasing her. She stretched out her hand and extended her middle finger.

"Eat shit, assholes!"

The top of this median was also lined with weeds and dead shrubs. She pushed through the nearest ones and stared down at the parking lot of the mall's north side. Her heartrate increased when she saw several cars parked at the curb in front of the entrance. One vehicle in particular snagged her attention. It was black and had the LOST PLACES logo painted on its side. As soon as she saw it, she began to simultaneously laugh and cry. This was it, the thing she'd desperately been hoping for, a way out of this nightmare.

Salvation.

She'd never watched Lost Places, but she'd heard of it, and had friends who subscribed to the channel. One of her sandals caught a root, and Tara nearly tumbled headlong to the pavement below, but a last-second correction allowed her to keep her footing and continue to the bottom without incident.

Fuck it, she thought. I'll mash that like button a thousand

goddamned times if you help me. I'll buy all your merch, too.

Dropping the skateboard, she waved her hands over her head as she started down the slope, shouting for help.

Panting and relieved, she jogged toward the van.

TEN

Celeste frowned in confusion as they emerged into what appeared to be the former Macy's department store. The location directly contradicted what their guide had told them about where they would be after exiting the service corridor.

Immediately prior to entering the department store, they'd passed through some smaller areas she guessed were once stockrooms. The walls of these rooms were lined with cubby hole shelving, probably once filled with clothing items wrapped in plastic. But the way Hereford had explained it, she thought they'd be entering via a smaller clothing store. Then, once the roller gate at the front of the store was unlocked and opened, they would step out into the main part of the mall.

Okay, she thought. So what? Hereford probably just got turned around. It's easy to do in here. Just look at this place.

She turned her attention back to her boyfriend and their guide. Mark Hereford's presence was clearly making Bradley feel insecure. Every knowledgeable remark from Hereford about the history of the mall triggered some snide retort from Bradley. Even to someone like Celeste, who truly couldn't have cared less about the subject, it was obvious there was little to no substance in his refutations. He simply couldn't abide the idea of anyone at all—especially some other dude—coming off as smarter than he was.

To his credit, Hereford mostly ignored Bradley's remarks. He radiated a kind of easy, unaffected, unruffled confidence.

Which was why it was so disappointing to now suspect that Hereford wasn't as confident and knowledgeable as he'd first seemed. Either he didn't know the interior layout of the mall as well as he professed, or he'd deliberately misled them about where they were going. The latter possibility struck her as unlikely because what would be the purpose in doing such a thing? Celeste could think of no good reason for it.

The longer she thought about it, the stronger her paranoia became. It bothered her that no one else in the group seemed to be noticing that something wasn't quite right. As a rape survivor, it was possible that she was more attuned to the inherent risks that came with men's shady behavior. Hereford was a stud for sure, but he no longer felt trustworthy to Celeste.

She cleared her throat, interrupting the two men. "Excuse me?"

Hereford and Bradley both glanced back at her as Chuck swiveled the camera around. There was a pained crease across the center of Bradley's forehead, and she could see how hard he was gritting his teeth behind his forced smile. He was angry at what he perceived as his girlfriend's rudeness.

Well, fuck you, Celeste thought.

She made a decision then—in the same instant she saw that look on his face. Whatever faint appeal she'd once perceived in Bradley had faded to the point of invisibility. She couldn't even squint at him and see it anymore. He was just another condescending dude-bro who wanted his bitch to know her place and just be fucking quiet wherever he felt it appropriate.

Fuck you a thousand times over, dude. Fuck you to infinity and fucking beyond.

She watched him unclench his teeth with obvious effort and glance at Chuck.

"You still taping?"

"Hang on." Chuck sighed and fiddled with the camera. The light went off. "Okay, I stopped."

Bradley turned to her. "All right, Celeste, what's so fucking important that you had to interrupt us this time?"

Audrey snickered in the shadows.

The urge to verbally go off on both of them was intense, but Celeste forced herself to hold her tongue. She shifted her gaze to Hereford, who was regarding her with a mildly curious smirk. The flirty impulses she'd felt toward him earlier were gone.

"I've got a question for our guide," Celeste said. "Why did you lie to us?"

His smirk turned into a frown. "What do you mean?"

"You told us we'd come out inside the mall, where all the shops are, not in a department store. You were very clear about that, but obviously it didn't happen, because here we are, in goddamned Macy's. So what's the deal?"

Hereford's only response was to snort and shake his head.

"You did say that," Stuart agreed.

"What is this bullshit, Celeste?" Bradley sighed in exasperation. "The guy decided to bring us out in another part of the mall. So what? We were getting great footage, but you ruined it for no good reason. Personally, I'm happy for the chance to poke around in here a bit before getting into the real guts of the place. Shit, look at that mannequin over there, for example."

He pointed to a spot off to the right. Celeste and the others turned in that direction. A pale white form lounged atop a dusty display table.

"Fuck me," Stuart whispered. "That thing looks real as shit!"

"It would look great on camera," Chuck agreed.

"Exactly," Bradley said. "Mark, you watch our channel. I'm sure you brought us this way for the ambience and visuals like that, right?"

Before Hereford could answer, Celeste interrupted again.

"So why didn't he say anything about it first?"

Bradley groaned. "Didn't I just cover that?"

"Actually, you didn't, probably because you have about the same amount of brain power as that fucking mannequin."

"Celeste…"

"Oh, don't look so hurt, Bradley. You know it's true, because if you had any brains at all, you'd be wondering why this Crocodile Dundee-wannabe motherfucker still hasn't said anything about this. Are you so worried about losing one fucking subscriber that you can't see what's going on? Look at that fucking smirk on his face."

Hereford winked and shrugged as they all glanced at him.

"I guess that's it," he said. "Celeste found me out. I live here with a bunch of killers, and you're our dinner."

Bradley gaped at him a moment, and then laughed. Chuck and Stuart did the same a second later. Audrey, Celeste noticed, stayed quiet, and seemed to hug the wall.

"There's something wrong here. I can see it in his goddamn eyes."

Bradley whirled on her. "Leave it alone, Celeste."

"She's right, actually," Hereford said. "I wasn't kidding. I've intentionally misled all of you. This urban exploration guide thing is a total sham. The mall is my home. And it's time you met the rest of the family. The doctor is waiting."

He yanked a long-barreled pistol from the holster at this hip, pointed it at the ceiling, and squeezed the trigger. The explosion of light and sound that followed made them all flinch and shout in fright.

Stuart ducked, holding his hands protectively over his head. "What the f—"

Celeste's ears rang. Her first instinct was to look away from the gun as Hereford lowered the weapon and pointed the still smoking barrel at them, so she glanced toward the old mannequin…

…which had hopped down off the old display table and was now loping toward them with a bizarre, spasmodic gait.

Celeste opened her mouth to scream, but could only manage a small, plaintive wheeze. She stood transfixed, unable to warn the others as the thing crept closer. Its skin was albino-white, with the exception of several places where the flesh was marred by large, tumorous sores that oozed infection. It had a strangely shaped mouth that projected outward like a snout, with long teeth at the corners that resembled the tusks of a walrus. Clasped in the creature's right hand was the handle of a long-bladed implement.

"What the fuck, Mark?" Bradley did a strange sort of hop. His voice had risen several octaves. "What is this shit?"

"I told you already," Hereford replied. "Boy, Celeste is right. You really are dense."

It was a machete. That's what the albino was carrying. Celeste saw that now, as it crept closer. Again, Celeste tried to call out a warning, and again, her voice betrayed her.

It was too late anyway.

The albino slid up behind Chuck, reached around, and ripped the long blade across the cameraman's throat, unleashing a torrent of blood that splattered across them all—all except Hereford, who neatly side-stepped the arterial explosion—and quickly soaked the front of Chuck's blue hoodie.

Shrieking, Celeste wiped Chuck's blood from her eyes. Her lids felt sticky and warm. She thought she was crying, but then realized it was just more of his blood, slipping down her cheeks. Her vision cleared in time to see Audrey vomit, and then back away. The woman's headlamp disappeared in the darkness.

The albino propped up Chuck's jittering form and continued sawing away at the dying man's neck. Chuck sputtered, trying to yell, but more blood bubbled out of his mouth. Slowly, the albino allowed him to sink to his knees. Then it went back to work, and quickly removed Chuck's head from his body. The thing hoisted the grisly trophy by the hair and raised it high. It then tossed the head at the group.

Screaming, they scattered.

Chuck's severed head landed at Celeste's feet and rolled to a stop. He stared up at her.

Then he blinked.

Shrieking, Celeste kicked his still-conscious head away from her. Chuck rolled over Stuart's foot and came to a rest face down against the filthy floor.

"Okay," Hereford raised his voice over their cries. "Don't any—"

In one quick motion, Stuart bent, grabbed Chuck's head, and flung it like a football at Hereford. The gruesome missile smacked face first into the guide. Chuck's bloody lips grazed Hereford's in a momentary kiss. Before their abductor could react, Bradley struck out, grabbing his wrist and forcing the gun down.

The albino snarled, and lunged at Stuart with the machete.

Celeste backed away, but stopped, turning in a panicked circle as more creatures emerged from hiding places and began to close in around them. They crept slowly at first, but when Hereford fired his pistol again, they raced forward. Celeste swatted away a grasping hand, even as another snatched the lamp from her head, taking a fistful of her hair with it.

Wheeling away, Celeste fled into the darkness.

Lorok liked to look at the moon and the stars, so Curd had accompanied the youngster outside. The boy might be as big as his father Noigel had been, but his mind was still that of a child. It wouldn't do to have him wandering off into the outside world. Scug would be furious, and rightfully so. The outside world would destroy Lorok as soon as they saw him.

They sat on a concrete loading dock at the rear of the mall. It overlooked an empty, overgrown field and a small stand of trees. Lorok stared up at the night sky, drooling and smiling with happiness. Curd tried to focus, but the noises from the other side of the mall kept distracting him. Car engines. Screams. Something was going on over there. He wondered what it was.

The mall was busier than usual. Of that much, he was certain. It made Curd uncomfortable. He didn't like this place, even on quiet nights. He missed their home. Scug kept promising that they would move on, and find a new place, but they never did.

He missed the rest of their family, as well.

"Your father and I saw a night like this once," he said.

Lorok turned to him, his expression curious.

Curd nodded. "Perfect night, just like tonight. We had gone to the surface to do some hunting. The clan was low on food. We found some. Four of them, in a parking lot not that different from this. We took our time with them. Shared. The air was cool like it is tonight, but when we opened them up, they were warm inside. It was nice."

Lorok turned his attention back up to the moon. Curd saw a single tear slide down the youth's misshapen cheek. He was about to reach out and comfort his companion when they heard a shuffling footstep to their right. A moment later, one of the insiders—one of Doctor Midnight's people—stepped into view from around a garbage dumpster. Curd didn't know his name, but had seen him before, hanging around the old arcade. He was noticeable for his three arms.

"What are you doing out here, Cyclops?"

Curd frowned. Since fleeing Philadelphia and living here in the mall, he had come to understand that word was meant to be an insult. He pointed at the sky.

"Stargazing."

The three-armed man snorted. "Stargazing? The fuck does that dummy know about stars?"

"Watch your mouth."

"You watch your mouth, you ugly fucking turd. I don't care how big you are. I'll put out that fucking eye and blind you. Don't forget your place in the pecking order."

Lorok growled, obviously upset by the man's tone.

"Leave us alone," Curd said.

"Fuck you. Both of you get your asses back inside, or I'll tell Captain Rat and we can let him settle things."

"Tattletale." Curd smiled, pleased with himself. He had only recently learned the word, and had been eager for a chance to use it.

The three-armed man sputtered with anger. "Okay, you just signed your death warrant, Cyclops. You and the dummy bo—"

Klavo leaped out of the darkness, jumped into the air, and buried a meat cleaver in their antagonist's head. Then he dropped to the ground and sprang back up, watching. The three-armed man stood there, mouth still working, but no sound came from his throat. Blood ran down his face in rivulets. He sighed once, and then toppled over to the side. Grunting, Klavo waddled over to his still twitching corpse and pulled the meat cleaver free. Then he looked up at them and nodded.

"You shouldn't have done that," Curd said, getting to his feet.

The dwarf pointed at the dead man and then at Lorok.

"I know," Curd agreed. "He was being mean. But this will cause trouble if we are found out. Scug will be mad. We have to get rid of him."

Grinning, Klavo rubbed his belly.

"Yes," Curd replied, "I'm hungry, too. Come on Lorok. Let's eat."

The giant youth picked up his massive hammer and gazed at Curd expectantly.

Curd shrugged. "Klavo already split the head, but you can smash the rest."

Hooting with joy, Lorok did just that.

Curd smiled, watching him, and was filled with nostalgia for better times.

ELEVEN

There was a slight lean to the Pillar of Souls. Lizzie hadn't perceived it from her previous supine position on the table, but she noticed it now, tilting slightly in the opposite direction. It was nowhere near as precarious as the famous Tower of Pisa. Indeed, if one wasn't looking at it from just the right angle, the lean was almost imperceptible. She supposed a design flaw in a tower constructed primarily of human flesh couldn't be helped. Bodies were less pliable and harder to mold than other, more traditional building materials.

A droplet of something warm and wet fell on her head. She looked up and saw living human faces contorted in unimaginable levels of agony staring down at her. Their eyes followed her every movement. The suffering moans rose in volume as she moved a few steps closer.

Lizzie stood in front of a woman sewn into the column at its base. The woman's flesh was yellow in some places, but black and rotting in others, particularly along the edges, where the flayed skin had been stretched taut in order to be attached to the flesh of her neighbors. Her lips were sewn shut, but her agony shone through in her eyes, along with a terrible awareness. The pain hadn't thoroughly broken her mind just yet. She was still cognizant of where she was and the impossibility of escaping her predicament.

The woman stared at Lizzie. Her lips moved, but the stitches rendered her words impossible to discern. Lizzie shuffled closer and turned her head, putting an ear almost against the woman's mangled mouth. The stench was unbearably oppressive—a miasma of shit, putrefaction, urine and blood—but Lizzie's morbid curiosity and desire to live overrode her disgust. It was a bit like trying to listen to someone speak from behind a waterfall. Shuddering, Lizzie pressed her ear completely against the woman's mouth, cringing when she felt the rough ends of the crude stitches move against her cheek. At last, the doomed woman's pitiful plea became discernible.

Kill me…kill me…kill me…kill me…

"Get away from her."

Flinching, Lizzie immediately retreated from the pleading woman, and turned around. She was surprised to see someone other than Dr. Midnight. The stranger was dressed in a fashion similar to the doctor—a white lab coat worn over blood-spattered green scrubs. Unlike the doctor, however, he was not tottering around on precarious high-heeled shoes or wearing a Richard Nixon mask. He was young, perhaps a decade older than her, maybe less. His physical appearance was normal, with no visible deformities. Wash away all the blood and grime and put him in some normal clothes and he'd look like any regular guy. He had piercing blue eyes, short but wavy brown hair, and a thick goatee. Both the hair and the beard had clusters of dried blood in them. He stood around six feet tall, and he had a slender but not scrawny build.

"Hope you're not thinking of offering that bitch an act of mercy," he said, lifting his chin. "You wouldn't want Dr. Midnight to see you do anything like that. Trust me. It'd be the worst mistake you could make at this critical juncture."

Lizzie studied his body language for a moment. He didn't seem intent on causing her harm, so she spoke.

"And why is that?"

He shrugged and spread his hands in a vague gesture. "The doctor is not a proponent of mercy in general. In fact, it's fair to say he has utter contempt for even just the concept. He revels in suffering. Gorges on it. He'd take anything done to alleviate or end the misery he causes as an unforgivable offense. Your punishment would be harsh, even by his standards."

"Thanks for the warning."

He nodded at the Pillar of Souls. "I know you were pretty out of it when they brought you in, but by now it should be obvious that when it comes to dishing out punishment, the doctor has no rivals anywhere in the world. He's a true master of pain. A majestic artist of misery."

"It sounds like you almost worship him."

He shrugged again. "You're new here. I get it. I felt that same doubt once, as well. In time, however, you will come to feel differently."

"I doubt that."

He smiled. "Right now, you'll do anything we want just to stay alive. But eventually, once you begin to understand and appreciate what the doctor is working to achieve here, you'll see that I'm right."

"Where is he, anyway?" Lizzie cast a quick glance around the interior. "He was showing me around just a minute ago. Then I turned my back to look around, and got distracted, and he was gone."

"He does that a lot. You'll see him again, soon."

"But where is he?"

"Working. This isn't our only project. There are many."

"Like what?" She gestured at the Pillar. "What's this supposed to achieve, anyway?"

"That's a matter best left for the doctor to explain. We're working toward a higher purpose. Despite appearances, our work here isn't just about murder and sick thrills."

"What kind of higher purpose?"

"Like I told you, that's for Dr. Midnight to say, if he so chooses."

Lizzie frowned. "If he chooses?"

"Correct. Look, I get that you want to know more, that you want me to tell you everything there is to know about this place and what we are doing, but that's not going to happen. Just know that I don't intend to hurt you. Indeed, it's nice to talk to someone new. Behave, and I'll behave, as well. Fair?"

Lizzie crossed her arms over her bare breasts, belatedly feeling a twinge of self-consciousness. "Uh-huh. Fine. But surely you can at least tell me your fucking name."

He chuckled. "Of course. My name is Conor. And we already know from a check of your belongings that your name is Elizabeth."

"Nobody's called me that since I was a little girl. People call me Lizzie."

"Okay, then. I'd say it's a pleasure to meet you, Lizzie, but given the circumstances, I doubt you'd agree. Hopefully, things will progress in a positive enough direction to change your mind."

"I don't see how that's possible."

"Keep an open mind." He turned partly away from her, the tail of his lab coat swinging as he swept a hand toward one of the tables. "This way, please. It's time we begin your indoctrination. Doctor's orders."

Conor turned fully away from her and walked toward the nearest metal table. Lizzie stayed where she was, arms still over her breasts. When he realized that she wasn't following, Conor turned around to face her again. His expression was stern.

"Lizzie, as I said…I'd prefer not to hurt you. I really have to insist that you come with me. It was your decision to volunteer in exchange for your life. If you're having second thoughts about it…?"

She stared into his hard, pitiless eyes. They reminded Lizzie of her father's eyes. And like him, Conor was probably a sadist.

She glanced at a bloody scalpel on a nearby table, and

considered suicide. Taking her own life might be the best option. Thinking of reasons not to wasn't easy. In truth, they hadn't been easy before tonight, either. She had no one and nothing. Logan was the closest thing she'd ever had to a real boyfriend and she barely felt anything even for him, maybe a vague fondness, but certainly not anything remotely like love. He was probably out there, worrying about her, but would anyone else be?

Worse, she hadn't thought of him until now. If their roles had been reversed and it was Logan who had disappeared, she wouldn't have let it affect her much. Lizzie knew this didn't say much about her as a human being, especially in light of how Logan unabashedly adored her, but she'd never found anything endearing in his devotion. It was more annoying than anything else.

"Don't do it," Conor warned. "I see you looking at the scalpel. I know what you're thinking. Don't."

"Why not? I don't see how I have anything to lose."

"Because no matter how quickly you slash your throat or cut your wrists, I can save and stabilize you. You'll live. And suffer." He smiled. "And you're wrong, by the way. You have everything to lose. Immortality is within your grasp, if you join us, and are found worthy."

"Worthy." She spat the word.

"Indeed. You told Dr. Midnight that you wanted to be his assistant. Many who come here say such things in moments of desperation, but in all these years, I've only seen three granted an actual opportunity to be a part of the work we're doing here. The doctor must have sensed something special inside you, a rare potential just waiting for the right chance to blossom. This is that chance. You can embrace it, or throw it away."

Lizzie stood absolutely still. Her first thought was that Conor was like one of those crazy Qanon assholes who hung out on internet forums like 4chan and Godlike Productions, parroting bizarre meme-inspired sentiments that any sane, rational person could clearly pick apart under the light of day. He sounded like the former cult members she'd seen in various documentaries, reciting half-baked, pseudo-mystical, self-help nonsense that had been drilled into his head by a more charismatic leader. But she hesitated in discounting what Conor was saying, simply because Dr. Midnight didn't fit the stereotype of any cult leader she knew about. Unlike Jim Jones, Heaven's Gate, or any of the others, what he was up to here seemed to have nothing to do with sex, money or influence. It constituted an extremely elevated level of bizarre and macabre. The Pillar of Souls, for example—who would devote so much effort to constructing and maintaining an edifice like that? It seemed more like the handiwork of Albert Fish or Jeffery Dahmer than it did David Koresh. Convincing others to willingly go along with such an endeavor would take a level of charisma that Midnight—from all indications—didn't possess. And yet, Conor obviously believed in it, and she'd seen the throngs of others living in this place. They must be true believers, as well.

Could there really be something of genuine substance to it all? Yes, Conor reminded her of her father, and yet, he hadn't harmed her the way her father had over and over again. Perhaps whatever the doctor was doing here had changed him. Made him a better person. Maybe the doctor truly was privy to some arcane knowledge that could be used to effect some manner of transcendence.

Having never believed in much in her life, Lizzie was surprised now to find a small flicker of yearning awakening inside her. She wanted to believe in something bigger than herself. She wanted to find someone worth following. Someone worth giving a shit about. If—and she acknowledged it was a far-fetched if—everything Conor was telling her somehow proved true, the reward for being a part of it might be more amazing than anything she'd ever imagined.

She might finally be happy.

That was reason enough to go on living, at least for a little while longer, rather than ending it all here and now.

Lizzie exhaled, realizing only then that she'd been holding her breath. "I'm sorry. I'm just…this is a lot to process. I'll do better."

Conor's smile grew wider. He gave her a curt nod. "Very good. Let us begin."

She followed Conor to the nearest table. What she hadn't noticed before was that there was another person strapped to it—a nude man. He was gagged and bound, but not blindfolded, and his eyes widened at their approach. He stank of piss. Judging by his whiskers and the length of his fingernails, he hadn't been here long.

At Conor's instruction, Lizzie took up a position at the side, overlooking the naked man's face. She wondered how he had ended up here, but not about who he was.

Conor clamped two metal clamps to the man's hairy nipples. The prisoner yelped beneath the gag. The clamps were attached by wires to an old-looking machine resting atop a metal cart. The machine had dials and what she guessed was a wattage indicator. She remembered seeing one like it in high school science class.

On the opposite side of the table was a small flatscreen monitor, bolted to one of the garage's steel support girders, and tilted at a downward angle for optimal viewing. The blank screen abruptly came to life, filling with an image of the doctor's mask-obscured face. Lizzie's heartrate increased at the sight of him.

At the same moment, Conor touched her from behind, squeezing one of her buttocks while groaning in a way that indicated arousal. Lizzie stiffened, eyes widening in shock.

"Pick up the scalpel, please." Midnight's voice sounded muffled through the flatscreen's speakers.

Conor squeezed harder. Lizzie thrust at him, trying to shoo him away, but he must have taken the movement as an invitation, because he redoubled his efforts. If Midnight noticed, he gave no indication. She did her best to ignore Conor's groping and focused instead on the doctor's step-by-step instructions.

Breath quickening, heart racing, she pressed the blade of the scalpel to the man's sternum. After a hesitation of no more than a full second, she pressed the blade through the flesh. She felt a little flutter in her stomach as blood welled up from the wound, but that faded an instant later when Conor began to stroke her clitoris and labia from behind, using all four fingers. Simultaneously, his thumb gently probed her anus.

She gasped, but did not pull away.

Then she resumed cutting the flesh, and was pleasantly surprised at how the writhing man began to transform as she sliced and parted the skin and changed his form.

TWELVE

As he did every time that he descended into Dr. Midnight's subterranean realm, Scug sighed with weary trepidation.

A moment later, Gax breathed a diminutive sigh of his own from Jax's shoulder.

"I don't like it down here," Gretch said.

"I don't either," Scug admitted. "We'd like it even less if we were alone. That's why you three are with me."

"Midnight's people, they are…" Jax paused. "Dangerous."

"So are we," Scug reminded him.

"But they're not like us." Gretch tugged at the hem of Scug's dress. "They scare me."

Scug frowned. The truth was that Doctor Midnight and his acolytes scared him, as well. That wasn't something he could admit to out loud, however. He was the leader. The patriarch. They had a family to rebuild, and he was determined to see that happen.

Which was why they now occupied this mall with Midnight and his kind.

"You should be scared," Scug told her. "But not of Midnight. Be scared of what could happen. There's too much going on tonight."

"The Boseman-Kline man?" Jax asked.

"He was fine," Scug replied. "It's all the people who have showed up after him. Do any of you ever remember the mall being this busy?"

Jax and Gretch shook their heads. Gax gibbered.

"This many people," Scug continued, "things could get out of control fast. More victims means more chance of being found again. Last thing we need is for one of them to get away and talk about what they saw here. We don't need that. Neither does Midnight."

Jax frowned. "Why be here at all? We could find our own place?"

"Not yet." Scug shook his head. "We're not strong enough yet."

"It's been eleven years…"

"Yes," Scug agreed, "but not all the children grow as fast as Lorok. We have to rebuild before we strike out on our own again. When we do, it will be some place far away from the cities and the suburbs. A farm. A nice farm. Of our own. Until then, we need Midnight. And he needs us. We bring him livestock for his projects, and he lets us live here."

"But they're not like us," Gretch repeated.

Scug's first urge was to backhand her, but he showed restraint, and kept his tone calm.

"No, they aren't. Some of them even look like the outsiders. But that allows them to lure more livestock."

Gax murmured something unintelligible.

"What did he say?" Scug asked.

Jax translated. "He asked if Midnight's people are bringing in outsiders for him, then why does he still need us?"

Scug didn't answer because he genuinely didn't know. It was something he'd asked himself, as well. There were a lot of mysteries concerning Doctor Midnight, and his reasons for allowing them to live here was only one of them.

Midnight's fortune was another mystery. Scug and his people had no use for money in all the years they'd lived beneath Philadelphia, but they'd since learned to adapt and change.

Scug now understood money's value, and the power that it provided. But the source and size of Midnight's fortune were unknown to him. They must be considerable. It was more than enough, for instance, to purchase the handful of automobiles Midnight's more normal-looking minions utilized. Someone at the power company was being paid to keep the electricity flowing through the mall.

He didn't even know the man's real name, or what he really looked like beneath that plastic mask he wore at all times. Scug had caught a glimpse once, but what he had seen was the face of an outsider—a visage unmarred by deformity or squalor or genetics. Maybe that was the point of the mask—to help maintain that air of mystery and intimidation. But if so, then why that mask? Scug hadn't known who Richard Nixon was when they arrived here. Midnight had explained it to him, in his condescending way, but afterward, Scug still didn't understand the symbolism. Maybe he wasn't supposed to.

Scug didn't understand the man's projects, either. When Scug and his kind butchered livestock, it was for things they needed, like food or clothes or to protect the family. Midnight and his people didn't kill outsiders for those reasons. The tower in the basement, for example, with livestock sewn to it and kept alive. What was its purpose—or the purpose of any of the other activities Midnight and his followers were engaged in? It all seemed so…wasteful. And Scug hated wastefullness.

Scug had a theory, however. He suspected that Midnight served a dark god or entities. While Scug might not have known about money or the moviegoing experience before coming here, he knew a lot about old gods. His people had paid reverence to the Thirteen since time immemorial, particularly Ob and Meeble. It was said that Meeble had even appeared to Scug's great-grandfather.

But the doctor and his followers? They worshipped something else.

He just wasn't sure what.

"Scug?" Jax gently tapped his shoulder with a sausage-like finger.

"I heard you." Sighing again, Scug smoothed his dress, pausing to flick away a tiny fragment of the realtor's skull. "That's what we are going to find out tonight. If it is safe for us to stay here."

They stopped at a set of double doors which led into the former parking garage. The sounds of moaning livestock were audible even through the thick walls. Scug gritted his teeth, annoyed at the noise.

"Okay," he said, turning to them. "Let me do all the talking."

Then he steeled himself and pushed the doors open.

The two vehicles parked near the Lost Places van were obviously unoccupied, but the van itself had tinted windows, and Tara couldn't be sure about it.

Please, she thought. Please, please, please, please...

She tried the driver's side door, but it was locked. She pounded on the window with her palm, but there was no answer. She slapped the van harder, hoping to set off the alarm and possibly arouse someone within earshot, but again, there was only silence. Tara choked in frustration. She would have screamed, but her throat was raw and sore and when she spat, her phlegm was flecked with blood.

Sobbing, she squatted down on her haunches alongside the vehicle and rubbed her eyes. Her palms came away streaked with black mascara. A disturbing possibility occurred to her. What if the drivers were all inside the mall? She glanced around, and saw no sign of her pursuers. She was alone. Instead of calming her, the emptiness of the big parking lot only fueled Tara's paranoia and sense of isolation and hopelessness.

Tara heaved herself upright and slumped against the van. Then she shuffled around it, trying the rest of the doors, and finding them all locked. She kicked the rear bumper in frustration, scuffing the faded Bernie Sanders For President bumper sticker. She then decided to check the BMW. It was a recent enough model that it should have a car alarm, but—traumatized and resigned—she decided that it didn't matter. If she triggered the alarm, nobody would hear it.

But then again, her pursuers or Cam's killers might hear it instead.

She carefully tried the doors, and found them locked, as well. Tara stood there, debating what to do next. Fleeing should be her top choice, but it was a relief to just be still for a moment, and quiet, after the night's events. She reached for her phone out of habit, and then remembered that it was broken. She considered prayer for a brief second, but that was as useless as the broken phone. Tara didn't believe in what others thought of as God, but she did believe in the idea of a benign force of creation—a power that allowed good things to happen even when all seemed dark, all hope lost. It didn't answer prayers. It didn't punish. It just was. The universe wasn't good or bad by nature. Nor was it governed by some unseen, intelligent force. No, the universe was neutral. Only the living things residing within it were good or bad.

She thought of something her grandma used to say—God helps them what helps themselves…

Prayer wouldn't work, but resolve and wits might. They'd helped so far, hadn't they?

The vehicles were useless to her. Even if she smashed out a window, she had no way of starting them to drive away. She supposed she could hide inside of one until daybreak, or maybe find a weapon to defend herself with, but there were no guarantees.

Before resorting to property damage however, she decided to investigate the red Chevy. She tried the passenger side door and gasped when it opened. The hinges creaked. There were no keys dangling from the ignition, but maybe she could find something useful. Tara leaned into the car. The dashboard was coated with enough dust and grime and dead insect carcasses that she could have drawn pictures on it with her index finger. The floorboards were littered with empty soft drink bottles and fast food wrappers. The shaft of the gearshift was covered in sticky grime. She pulled down the window visors and checked the glovebox, but found only an array of crumpled receipts and other papers.

Tara backed out of the dirty vehicle and knelt in turn at each of the tires, feeling around in the wheel wells for a magnet box clamped to the metal. This was something she'd seen people do in movies, though she'd never known anyone in real life who stored their spare key this way. Unsurprisingly, this search also turned up nothing.

She scanned the parking lot again and confirmed that she was still alone. She was acutely aware of time passing, and knew that her relief was achingly fragile. At any second now, a horde of killers could come hurtling toward her from the top of that median.

Tara circled around to the Chevy's driver's side, opened the door, and leaned in again to pull the trunk latch. Hearing the lid pop open, she backed out of the car and hurried to the rear, where she lifted the trunk lid fully open and peered inside. She saw a tire jack, a dirty blanket, and a wooden croquet mallet with faded paint. She grabbed the latter and hefted it with both hands, giving it a few experimental swings. The weapon felt good. Her spirits lifted.

Then she heard the sound of a motor.

Tara looked up and saw headlights in the distance, swinging into this section of the parking lot. A second later the cargo van rolled into view, followed on foot by the attackers she had just escaped.

"Shit..."

She hunched down slightly and crab-walked over to the Lost Places van. Then she peered around the side. The van cruised slowly, and the horde spread out behind it, covering more ground. She heard voices from the median, and glanced in that direction as several more pursuers pushed through the dead shrubs and weeds at the top, and began a rapid descent to the parking lot.

The two groups were heading right toward her.

Tara felt frozen in a moment of indecision about what to do next. The skateboard was out of reach, but she could bolt from behind the van and run toward the next median over, trying again to find sanctuary of some kind on yet another side of the mall, but she was exhausted and didn't know if her legs would carry across the pavement fast enough to elude her pursuers this time. She could smash the van's window and crawl inside, but her tormentors were close enough that they'd see and hear her. She might be able to fight one or two of them off with the croquet mallet, but they would overwhelm her soon enough.

There was only one thing she could do.

Tara dropped to her stomach and flattening herself at the edge of the curb. Still gripping the mallet, she then crawled beneath the van. She was slender enough to fit between asphalt and the vehicle's undercarriage. She just hoped she hadn't been spotted before trying it. She held her breath, waiting for an outcry, but there was none. Slowly, she exhaled and wriggled further. Her wrist slid through a small pool of viscous fluid. Tara cringed in reflexive disgust, but relaxed when she realized that it was just motor oil. The van had a slow leak. That was all. Another drip of black oil hit the back of her hand even as she realized this.

She curled up in a tight ball as the other van drew closer. She held her breath again as several pairs of feet appeared. Then the other van's tires squelched on the pavement as it came to an abrupt stop. She heard its door open, and then saw a pair of boots touch the ground. The engine idled loudly.

Tara's heart hammered as the boots came closer to the Lost Places van and then stopped. The toes were pointed right at her. She had to grit her teeth hard to keep from gasping out loud. For a wild moment, she considered crawling out from under the van and attacking the driver with the mallet. The cargo van's engine was still running. She could knock him down, hop in the van, and drive the fuck out of here before the others could catch her.

But then the driver dropped to his hands and knees and peeked under the van.

Tara moaned in abject despair. It was the same guy from before—the gaunt face with the sunken eyes, pointed chin, and fish-white pallor. He grinned, confirming her earlier suspicion that his teeth were indeed filed and pointed. He licked his wormy lips with a tongue that almost looked forked at the tip, though that may have been a trick played on her eyes by the shadows.

"There you are, pretty thing." He chuckled, a dry rasping sound. "Hide and go seek is over now, yes?"

Tara sobbed.

He stood up and said. "Get her."

Tara screamed as multiple hands reached beneath the van and grabbed at her. She tried to swing the mallet, but there wasn't enough room. She lashed out with a foot and felt something soft yield beneath her sandal. This was followed by a squeal of pain. The victory was short-lived, however. They seized her legs and began dragging her out from under the van. Tara did not go easily. She slapped and shrieked and tried to writhe out of their grasp.

They yanked her out in the open and rolled her over onto her back. With this close proximity, Tara was stunned by their numbers. There were more of them than she had realized. The stench roiling off them was revolting, and their various deformities were visually staggering. She noted, however, that some of them could pass for normal.

They all gathered around her, laughing and leering as they knelt beside her, holding her down and tearing at her scant clothing. Her skimpy top ripped away, exposing her bare breasts to the chilly night air. One of her tormentors—a filthy kid who looked more or less like a regular human—rubbed the garment over his face before plunging it into his shorts. Another pried the mallet from her weakening fingers. Others pulled at her denim cutoffs until they slipped off over her legs. Her underwear was ripped away next, leaving her completely nude on the rough pavement.

Tara gazed up through a film of tears and saw them leering lustfully at her. As another of the relatively regular-looking ones positioned himself between her legs, she became certain she was about to be violently gang-raped.

"Don't," she pleaded. "Just don't! Not that..."

"Agreed," the ghoulish driver said, raising his voice over the clamor. "Away from her now."

The underlings backed off, albeit with some obvious, grudging reluctance. Tara cringed at the shape of several erections visibly straining the fabric of their frayed, dirty garments. Their intention to rape her was there, no question about it, but the driver was forbidding it.

"T-thank you," she rasped.

"Do not thank me." He knelt beside her with a long length of heavy chain. "We do not need you. The doctor is busy with other things, and has given you to us as a treat. But I am more imaginative than the others. You see?"

She craned her head around and saw the other end of the chain was connected to the rear bumper of the cargo van, the engine of which was still idling.

Deducing that she was about to be dragged across the parking lot, Tara found a last inner reserve of strength and defiance. She tried getting to her feet with the intent of running again, but she was knocked back down. The driver leaped on top of her, pinning her to the pavement.

"You prefer to be raped then, yes?"

"No!"

He leaned close to her, his foul, rancid breath making Tara gag as he wrapped the chain around her left wrist, cinching it tight. Still straddling her, he sat up straight again and began snapping orders at his underlings. They responded to his commands with bursts of manic laughter and howls of delight.

"You see? They understand that Captain Rat's idea will be more fun."

Despite her peril, Tara was bewildered by the driver's name. Captain Rat? It was bizarre and yet strangely appropriate.

Her tormentors bashed out windows of the BMW and the Lost Places van. A car alarm immediately began to blare, but a short inbred crawled through the window of the BMW and after a moment, the alarm fell silent. Tara could only watch in confusion as they bustled about. Unless she was mistaken, they seemed to already know that the Chevy was unlocked, because one of them simply opened the driver's side door and slid in behind the wheel. The Chevy's engine started up seconds later and its lights came on as the person driving it pulled the vehicle away from the curb. Tara wondered how they'd started it. Was there a spare key that she'd missed? Had they hotwired it, like in the movies? Or did they already have a key?

The driver steered the Chevy in a wide loop around the cargo van before backing up alongside it and putting it in park. The back door of the cargo van swung open and another figure emerged with a second length of heavy chain, which he immediately fastened to the back of the Chevy.

Tara's eyes widened as he then approached her with the other end of the chain. Shrieking, she squirmed beneath the weight of the ghoul. Despite his rail-thin frame, Captain Rat was far stronger than he looked. He kept her pinned as they cinched the chain around her flailing right wrist. Then, grinning, he stood up and stepped back.

"There,' he said with a tone of satisfaction. "Now you will not be running off to play more hide and seek."

Tara raised her head and saw another mutant behind the wheel of the Lost Places van, the door to which was standing open. He hammered the side of the steering column. A companion standing outside the vehicle handed him a screwdriver. He ducked beneath the dashboard, and then popped back up again. The engine made a whirring sound, and then thrummed to life. The mob roared with raucous approval. Slowly, the driver pulled the van away from the curb.

"Ah," said Captain Rat, his dark sunken eyes seeming to float in their sockets. "Now we are cooking with gasoline, yes?"

Tara arched her back and wailed until something tore at the back of her throat.

The ghoul raised his long, pointed chin and nodded. The engines of the Chevy and the cargo van revved and suddenly Tara was jerked across the asphalt. The skin on her back and legs was scraped away. She felt a tug at her hair and raised her head just in time to keep her scalp from being ripped away, as well. At this angle, she saw bits of herself that had been left behind in her wake—red and wet and glistening in the dark. She screamed and screamed but all that came out of her was a dry rasp. Blood welled up in her throat and burst from her gaping mouth.

The vehicles slowed but were still moving. Now her back felt like it was on fire, as the asphalt dug into her muscle tissue. She craned her head up farther, staring at the impassive black sky. Tara abandoned all hope at that moment. The benign universe would not intervene on her behalf. She could not free herself from her dire circumstances, nor would any last-second miracle rescue be forthcoming. The mall was in the middle of nowhere. The convenience store might as well have been located on Mars. A car passing by on the highway wouldn't notice what was happening.

The vehicles stopped in the approximate center of the parking lot. This brought a new kind of agony. Her raw tissue and exposed nerve endings grated against the pavement. Tara lifted her head again and squinted against the red glare of two more sets of taillights. The BMW and the Lost Places van had been backed into position near her feet. Her vision blurred. The air stank of her own blood. She tried to breathe but inhaled engine exhaust.

Tara closed her eyes and imagined that she was home—not at her apartment, but her parent's home. She thought of her bed there, and imagined being safe and comfy in it, tucked away under soft blankets.

The vision was shattered by the sound of more heavy chains clanking on the pavement. She kept her eyes closed. Her lips quivered, swollen from shock. Surprisingly, the pain began to fade. She imagined the bed again, pretending she was there rather than lying naked and trembling on cold asphalt while murderous fiends leered and cheered her imminent demise.

Tara felt hands close around her ankles. She tried kicking, but it hurt too much to move. Instead, she could only lay there, limp and moaning, as the chains were fastened around her ankles.

All four engines revved. Tara's eyes fluttered open, wide with terror. The ringleader stared down at her.

"See? This is much better than being raped, yes? More fun for us. Less invasive for you. Everybody wins."

He raised a hand high over his head and backed off a few steps. Then he glanced back down at her again.

"You must forgive my manners. I just realized that I never introduced myself. I am Captain Rat. And you…? Well, it does not matter. I will call you roadkill."

Tara closed her eyes again, and resolved this time not to open them. She thought of the room, the bed, the blankets. She ignored the sounds coming from her own injured throat. She thought of her parents, and her little sister, and her cat who had died her senior year of high school. She kept her eyes shut even as reality intruded. She kept them closed as the engines revved louder, and chain links rattled on the pavement and then grew tight. She kept them closed as she heard the terrible suction sound her raw and bleeding back made as it was lifted up and away from the asphalt. She even kept them shut while she hung there, suspended.

But as the engines revved louder still, Tara heard a cracking and popping sound. She opened her eyes in time to understand that it was her own ligaments and muscle tissue snapping and pulling apart.

Strangely, there was no pain.

Her eyes remained open as her arms and legs were simultaneously torn away from her body. They remained open as her now limbless torso abruptly dropped back to the pavement. They remained open as her own blood splashed into them.

Instead of suddenly blacking out, consciousness lingered a few horrible moments longer. A single engine was still revving in overdrive as the cargo van sped away from her drawing and quartering. It made a circle in the lot and then crept toward her again.

Tara tried to close her eyes once more, but they no longer obeyed her brain's command. She watched, helpless and all-too aware the front tire drew closer and closer. Slowly, it rolled over her head.

And then her open eyes burst from her skull.

THIRTEEN

Audrey ran—not only from Mark Hereford and the other killers—but from Chuck's final moments. She couldn't shake the image of his head separating from the rest of his body, and how he had still been aware. In the darkness, she kept seeing Chuck's eyes, blinking, as the albino held his severed head aloft and bathed in his blood.

It had all happened so quickly, and although she'd seen it go down, she couldn't quite believe it. Chuck—someone whom she had been intimately involved with both physically and emotionally for years—was now gone. Just...gone. He was no more. She would never speak to him or hear from him again. Her relationship with Chuck had been the longest of her life. With the one notable exception of her bisexuality, they'd shared everything together. No one had ever known or understood her as completely as Chuck. How could he be gone? And how could it have all happened so quickly? And why?

She thought back to their last private conversation, in the parking lot of the sports bar. If she had known then it would be their last, she would have talked about something different. She would have told him what he meant to her.

No amount of praying or magical thinking would bring him back. The enormity of the loss was staggering, almost more than Audrey could take. A part of her wanted to give up and die, just lie down on the dirty floor of the empty department store and let the rampaging savages take her.

The larger part of her, however, wanted to live.

More than that, she wanted blood.

Vengeance.

Audrey stopped running, crouched down, and remained still. She held her breath and waited. She had already removed her headlamp, and was now concealed in total darkness. She listened for sounds of pursuit, but all of the action seemed to be further away from her current location. It was hard to tell. The bizarre makeshift architecture and the darkness and shadows all combined to do weird things to sound and sight. She heard screams and echoes and laughter, but couldn't tell who it belonged to or how far off it was.

Again, the slack features of Chuck's face as his murderer held his head aloft came to her mind. She pushed the thoughts away with a shudder and focused instead on the gun in her backpack. The Sig Sauer had a fully loaded magazine, and she'd had the presence of mind to pack half a box of spare ammunition, as well. She might not have quite enough bullets to kill every one of these savages—their numbers, from the brief glimpse she'd seen, had been stunning—but there was definitely enough to send a whole bunch of the nasty motherfuckers straight to hell.

Slowly, Audrey unzipped the backpack, holding her breath again as she did. The zipper sounded impossibly loud, and she half-expected one of their attackers to hear it and come lunging out of the darkness. When none did, she pulled the weapon free. Relief washed through her as she felt the comforting weight of it in her hand. She chambered a round, pensive again that someone would hear it, and then closed the backpack and re-slung it over her shoulders.

Next, she reached in her back pocket with her free hand

and pulled out her cell phone. She held it low to the floor so that the light wouldn't easily be seen, and then thumbed the screen, bringing it to life. She had no service inside the abandoned mall's confines. A thought occurred to her—maybe she couldn't call or text anyone for help right now, but she could type up a text and hit send, and then, when she reached an area where the phone reconnected with the network, it should automatically go through.

She muted the device so that no one would hear her typing, and quickly sent a text message to her brother, explaining that they were inside the Westgate Galleria in suburban Lancaster, Pennsylvania, and that Chuck had been killed, and that this wasn't a joke or a prank for YouTube, and that as soon as he got this message he should call the police. She hit send, and saw the little progress bar stall out as the phone searched for a signal. Maybe it wouldn't find one just now, but if she moved around, it was sure to connect. Satisfied, she shoved the phone back in her pocket.

Taking a deep breath, Audrey scuttled ahead, remaining crouched as low as possible, threading her way between and around old display tables and cash register stands. More than once, she encountered old mannequins that had been left behind after the store shut down. Each time, she nearly screamed, thinking it was Chuck's killer.

The other members of the team had scattered in different directions. She wondered how they were faring. As she did, another scream echoed through the store. This one sounded even further away. Judging by the sound, it was a male.

Audrey continued onward, and eventually emerged into a wide main aisle that ran through the center of the store. She was about to cross over it when she heard footsteps pounding toward her in the darkness. She shrank back, ducking beneath an old glass display case. Once it had probably held cologne or jewelry. Now, it held teeth. Thousands upon thousands of human teeth had been shoveled inside. Audrey's hand went to her mouth. She shuddered in revulsion.

Two figures ran by. She was shocked to see that it was Bradley and Stuart. She was about to call out to them, but then their pursuers came charging by. Audrey remained hidden until the procession had passed.

Audrey moved again, creeping in the opposite direction of Bradley and Stuart, sticking to a darker, narrower side aisle that ran parallel to the main aisle. The way in front of her appeared clear for one tantalizing moment. Then a shadowed figure popped up from behind a register stand. There was a dazzling flash, followed almost immediately by a deafening boom. Audrey felt the bullet zip by her, cleaving the air next to her shoulder.

Mark Hereford stepped out of the shadows. Smoke curled from the barrel of his gun.

"The doctor would have preferred to have you alive, but I guess we'll just have to settle for your corpse. We can use it for other stuff."

Audrey froze. She forgot how to move, forgot about the pistol in her hand, forgot how to breathe. Terror overwhelmed her, but beneath it, she felt a deep disappointment with herself. She had always thought of herself as capable and able to deal with high stress situations, but it seemed now that she'd been wrong about that. This disappointment was made worse by the regret she felt at having failed to exact even one iota of vengeance on Chuck's behalf. All she could do now was stand here like a fucking statue and wait for the next bullet to punch a hole through her.

Then a miracle happened.

A miracle in the form of Celeste.

The Instagram model popped up behind a stack of moldering wooden pallets to Hereford's left. She grabbed him by the throat with one hand and yanked him close. Hereford stumbled, off balance, and fired another round. Audrey gaped, watching the two opponents struggle. Then she realized that Celeste clutched a nail file in her other hand.

"Bitch," Hereford grunted.

Audrey's ears still rang from the gunshots. His voice sounded like a whisper.

Teeth bared in a snarl; Celeste jabbed the nail file deep into Hereford's left eye. A spurt of blood dribbled down Celeste's wrist. The pistol slipped from Hereford's grasp and clattered on the floor. Shrieking, the injured man reached for his face with one hand and tried to break Celeste's grip with the other, but the woman hopped on his back, hooking her legs around him. Hereford doubled over, swatting ineffectively. More blood splattered the dirty floor. His shrieks grew even more frantic as Celeste drove the nail file deeper into his head. Hereford spun about, crashing into empty displays and wailing, but Celeste held on with the tenacity of a wild animal.

Then Hereford went quiet and abruptly collapsed, like a puppet with its strings cut.

Audrey let out a breath she hadn't known she was holding and shook her head in utter astonishment.

Panting, Celeste stood up and eyed her. Then she flicked her hands, trying to get rid of the excess blood.

"Holy shit," Audrey exclaimed. "That was...you saved my life!"

"Keep your voice down," Celeste whispered. Then she smiled. "Didn't you know? All Insta-models are born killers at heart."

Audrey stared at her for a moment, and then began to laugh. She couldn't help it. Humor in the midst of all this carnage seemed so strange, but it felt good. She clasped a hand over her mouth to muffle the sound.

Celeste's blue eyes widened. She raised a finger and pointed at Audrey. "Look out!"

As Audrey ducked, she felt something swing overtop her head, close enough to ruffle her hair. She flung herself to the floor and rolled over on her back. Above her loomed a filthy man dressed in a pair of underwear and a frayed flannel shirt. His bald head was a big, veiny dome and he had an elongated, almost horse-like face with lips swollen to the size of hot dogs.

He clutched a machete in his right hand.

This time, Audrey didn't freeze. Before her attacker could recover from his swing and raise the machete again, she snapped her pistol up in both hands and shot him in the face. His mouth exploded, showering her with bits of teeth and gore. As the force of the bullet jerked his head backward, Audrey fired again, punching a hole in his throat. He toppled backward. One leg jittered as he bled out.

Audrey lay there, gasping.

"Fuck..."

Celeste loomed into view above her and stuck out a hand. "Come on. Those gunshots were like ringing a fucking dinner bell."

Audrey groaned as Celeste helped her to her feet. As soon as she was upright again, she saw more shadows rushing toward them. Celeste ducked low and snatched up Hereford's gun.

"How does this work?"

"Point it and shoot," Audrey said.

"That's helpful."

A strange sense of calm came over Audrey. Gripping the Sig Sauer with both hands, she stood with her feet apart, and took aim on the closest figure. She inhaled, exhaled, and slowly squeezed the trigger. The gun barked. The shadow fell. She shifted her aim and repeated the process. Another onrushing attacker dropped. A spear hurtled out of the darkness only to fall short and clatter across the floor. She took aim on yet another shadow, but Hereford's gun discharged at that moment, causing her to jump. Celeste yelped. The rest of the mob disappeared back into the darkness, and as the echoes of the gunshots faded, silence returned.

"I nearly broke my fucking hand," Celeste said.

"Hold it with both hands next time," Audrey advised.

"Did we get them all?"

Audrey shook her head. "They've fallen back."

"We need to get out of here."

"I saw Bradley and Stuart go that way." Audrey nodded her head.

"Do you care about saving their stupid asses or do you want to get out of here? It's their fault we're in this fucking mess in the first place. Bradley should've done a better job of vetting this dead piece of shit. Fuck that second-rate Matthew McConaughey."

"Jesus Christ, Celeste. He's your boyfriend."

"My boyfriend. Your co-worker and friend. But he abandoned us both. He'll abandon Stu, too, if he doesn't keep up. We're on our own here, Audrey."

Audrey nodded. "Okay, let's go. Stay low."

They crept through the abandoned store. Audrey took the lead. Celeste followed close behind. Several times they cowered in the darkness when their hunters drew close. Eventually, they reached the back room of the menswear department.

"This is where we came in," Audrey whispered. "You okay?"

Celeste nodded.

Audrey led them out into the service corridor. She quietly closed the door behind them. Then they stood up and hurried into the darkness.

Scug scowled impatiently. They'd been forced to stand in the corner and wait, while Dr. Midnight supervised his minions via a computer screen. One of the assistants was Conor. The other was a nude woman whom Scug had never seen before. At first glance, he assumed she was nothing more than livestock—a prisoner that had been turned into a pet and allowed to roam free. But as he watched, he realized that this was something more.

Gretch's stomach growled loudly. Scug glanced down at her, and then followed her gaze. She stared at a table to their left, on which was strapped a human bedsheet. Scug couldn't determine the specimen's gender. Indeed, were it not for his own adept skill at skinning people, he wouldn't have even been sure that this was a human being. The person had been completely flayed and stretched out.

A series of tubes connected the flattened skin to their raw, glistening body. Amazingly, the specimen was still alive. He stared harder, taking it all in. He finally found the human bedsheet's genitalia, and saw that it had once been a man. Scug didn't understand the purpose of what had been done to him, but he admired the man's flesh. He would have made a fine dress.

Gretch's stomach growled again.

"We'll eat later," Scug muttered.

"I hope soon," she replied. "I'm starved."

The assistants ignored Scug, Gretch, Jax and Gax, focusing their attention instead on a woman strapped to a table near the human bedsheet. A large aquarium filled with murky brownish-yellow liquid rested atop a metal cart next to them. It looked barely capable of sustaining the aquarium's weight. Two foldable metal step ladders sat open on the floor in front of the enormous tank. The section of concrete floor between the ladders was wet.

Gax chittered from Jax's shoulder.

"He wants to know what they're doing," Jax whispered.

Scug frowned. "So do I."

He turned his attention back to the woman on the table. She had been arranged in a position similar to the one that women adopted when about to give birth. The primary difference was that this procedure did not involve a new life emerging from the woman's vagina, but rather the insertion of a life into her vagina.

The tentacles of an octopus squirmed and thrashed on the table between the woman's legs. A metal spreader of some sort had been used to hold her vagina open to its furthest possible extent. Scug searched his memory. He thought the device might be called a speculum. Or perhaps a spatula? While he'd learned a lot about the modern world since fleeing Philadelphia, there were still small gaps in his knowledge, and that frustrated him each time he encountered one.

The squishy, malleable head of the octopus had been pushed up inside the woman's vagina, leaving only its tentacles visible. To prevent the creature from wiggling its way back out of the orifice, numerous large staples had been used to connect sea creature and human.

What was the point? Again, it all seemed so pointless. So wasteful. The flayed man's skin could clothe at least two of Scug's people. Both the woman and the octopus could fill their stomachs for several days. Their bones could be fashioned into weapons and tools. Their hair could be used for pillows or as kindling for a fire. Try as he might, Scug couldn't see the value of jamming an octopus up a woman's vagina and then sewing them together.

The insanity of it frightened him. He didn't like that feeling. Scug had lived his life inspiring fear and dread in others. Things had been so much simpler then. He missed the crumbling, sprawling house in Philadelphia and the endless tunnels beneath. He liked the aura of fear it had radiated out into the surrounding environs. He didn't like being on the other side of that dread equation.

A breaking point was near. The mall had become unstable—a place of barely contained chaos. If the situation could not be brought under control, then Scug and the members of his clan still willing to follow his lead would have to find a new home.

"Let's go," he muttered. "We'll come back later."

As he turned back to the door, Dr. Midnight's voice echoed from the speakers.

"Is our tenant still there?"

"Yes, doctor," Conor replied.

"I will see him now."

Growling, Scug turned back around to face them. Conor waved him over, his expression congenial. The new woman stared impassively.

Scug motioned to the others to stay where they were. Then he approached the table alone. At this range, the air stank of brine and blood. He moved opposite Conor and the girl. Midnight was turned away, looking at something off camera that Scug couldn't see. Scug cleared his throat.

"A moment, my friend," Midnight said, without looking at him.

Scug glanced down at the woman on the table. From his previous vantage point, he had only been able to see her legs and octopus-embedded groin. Now, he could see the rest of her, and it was enough to make even Scug pause. The subject's abdominal cavity gaped open from her sternum to just above her pubis. The flesh on both sides of the incision had been peeled back and was held in place by clamps. Smaller clamps were clipped inside the cavity, preventing the woman from bleeding out of several severed arteries. Her internal organs glistened in the light.

So did a pair of eyes.

Scug frowned as he tried hard to make sense of what he was seeing. He stared.

The octopus stared back at him.

As he watched, the nude girl reached into the abdominal cavity with her bare hands and worked to pull the creature's head up through the opening in the woman's flesh.

He glanced up, squinting at the girl. "Why are you doing that?"

Without looking up from her work, she said, "Because they told me to."

Standing off to the younger girl's side in his blood-spattered scrubs, Conor nodded and chuckled. "Lizzie, this is Scug. He and his people live in the old movie theater. They…rent from us, I guess you could say. Scug, this is Lizzie. She's a very attentive student. Takes direction well. She didn't even mess up too terribly when I was fucking her from behind."

"I don't care." Scug couldn't keep his contempt for the man hidden. "What's the point of this?"

"We're getting the cephalopod's head pulled up high enough to suture the patient's flesh in place around it. By doing this, both subjects will be viable as a single living organism, albeit for a fairly short time, probably. Cool, huh?"

Scug shrugged.

Conor smirked. "You have no idea what I'm talking about, do you?"

Scug stared at him for a moment. There were over twenty different items within easy reach that he could use to kill Conor right then and there. Instead, he dismissed him with a wave of his hand.

"I'm here to talk to the doctor. Not to you."

"Yes, yes," Midnight agreed. "Enough of this, Conor. Continue with the work. What is it you wish to discuss with me, Scug?"

Scug turned toward the pole-mounted monitor. "Lot of trouble tonight. Too many outsiders. There's a lot of noise—gunshots and screams."

"Granted, we've had an influx of visitors tonight, but gunshots and screams are common here."

"Inside, sure," Scug said, "but there's fighting outside. In the parking lot. Captain Rat is out of control. It's going to attract attention."

Midnight stared at him through the monitor. As always, his mood was impossible to gauge due to the Nixon mask hiding his features. His silence seemed to indicate displeasure. Scug mentally gauged the distance between himself and Conor. If the doctor reacted badly, and the situation turned dire, he'd leap across the table and tear the assistant's throat out with his teeth before anyone could react—but he hoped it wouldn't come to that. Much as he would have enjoyed it, Scug needed to think of his family first.

"We don't want attention," Scug prompted.

Midnight stirred, tapping a forefinger against the plastic chin covering his mouth. "Scug, my friend, I pride myself on maintaining a keen awareness of all factors potentially affecting both my work in this place and the continued viability of the mall habitat, which in itself functions as an ongoing social experiment of great interest to me. I am aware of no serious threat to either the habitat or my operation, and to put it quite simply, if I am unaware of such a threat, then it simply does not exist."

Scug frowned, shaking his head as his anger began to mount again. "The threat is everywhere. Always! It's right outside."

"Nonsense. Captain Rat has it well under control. The outside world is currently dealing with a pandemic that ultimately means less passerby and fewer eyes on this location than ever before."

Now it was Scug who stood silent. He chose his next words carefully, and spoke slowly.

"I think it's time my people left."

Midnight laughed. "And where would you go, dear Scug? Are you Moses of the Mutants, leading your people to the promised land?"

"I don't know who that is."

"Of course you don't. My point is that there is nowhere for you to go, Scug. You would leave this place, and risk the fate of your clan on the outside—a place you yourself just expressed a fear of?"

Scug balled his fists. "We'll take our chances. I won't see my family butchered again just because you're too stupid to—"

"Enough!" The doctor pulled back from the monitor, his masked face no longer quite filling the screen as he made a sharp cutting gesture with the flat of his hand. "You're fortunate I respect your position as the leader of your people, because otherwise I would not abide being addressed in this manner. How dare you imply shortsightedness or inattention of any kind on my part! If you were anyone else, I would have your intestines pulled out of your body via your slanderous mouth with a harpoon!"

"Try it."

Conor gasped. Behind him, Scug heard Gretch and Jax stir.

"I beg your pardon?"

"You heard me. Try it."

There was another pause. Then, Midnight threw back his head and laughed again. "Oh, Scug. You amuse me so."

"Why?"

"Because I don't have to try it. While you are standing here whining, I can have the rest of your precious family slaughtered. Do you really think that dim-witted young giant, or that mute dwarf, or your cyclopean friend can defend the rest of your children against my acolytes?"

"I…"

"You have a use, Scug. Pray that you do not outlive it. The next time you challenge me like this, I will see each and every one of you butchered. Now, get out of my sight before I change my mind and have it done anyway."

Scug slowly turned away from the monitor and stared angrily across the table. Conor was watching him with a cocked eyebrow and an amused expression. Scug sighed with resignation.

So be it.

He stalked across the room and past his companions. Together, they exited again through the double doors and out into the dark corridor that terminated in a stairwell leading back up to the mall.

"What now?' Jax asked.

"Hell." Scug's hands clenched into fists. "Hell is what happens now."

"More of them than there are of us," Gretch said.

"Maybe," Scug agreed, "but it's war either way. You three go back to the theater. Tell the others. Keep everyone together. I'm going to try to even the odds."

"How?" Jax asked.

"Annie," he said.." Going to talk to Annie."

He ignored their three simultaneous gasps, and stalked on.

FOURTEEN

Gunshots echoed as Bradley kept running. He assumed it was Hereford, shooting at Celeste or Audrey. He couldn't be shooting at Stuart, because he was plodding along behind Bradley, alternately sobbing and gasping for breath and begging Bradley to wait for him. And Chuck couldn't be the target because Chuck was…

Don't think about it. You'll start seeing his head again, and…

As far as Bradley was concerned, dying simply was not an option. He viewed his life as precious, perhaps more so than the lives of nearly everyone else on the planet. Many would see this as a gross overestimation of his own importance, but Bradley truly believed his death, should it occur while he was still so young, would be a terrible loss. He was destined for more. He was supposed to be famous. He possessed a rare and particular kind of genius. He was a visionary, a documentarian with the soul of a poet. Via his YouTube channel, he was able to offer valuable insight into humanity's future by exploring the decay and ruin of so many once vital things from its past. He was a digital-era archaeologist, exposing shocking examples of shameful waste and rot.

Dying is not an option. I've got too much left to do.

"Bradley! Wait up…pleeeeease…" Gone was Stuart's swagger and sarcasm. He sounded nothing like himself. Indeed, this was a Stuart that their online followers were unfamiliar with, as was Bradley himself. He didn't know this blubbering, shrieking guy.

And if he didn't know him, then there was no reason to wait for him or help him.

Sorry, bro. It's every man for himself because dying is not an option.

He did slow down though, and risk a glance over his shoulder. It was hard to tell from the darkness and shadows and debris, but he was fairly certain that the number of deformed people chasing them had somewhat lessened. There were still some back there, ragged clothing flapping around them as they hooted and hollered and closed the gap between themselves and Stuart. But it appeared that the gunfire had drawn more of them away from the pursuit.

His lungs ached, and his pulse thrummed so hard in his neck that he worried he was having a stroke. The heel of his left foot grew numb, and the calve above it started to cramp. Bradley gritted his teeth and pushed on.

Dying's not an option.

The phrase kept looping through his head, a motivational mantra that pushed him to run harder and harder, digging deeper again and again for extra reserves of energy as he fled through the store, abruptly cutting in different directions to throw off the horde on countless occasions. Several times, the manic zig-zag approach enabled him to narrowly elude capture. It also elicited more shouts of plaintive protests from Stuart Carlson, who was chugging along and doing his damnedest to stay with Bradley every step of the way. Bradley didn't understand how the fat bastard hadn't been taken down yet. Maybe their pursuers were toying with them to some extent?

He felt a twinge of something, deep down inside. Doubt? Conscious? Guilt? Stuart was his oldest friend. How could he think this way?

Dying's not an option the voice inside his head answered.

After another near collision with a squat, rotund pursuer dressed in a black garbage bag, and no sign of anything resembling salvation, Bradley tried a new approach. He kept an eye on the perimeter of the store as he ran, looking for potential exits. He spotted places where doors or open passages had once led into the back rooms of various departments within the store, but nearly all of these had been sealed off by the inhabitants of the mall, boarded over with stray pieces of wood and other debris.

He yelped, nearly colliding with another person, before realizing that it was just a mannequin. An easy mistake to make, given how uncannily lifelike the thing looked. Then he realized why it appeared so realistic. Parts of the mannequin—an arm, the eyeballs and lips, an ear, a foot—had been replaced with real human parts. He pushed the gruesome display over and continued running.

Finally, Bradley spotted the exit into the main part of the mall. His breath came easier and his cramps subsided when he saw that this exit wasn't blocked. The glass doors were smudged and caked with years of dirt and grime, but they weren't boarded over like many of the others. He darted toward them, gasping with relief. He slammed into them with a loud bang. The glass shuddered but held. He pulled the handle, but the door didn't budge. Straining, he yanked harder, but still had no luck. Then he tried the door next to it. This one was also locked. Screaming, Bradley pounded a fist against the glass. It vibrated again and made a sound like a gong being struck.

Dying is not an option.

Not now, not fucking ever.

Stuart slid up beside him, panting and heaving, his face beet red. Undeterred, the bigger man kicked a booted foot against the glass in an effort to smash through it. The attempt proved just as unsuccessful as Bradley's own efforts. The glass panels were thick and strong.

Bradley was about to suggest they try it together when he caught a glimpse of movement in the glass. There was very little ambient light, yet he saw shadows reflected in the doors as their pursuers came to a halt behind them. He turned, slowly.

"Shit..."

Stuart glanced to him, breathing so hard that he couldn't speak. Bradley nodded at the horde. When Stuart turned in their direction, he yelped.

"Shit," Bradley muttered again.

"You're...an..." Stuart gulped several deep breaths. "...asshole..."

Sighing, Bradley pushed his back against the glass as the mob inched closer. They carried a bizarre array of weaponry—everything from machetes and fire axes to crudely-fashioned spears, bone clubs, and broken bottles. There were too many of them, spread out and cutting off every conceivable route of escape. He would never be able to slip past them and weave his way back to another part of the store. This was it.

His defiant mantra—dying is not an option—had won him nothing.

He glanced at Stuart, who'd also slumped with his back against the glass doors turned away from the glass doors and now stared straight ahead, mouth agape. Tears and sweat streamed down his puffy, red face. The Lost Places baseball cap he perpetually wore wedged down tight over his voluminous mane of frizzy hair now hung at an angle across one side of his face.

"Remember when we used to play football?" Bradley asked.

Stuart nodded. "Y-yeah..."

"Senior year? Homecoming? Remember? We played against Columbia."

"We're gonna die, dude..."

"Remember the third quarter?"

Stuart suddenly stopped panting. "Yeah?"

Bradley nodded. "Yeah."

Then he broke, running forward and to the right, praying that Stuart had understood the reference. A second later, his prayer was answered. With a breathless whoop, Stuart broke left and charged.

"Yeah," Bradley bellowed. "Fuck yeah, motherfuckers!"

He barreled ahead, barging between two misshapen forms in front of him, elbowing them both aside. They staggered sideways and one fell to the floor. Bradley didn't slow. The others reacted in confusion, allowing him to weave his way around them and emerge into the clear. Laughing, he darted out into the main aisle and sprinted away.

He'd gone about eight feet when he tripped over a rope that had been stretched across the aisle at ankle height. Bradley's shout of triumph sputtered into a squawk of surprise and dismay as he fell face first, hands outstretched, onto the floor. He raised his head in time to see Stuart plod past. His friend's mouth was open wide in terror and his arms and legs pumped hard. His face was so red that he looked on the verge of a heart attack. And somehow that goddamn ball cap was still atop his head, although at an even more precarious angle than before. A horde of attackers chased after him, grasping for his hoodie.

"Stuart," Bradley yelled, reaching for him. "Stuart, don't—"

His pursuers fell on him then, crushing him with their body weight, and pressing the air from his lungs. Bradley's eyes bulged. He wheezed, desperately trying to breathe. Then, the weight subsided somewhat. Dozens of pairs of hands flipped him over on his back. The horde pressed close, pinning his arms and legs to the floor. He looked up at the leering, hungry, savage faces arrayed around him and screamed.

Dying's the only option...

He heard footsteps approaching. Unlike the others, these were slow and measured—an almost leisurely pace. Bradley's captors fell back as a man came into view. He looked like a human ghoul. Bradley shuddered at the sight of him.

The man had a sledgehammer slung over his shoulder.

He smiled, revealing pointed, gray teeth. Then he licked his wormy lips and knelt.

"Hello there. Welcome to the Westgate Galleria. I am Captain Rat. Please forgive me for not being here to greet you earlier. I was occupied elsewhere."

"What do you want?" Bradley wheezed.

"Well," the man grunted as he stood back up, "what I want and what my master wants aren't always the same. He graciously allowed me to have some fun, earlier, but now I've been ordered to come back inside and deal with you and your friends. I would prefer to torture and kill you. But this is your lucky night. He has other plans for you."

"W-what?"

"You will be made part of something bigger. Something miraculous. Doesn't that sound nice?"

"No," Bradley cried. "That doesn't sound nice at all."

Captain Rat made a mock sad face. "Perhaps you will feel differently after a brief tour. But first…I'm afraid I must eliminate the possibility of further attempts at flight. I'm told that you've given our people quite the chase, yes?"

He lifted the wooden handle off his shoulder and raised the sledgehammer high over his head. Bradley turned his head away, trying to press himself into the floor.

"Please...please don't hurt me."

Captain Rat's smile vanished. His features tightened as he swung the sledgehammer, smashing it into Bradley's right knee. Bradley wailed and thrashed. The pain was so intense that he puked, choking on his own vomit. Then came a second blow, which turned his other kneecap into red paste.

"A good start," Captain Rat mused, "but we must make sure, yes?"

He swung the hammer down again.

And again.

And again.

After that, things got worse.

Dying was not an option.

As she assisted Conor on nearing the end of the extensive suturing work, Lizzie was amazed that the woman on the table was still alive. Her heart had stopped beating multiple times throughout the procedure. Each time, the monitor tracking the woman's vitals displayed the flat line Lizzie was familiar with from countless medical dramas. Every time that happened, Conor got her heart going again with a pair of defibrillator paddles. The one time that didn't work, he resorted to injecting a dose of adrenaline straight into her heart with a monstrous syringe. The woman gasped and the beeping from the heart monitor resumed. Conor pumped a fist in the air and let out a whoop of triumph. Lizzie released a breath she hadn't realized she was holding and resumed her suturing work after taking a moment to wipe sweat from her brow. In those moments, she felt a bit like the star of some bizarro world version of Grey's Anatomy.

Of course, the reality of the situation was far more deranged than that. She was a prisoner in the underground lair of a mad scientist with a penchant for strutting around in glittery high-heeled shoes while wearing a cheap Presidential Halloween mask, performing an unorthodox and insanely complicated surgical procedure with no prior medical knowledge or training whatsoever, in an environment that was the antithesis of sterile. The coronavirus was the least of her worries in this place. The cutting. The cephalopod insertion. The suturing. She hadn't paused to think about any of it while she did it—knowing that if she had, her resolve would have snapped, and her mind would have probably snapped with it. She was in this insanity now, spinning at the heart of the whirlwind, and all she could do was go with it. Every goddamn bit of it. She'd taken part in a grotesque and horrific thing—an atrocity that would make many of history's most notorious sadists blanche.

Part of her felt sickened by her actions. Another part simply felt numb. But there was a third part of her, deep down inside, that experienced a strange and unexpected degree of pride. She'd worked hard at a task assigned to her and she'd completed it successfully. She'd accomplished something, which wasn't a thing she'd done often in her life. In the moments immediately following the conclusion of her work, the awful nature of what she'd done didn't even matter. The strange sense of euphoria that overcame her then was a revelation, a high rivaling any she'd ever derived from booze or drugs.

She just wished she understood why they were doing what they were doing.

Two more of the doctor's assistants emerged from the darkness beyond the circle of tables. Like Conor, they were clad in blood-spattered lab coats and green scrubs—but unlike him, they wore cheap Halloween masks similar to the doctor's. Lizzie guessed that the one in the Star Wars Chewbacca mask identified as a woman, given her ample breasts. The man next to her wore a Marilyn Monroe mask. Both plastic facsimiles were artless, cheap knockoffs rather than officially licensed merchandise, so the design of each was a bit off, just different enough from the real thing to protect the manufacturer from copyright infringement lawsuits. The role reversal came as no surprise to Lizzie, as it was right in line with the off-kilter nature of everything else here.

She moved out of the way as Marilyn and Chewbacca took the table out of its locked position and wheeled it away into the shadows. Although sedated, the woman was conscious enough to let her head loll slightly. She directed a bleary, accusatory look Lizzie's way. Lizzie supposed it should bother her.

But it didn't.

Lizzie raised her hand and waved. "See you later, Octopussy."

She watched the woman get rolled away, and giggled at the last glimpse of the squirming tentacles between her spread legs.

Lizzie stifled another giggle.

Conor frowned. "What did you call her?"

"Octopussy. You know, like in that old James Bond movie?"

He laughed. "Shit. That is funny. Why didn't I think of that? It's so obvious."

"I know, right?"

"Would you like to get cleaned up a bit?"

Lizzie nodded. "I feel gross. And maybe…"

"What?"

"Maybe I could get some clothes? At least some scrubs like you and everyone else?"

He smiled. "That can be arranged. Although I prefer you this way."

"Well, I—"

Before she could reply to that, Dr. Midnight cleared his throat. Both of them turned back toward the monitor His masked face loomed in close-up.

"Congratulations to you both on a job well done."

"Thank you, sir." Conor nodded.

"Thanks," Lizzie said.

"Conor, please escort Elizabeth to her evaluation."

"Understood."

The screen went black.

Lizzie glanced at Conor. "Evaluation? What does that mean?"

The amusement he'd shown just a moment before was gone now. Conor's expression was blank as he took her by an elbow and steered her away from the operating theater and the Pillar of Souls.

"The doctor wants to talk to you in private." His tone was flat.

"About what? Conor, what's going on? I did everything you asked."

"You're about to find out whether or not you passed your test."

Lizzie's own expression sobered. Apprehension welled up inside of her as she allowed Conor to guide her into the murky darkness. She realized now that she'd let her guard down too far. The obscene sense of twisted safety she'd felt after performing the procedure was foolish. There was a very real possibility that Conor was taking her to her doom.

Which made all the things she had just done—all the atrocities that she's participated in—that much more unforgivable.

Despite this, she did not attempt to twist out of Conor's grip and flee. Lizzie knew any such attempt would be stupid. She'd seen enough of this place on the way in. The mall's interior was a bewildering maze. She'd end up hopelessly lost. Then recaptured, tortured and killed for her defiance. Or worse, she'd end up sewn into the Pillar of Souls, or with an octopus sewn into her snatch.

Another reason she didn't run was because of how she'd felt while cutting up the people in the operating room.

She wanted to do it again.

And she wanted to know the reason. She wanted to understand what they were doing here.

She smiled as Conor tugged at her elbow again, steering her down a narrow, dark corridor. Their footsteps echoed. Spiderwebs brushed against her face.

"I'm ready," Lizzie said.

"Ready for what?" Conor asked.

"For anything. Anything at all."

Up ahead, a faint glimmer of light appeared.

FIFTEEN

Once they were back out in the service corridor, Celeste and Audrey slowed down to catch their breath. There were no sounds of pursuit. There was also no illumination since both of them no longer had their headlamps. They cautiously crept around piles of debris and refuse. from banging into the walls or skidding into piles of debris.

Celeste paused for a moment and sniffed the air.

"What's wrong?" Audrey whispered.

"I smell…blood?"

Audrey's expression grew panicked. She raised her nose and inhaled. "I smell it, too."

"I know, right? But where is.." Celeste glanced down at her hands, still slick with Hereford's blood. "Oh, shit. It's me. False alarm."

"We probably both smell like it."

"All I know is that I'm taking a bath for seven days once we get out of here," Celeste replied. "And then I'm getting my nails done."

"You can't," Audrey reminded her. "The pandemic is still going on out there. The nail salons aren't open."

Celeste gestured down the corridor. "I survived this shit. Covid can go fuck itself."

They paused a few more times, listening for any sounds of pursuit, but the hallway remained quiet. They pushed on, and their eyes finally adjusted to the darkness. Eventually spotted the door through which they'd entered the mall. They could only make out the vague outline in the darkness, but to Celeste, it was the most beautiful thing she'd ever seen.

She slowed her pace as they neared it, however, sensing something wasn't quite right. It took her a moment to figure out what was wrong.

When they'd first entered the mall, they had left the door propped slightly open with a cinderblock. Now, the cinderblock was gone, and the door was closed.

Celeste opened her mouth to call out a warning, but it was already too late. In helpless horror, she watched as Audrey jammed the heels of her hands against the push bar inset in the middle of the door. Instead of depressing inward as it yielded to the pressure and unlocked the door, the bar failed to budge. There was a static snapping sound and then Audrey was abruptly jolted backward off her feet. She hit the floor hard and didn't move. Amazingly, she'd kept her grip on her gun.

Gasping in shock, Celeste rushed to her side. She place Hereford's handgun on the floor as she knelt next to the injured woman.

"Audrey? Hey! Hey, wake up, Audrey. Talk to me."

Unless Celeste was mistaken, Audrey had just been electrocuted. That would explain the sound she heard and the immediate aftermath. Fearing the electric shock had been severe enough to kill Audrey, she figured she should check for a pulse or try to administer some crude form of first aid in an attempt to revive her. The only problem with that was she remembered almost nothing of the basic instruction she'd received in such matters back in high school health class. During her school days, she'd always done just enough to get by, knowing even then her future was not tied to academic excellence or the pursuit of higher education. Her only goal in those days was to get that high school diploma while exerting as little effort as possible and move on to the glorious and glamorous future as a model and celebrity she knew awaited her.

She picked up one of Audrey's limp wrists and tried to feel for a pulse by emulating what she'd seen actors do on television. She felt nothing at first.

"Shit," she moaned. "What the fuck am I even doing?"

Then Audrey's eyes popped open and Celeste screamed. Audrey sat up quickly, sucking in a great gasp of air. Startled, Celeste tipped backward onto her ass.

"Jesus Christ," she gasped. "You fucking scared the shit out of me, Audrey! I thought you were dead. Are you okay?"

Audrey didn't respond right away. She remained in her half-seated position on the floor, staring blankly at the door. Her hair hung down in her eyes. She was alive, that much was clear. But her breathing sounded harsh and irregular, and she seemed locked in a state of shock, oblivious to any input from outside her own head.

"Hey," Celeste said, her expression pinched with concern. "Look at me."

Audrey expelled another big breath and turned her head slowly in Celeste's direction. "What happened?"

Celeste sighed with relief. "The door is electrified, I think. You got knocked off your feet when you touched it."

"What's that smell?"

"The blood on us both. Remember?"

Audrey shook her head. "No, not that. It's like…burnt hair."

Celeste leaned close and felt Audrey's hair. Sure enough, the ends were brittle and jagged.

"That's you."

"It burned my hair?" Audrey's voice rose. "Do I have any left?"

"Don't freak out. It doesn't seem too bad. The tips are just singed a little bit. That's all. You can get it cut out, just like split ends."

Audrey pushed her burnt hair out of her eyes and leaned forward to peer intently at the door for a moment. "It's electrified?"

"Yeah."

"Who would do that? Hereford?"

Celeste shrugged. "Maybe. I don't know. He wasn't the only crazy fucker in this place. I doubt Hereford was the brains behind all this."

"Sure," Audrey agreed. "He tricked us, but let's be real, we were easily tricked."

"We weren't tricked. Bradley was tricked. He was the one who hired the motherfucker."

They sat quietly for a few moments while Audrey recovered. Celeste winced. Every muscle in her body seemed to ache, as did her stomach and head. She wondered if it had something to do with the adrenaline that had no doubt flooded her system earlier. She wasn't injured. At least, not seriously. Her face hurt where she'd been hit, but that would heal.

"I guess they probably got Bradley and Stuart," Audrey said.

Celeste nodded, sniffling. She remembered the testy exchange between her and Bradley in the moments just before Hereford's revelation of deceit. That was the moment their relationship had ended. The two of them had been over and done then and there. She'd felt it strongly and was sure he had, too. Both of their shortcomings had been on display. And she was angry at him now for getting them into this mess. He'd failed to check Hereford's background. He'd led his team into danger without taking the most basic steps to protect them in advance. That was all on him.

And yet…they'd been in an intimate relationship together. She should feel something now. But she didn't. She didn't feel grief or worry or concern.

She only felt numb.

And that, in turn, made her sad.

But at least she felt something, finally, other than numb.

She sniffled and blinked tears from her eyes. "I'm sorry."

Audrey's dazed expression turned sympathetic. She twisted around and scooted closer to Celeste, drawing her into her arms. Celeste stiffened at first, but then surrendered to the embrace. She buried her face into the crook of Audrey's neck and wept. Her tears soaked through Audrey's shirt and slicked her skin. Audrey rubbed her back and whispered sounds of reassurance into her ear, telling her none of it was her fault and that everything would be okay.

Celeste gently broke the embrace and laughed.

"I should be the one telling you it will be okay," she said. "After all, you were just electrocuted."

"It's all good."

"I got snot on your shirt. I'm sorry."

Audrey glanced down at the garment, then back up at her. She smiled.

"That's okay. It goes well with the blood and dirt, don't you think?"

They both laughed.

"It's a nice top," Celeste said. "Where did you get it?"

"Chuck bought it for me. He…" She choked back a sudden sob. Her eyes grew wide. "Chuck's gone. Dead. He...he…how could…his blood is on this shirt, and he…"

"I know. I'm sorry."

Audrey clutched Celeste's hands and squeezed them tight, unable to speak.

Celeste was grateful for the ensuing moments of quiet. It gave her time to better absorb all that had happened and contemplate their next move. With this came the dawning self-realization that her attitude toward Audrey had always been decidedly unkind, and not even their shared traumatic experience had erased that slate entirely. In particular, she'd often voiced contempt for Audrey's unremarkable appearance, but now she could admit her nasty attitude was largely rooted in the woman's status as the only other female member of the team. She'd felt threatened by Audrey's higher level of competence as a better explorer and knowledgeable on-camera commentator, and the fact that the commenters and subscribers seemed to adore her.

Celeste frowned.

Face it, you've been a raving bitch to Audrey the whole time you've known her.

Well…she would make it up to her once they got out of this place and got help. They'd spent a long stretch of minutes here, seemingly removed from the immediate threat of mutilation and death, but she was under no illusion regarding the severity of their predicament. This little interlude had been nice and comforting, but they were still in danger. They needed to focus on finding another way out of the mall.

"Listen," Celeste said, "I know you loved Chuck and everything, but you can do better, okay? Maybe it doesn't seem like it now, but once we get out of here, and our lives go back to normal, you'll find someone. Hell girl, I'll hook you up! I'll hook us both up. Sound good?"

Audrey stared at her for a long moment. Then she shrugged.

"Good. Forget Brad and Chuck and Stuart. Fuck those losers." Celeste glanced in the direction of the electrified door. "Okay, that way's no good. And we can't stay here forever. So, what now? Any ideas?"

Audrey appeared to think about it a moment.

Then she said, "Where's my gun?"

"Right next to you. I thought you'd drop it when you got shocked, but you didn't. You sat it down when you felt your hair."

"Oh…" Audrey glanced down at the weapon. "Sorry. My brain is still a little…fuzzy."

"I'll bet."

Audrey picked up the gun and ejected the thing that held the bullets. Celeste wasn't sure if it was called a magazine or a clip. Then she rummaged around in her backpack and pulled out a second magazine or clip. She reloaded the weapon, and then looked up, seemingly satisfied.

"You still have Hereford's pistol?"

Celeste nodded. "Right here."

"Better let me check that, too."

Celeste handed the weapon to her. This one was different than Audrey's, Celeste noticed. A round thing popped out of the side. Audrey squinted, peering into it. Then she snapped it back in place, looked up, at Celeste, and smiled.

"All good?"

"Yep." Audrey nodded. "All good."

"So, what should we do now?"

Audrey drew in a deep breath and sighed. Then she lifted her head and looked Celeste in the eye. "I don't know about you, but I'm doing this, you fucking cunt."

Audrey leaned forward.

Celeste gasped. She glanced down and stared in confusion and disbelief at the barrel of the gun pressed between her breasts.

"Hey," she said, "this isn't funny."

"No, Audrey agreed, "it isn't."

Then Audrey squeezed the trigger.

Audrey was surprised by how little blood sprayed back on her. She had hoped that pressing the gun so closely against Celeste's breasts would help muffle the sound, and it had, but she'd steeled herself before pulling the trigger, expecting to be showered in gore. Instead, most of it blew out of the exit wound and painted the wall instead.

Celeste stared up at her. She tried to speak, but instead, she choked on her own blood. There was a wheezing sound from somewhere inside of her, like a balloon slowly losing air. Her eyes formed the question her mouth could not.

"I'll never do better than Chuck, you bitch." Audrey pulled the gun away and now there was blood—but still not a lot. A thin pool welled up and dribbled down between Celeste's cleavage. "I don't want you to hook me up. I want Chuck back. I can't believe I actually almost felt sorry for you."

Celeste coughed, struggling to raise her head. The wheezing sound inside of her turned into a rattle. Her mouth worked again, forming words.

"What are you trying to say? More stupid shit?"

Celeste's head drooped and the sound of her labored breathing ceased.

She was dead.

"Good."

But was it? Audrey had acted impulsively. She hadn't known she was going to return to her idea of murdering Celeste almost until the moment she did it.

And now it was done.

The muzzle flash had messed up her night vision. As Audrey waited for her eyes to adjust to the darkness again, her stomach cramped. Surprised, she leaned over and threw up all over Celeste's still warm corpse. Steam rose from both, mixing with the smoke from the gun barrel.

She had just murdered somebody. The realization made her stomach convulse again. This time, she thought she might shit herself. Audrey squirmed on the floor, trying to hold the nausea at bay. She'd killed someone. What if she got caught? What if Bradley and Stuart were still alive? In her head, a vivid and disturbing scenario formed. She pictured Bradley and Stuart come running down the hallway after narrowly escaping death at the hands of the mall freaks, skidding to a halt and gasping in shock upon seeing her in this position. She imagined trying to explain it away—coming up with a convincing lie. No, she hadn't killed Celeste. It had been one of the freaks. Then the real killer had stuck the still-smoking gun in her hand and scuttled off into the darkness. She was being framed.

They wouldn't buy it. Neither would she, if the situation had been reversed.

Audrey had killed one of her friends. Well, "friend" was stretching things a bit, but the point was the same. There was no going back from this. She could escape this place, but there would be no escaping her actions. Even if she got away with it, she would never be free of it.

She got to her feet and stared down at Celeste. Her eyes were still open, and now they seemed to stare at Audrey in an accusatory way. Audrey knew this was a false impression. Celeste was gone, her brain as sentient as a brick now. Those pretty eyes weren't seeing anything. Still, it bothered her, as did the shocked set of the woman's features. She couldn't help but read sadness and a sense of betrayal in that frozen visage. Maybe also a level of disappointment. After all, Celeste had extended an olive branch to a bitter rival only to have this happen to her. It was so very typical of her. Even in death, the shallow, narcissistic bitch had somehow managed to claim the moral high ground.

"I'm sorry," she said.

But she wasn't. Not really.

Audrey retrieved the spent bullet casings from the floor and stuffed them in the backpack. Then she stowed Hereford's gun, as well. She pulled out her phone and checked it. The text message that she had sent her brother still hadn't gone through, which was now probably for the best. She would try again when she got outside.

Glancing back down the dark hallway, she confirmed that she was still alone. Now that she was actively thinking about it, this struck her as odd. Maybe they hadn't followed her because they knew she couldn't get out this way. That meant they might be waiting for her.

She wondered if they were watching her right now. The door was booby-trapped, so obviously this place still had electricity. She looked up and craned her head around in search of security cameras. The ceiling was draped in spider webs—more than she'd ever seen in one spot. Audrey shuddered. She loathed spiders. The webbing seemed deserted, though. Maybe the spiders that had spun them were long gone.

After a few seconds, she caught sight of a security camera mounted to the wall just below ceiling level, but it looked like a dead piece of old technology, with no telltale red light to indicate it was in use. Most likely, it was left over from when the mall had still been operational. She felt no relief in noting this, however. There could still be more subtle monitoring systems in place, utilizing cameras so small hardly anyone would ever notice them. Things like that were no longer the exclusive domain of high-tech spies. You could buy that shit off Amazon these days.

Her foot collided with Celeste's corpse. As she glanced down, Audrey heard a strange, soft noise of indeterminate origin—a scuffling or scraping of some kind. She tensed, holding her breath. The sound was not repeated. She peered back down the corridor. When her ears began to ring, she slowly exhaled. Still, no sound came. She remained vigilant a few moments longer, however, searching the darkness for any sign of shapes moving furtively around out there.

Nothing.

Though she felt slightly less on edge now, Audrey knew better than to chalk up what she'd heard as a product of her imagination. She'd definitely heard something, but that didn't mean it had been one of their pursuers. It might only have been a rat rooting around in the debris. Also, because she'd been focused on searching for security cameras, she couldn't be sure the sound's source had come from inside. Maybe it was on the other side of the door, out in the parking lot.

Then she heard the sound a second time and realized she'd been wrong.

It was coming from directly above her.

Audrey turned her face toward the ceiling again. Her mouth dropped slowly open. The gossamer-like webs moved, as if stirred by an unseen breeze. Then, the webbing parted, and Audrey screamed.

Something that had a human head and a swollen spider torso emerged from the webbing and dangled upside down, grinning at her. As she stared at it in shock, the creature flexed its spindly legs. Its neck began to elongate, lowering to a point halfway between the ceiling and the floor. Malleable segments of mutated cartilage stretched and popped, making a sound like the breaking of bones.

Whimpering, Audrey turned to run, but tripped over Celeste and dropped her gun. She scuttled backward, hands scrabbling across the floor, trying to find the weapon.

Then the spider-thing dropped to the floor and she screamed again.

SIXTEEN

Bradley writhed in agony as the man with the sledgehammer finished obliterating both of his legs from the knees down. His fingers clenched and clawed at the hard floor, and several of his fingernails peeled back from the pressure. His mouth gaped, but he was beyond screaming. All he could manage was a high-pitched, whispering rasp. He'd never known pain like this before. Until now, he'd been fortunate in that way. Never once had he broken a bone. Now, he'd broken dozens. There was something like twenty-six bones in the human foot. He remembered seeing that statistic on a YouTube video. That meant fifty-two bones just in his feet alone. And now those feet looked like red and pink jelly.

The sound the sledgehammer made as it struck him over and over again was somehow the worst part. It accentuated the pain.

He thrashed, mouth still working soundlessly, and stared up at the hideous, leering faces gathered around him. Even the figures who were relatively normal in physical appearance had an element of the grotesque in their gleeful expressions.

"Okay. I think that is enough, yes?" Captain Rat stared down at him, inspecting his handiwork with a proud expression. "No more running for you."

Bradley saw bits of himself glistening and dripping from the sledgehammer's head. Two figures rushed forward and began to apply tourniquets above his knees, but Bradley couldn't feel their administrations. He stopped trying to scream because it was pointless.

Stuart screamed instead.

Bradley had briefly, mercifully passed out after his second kneecap was pulverized. He wished now that he could return to that blissful state of unconsciousness, but it eluded him.

Some of the faces ringed around him moved away as the focus shifted from Bradley to Stuart, who was being held down on the floor several feet away. Because he was no longer capable of rising to his feet or posing any threat, he was no longer being restrained. When the two applying his tourniquets were finished with the task, they left Bradley sprawled and quivering there on the floor. He realized then, through the haze of pain, that he was unguarded.

Stuart screamed again.

Bradley lifted his head off the floor and whimpered when he caught sight of his companion.

Stuart stared at him in a pathetically beseeching way. He'd lost his glasses and his Lost Places cap. The glasses were shattered and broken on the floor beside him. The hat was now perched atop one of their tormentor's misshapen heads, looking every bit as precariously placed there as it had screwed down over Stuart's bushy mane.

Captain Rat stood directly over Stuart, with the handle of the sledgehammer held in an almost languid pose over his shoulder as he grinned.

"Now it is your turn. Although, I suspect you could do with more running in your life, yes?"

"Please," Stuart sobbed. "We didn't fucking do anything to you people. I don't understand. Why are you doing this?"

Realizing this moment of distraction might represent his last, best hope of survival, Bradley decided he would try crawling away in search of a place to hide. Making it over to the menswear department and the exit out to the service corridor was out of the question, but maybe he could curl up inside one of these old register stands. They were U-shaped and clearly a better option for hiding than any of the barren display kiosks. Maybe he could pull something over him to further obscure his location, a piece of debris of adequate size, a tarp, or whatever. A scan of the floor revealed nothing that would do the job, but perhaps he'd find something hidden away inside the stand that would work.

There was only one way to find out.

Crawl the fuck over there and find out.

But first he needed a moment to mentally prepare. Before he could crawl away, he would have to flip over onto his stomach. He didn't know if he could do that without screaming and drawing attention back his way. Hell, he didn't know if he'd be able to do it at all, a realization that sent more despair spiraling through him. What if he passed out from the effort? Or from blood loss?

What if I just lay here and die? That might be easier at this point.

Bradley closed his eyes and willed himself to die. When that didn't work, he tried holding his breath, hoping that he would pass out, but ultimately, his will to live was stronger, and he ended up gasping for air.

Oblivion, like unconsciousness, eluded him. Earlier, he'd been intent on avoiding death. Now, it was avoiding him.

Okay, then...fuck it.

After taking another deep breath and steadying himself as best he could, Bradley gritted his teeth and braced his hands on the floor. Before he could do that, however, maniacal cheers arose from the mob. Stuart's pleas for mercy were cut short by a wet, heavy sound. Bradley shuddered. He'd heard that sound before, when the sledgehammer had pulped his legs.

He glanced over at them, saw the sledgehammer rise, and saw it fall again. Stuart shrieked. The crowd cheered. None of them were looking at him. He had been forgotten. Realizing that this was his moment, Bradley gritted his teeth again. Then he shoved himself up and over onto his side. The pain was overwhelming. He bit through his bottom lip to keep from crying out.

He started pulling himself toward the register kiosk. His injured fingertips burned. The broken nails dangled from them via bits of cuticle and tissue. Despite this, he kept at it, flopping over onto his stomach and reaching out with his hands to slap at the floor and continue the excruciating progress. He slid slowly across the dirty tiles, leaving two trails of blood in his wake. Inch by painful inch, he paid a heavy physical toll for each fraction of ground he gained. Sweat broke out on his brow and slid down his temples into his eyes, stinging them. His arms and what was left of his legs quaked with the effort.

At one point, he must have blacked out, because when he looked up again to check his progress, he was surprised to see how close he'd gotten. The kiosk was only a few remaining feet away.

Meanwhile, behind him, Stuart continued to scream, and Captain Rat's freakshow mob continued to cheer each swing of the sledgehammer and subsequent sickening crunch of bone and cartilage. With each swing, however, there was less of that crunch and more of a sense of something heavy smacking into a pile of wet, mushy meat.

He wedged his bleeding fingertips into a seem between the floor tiles and pulled himself forward another inch. It occurred to him then that his tormentors would be able to follow his blood trail—and then cried out in terrified surprise when someone grabbed him by a leg stump and began to drag him back the way he'd come. He wailed, overcome with rage and disappointment as his palms repeatedly slapped at the floor in a desperate, futile effort to stay in place.

Another person hurried over and grabbed Bradley by his wrists, while at the same time the person who'd retrieved him grabbed hold of his other stump, roughly jerking both of his legs upward. Bradley screamed and began to blubber for mercy. His shrieks intensified as they lifted him into the air and began to swing his body back and forth between them. The louder he screamed, the harder they swung him. He rose higher and higher at the end of each upward arc.

During the next upward swing, Bradley caught a quick glimpse of Stuart. His friend had stopped screaming, but he wasn't dead yet. He whipped his head back and forth, but that was the extent of his reaction.

Captain Rat looked away from the ruin of Stuart's legs and back to Bradley. On Bradley's next swing up, he saw that the sadist had slung the sledgehammer back over his shoulder and was now returning to him.

"Now, now," Captain Rat called. "I think you should let him go."

He gasped as his two tormentors released him in nearly the precise same instant, at the height of another precipitously high upward arc. Bradley spun through the air and then plummeted back to the department store floor. The pain from the impact was even worse than what Captain Rat had wrought with his administrations. It felt like every nerve ending in his body exploded. He was wracked with convulsions as those electrical impulses sizzled through him. Coherent thought left him, and was replaced with hot, rushing fire. Bradley screamed and screamed and screamed and was aware of nothing other than the pain until, after several moments, he began to perceive the rumbling, throaty throb of a motorcycle's engine.

Bradley blinked, trying to clear his vision. Everything was blurry, and his eyes stung. Dimly, he realized that the blood vessels in his eyeballs had ruptured. He could still see, but everything had a haze over them—a film. It was like looking at something through wet cheesecloth.

Two freaks on motorcycles rode into the department store from deeper inside the mall. The painted-over glass doors had been opened and beyond them, he saw multicolored lights twinkling. They reminded him of old neon bar signs—except blurry. He felt a twinge of despair—which was a refreshing change from feeling only agony—when he spotted the open doors. The freaks had been in charge the entire time. They controlled the mall. Controlled the doors. Controlled the situation.

Bradley glanced down at the ruin below his knees.

They even controlled him.

The sound of the engines grew louder as the motorcycles rolled down the main aisle. Soon, they'd drawn close enough that Bradley could make out the features of the drivers despite his faulty vision. One was driven by a guy in a ripped-up old leather jacket and assless leather chaps over blue jeans. His hair was long and filthy, matted in places. Atop his head was a dented old Prussian helmet with a spike sticking up from the middle. He looked like some biker burnout from a long-gone era, but younger than a guy like that should be. Then again, his gear and the bike were probably stolen. The other motorcycle was driven by a completely hairless freak with scaled skin and swollen, tumorous growths bulging from one side of his face. He was clad only in a pair of shorts, and wore a pair of leather work gloves on his hands. His eyes seemed reptilian rather than human.

The latter motorcycle slowed, heading toward Bradley. The other swerved toward Stuart. The reptilian, as Bradley thought of him, positioned the rear wheel of his bike between Bradley's bleeding, splayed legs. Bradley watched in horror as the tire rolled over a dangling bit of meat from his foot, and shuddered when he realized that he couldn't even feel it.

His sense of dread intensified as he heard a rattling of chains from somewhere nearby. Gritting his teeth again, he craned his head as far around as he could manage and saw a man with tusks jutting from his face. Gripped in this figure's gnarled fingers was a length of heavy chain, with a hook attached to one end.

"Strip them," Captain Rat ordered.

Several figures scurried over to Bradley. He heard Stuart wail. The motorcycle engines revved louder, then idled again. He stared at the hook on the end of the chain, wondering about its purpose when his captors fell upon him again and began tearing at his clothes, casting them aside. His shoes and pants had melded with his flattened flesh in places, and ribbons of bloody skin were ripped away with the fabric. Again, he didn't feel it, even as he watched it happen. Bradley frowned in concern. He wasn't sure what that meant. Maybe he was in shock?

Of course I'm in shock. Also, my legs are paste now. There's probably no nerve endings left to feel anything.

Tusk-face knelt in front of him. Bradley's feelings of helplessness and vulnerability increased now that he was naked. His entire body—what was left of it—quivered. The mutant reached out with its free hand and cupped a palmful of Bradley's blood. Then, both it and the other hand holding the hook passed from Bradley's field of blurry vision.

Bradley sobbed as Tusk-face smeared his own blood between his ass cheeks.

A second later, the tip of the hook pressed against his puckered anus.

This Bradley felt. No amount of shock or blood loss or ruined nerve endings could block the horrible sensory input of this violation. His trembling increased at the first intrusion of the cold metal hook into his warm, tender flesh. He thrashed and screamed as Tusk-face slid the hook deeper with a surprising level of care, keeping the hook from piercing the interior of his anal canal until it was fully inserted. Bradley heard Stuart whimpering a little more loudly now and guessed the same thing was being done to him.

"I have good news and bad news," Captain Rat said, raising his voice over the idling motorcycles. "Which would you like to hear first?"

"F-fuck y-you…" Bradley spat.

"Very well. The bad news first then. There has been a slight change of plans. Scug and his…ilk, they are making trouble. Because of that, the doctor does not need you, as he is focused on other things. So, there is no need to keep you alive any longer."

Bradley worked his tongue, trying to wet his mouth enough to speak again. It was difficult to do given how hard his teeth were chattering.

"S-so k-kill usss, ass… asshole… G-get it… o-o-over with… already…"

"Ah, so you have changed your mind? You wish to die now? No more crawling away? No more hide and seek? This delights me. You are taking this unfortunate change of plans better than I thought you would. But… you have not heard the good news yet!"

Bradley's response was a mournful whine.

"The good news is that we promised you and your piggy friend a tour of our home. I am happy to say that has not changed. I will, unfortunately, not be able to give it to you myself, as I am needed elsewhere, but you will still get the tour before you die. So, rejoice, yes?"

Bradley flailed, shrieking as Tusk-face rotated the hook inside of him and jerked it savagely upward. At least two inches of sharp, solid steel pierced his innards. He felt a hot rush of blood flood his anal canal and gush out over the chain protruding from his ass. Worse, he could hear it splashing onto the floor, even over the jeers of the mob and the idling motorcycles. Absurdly, two competing, shock-induced thoughts occurred to Bradley in that moment. The first was to wonder how he possibly still had that much blood inside him. The second was that he would probably need a colostomy bag for the rest of his life.

Then he remembered that the rest of his life wasn't very long.

His crying intensified as he accepted that was what he was truly looking at here—the end of his life. No more denial. He was no longer able to find comfort in mindless denial. Cold, bleak reality decimated every last shred of magical thinking. This was it. The end.

And the worst part was that it was taking too long to happen.

Tusk-face gripped the chain and gave it a hard tug to test how well the hook was lodged inside him. Bradley screeched through gritted teeth, but did not beg. It was a small thing, a minor triumph, but at least it was something.

Behind him, Stuart yelled for his mother—a plaintive, pleading cry that brought only guttural laughter from their tormentors.

The reptilian backed the motorcycle up close enough that Bradley felt warm puffs of air from the chugging mufflers. The smell of exhaust was a pleasant distraction from the stench of his tormentors and the smell of his own blood. He closed his eyes, trying to enjoy the odor while Tusk-face wrapped the chain around his waist, and then weaved it through the ruins of his legs.

Bradley opened his eyes again, and saw the sadist checking the other end of the chain, making sure it was securely fastened to the back of the motorcycle. Then Tusk-face gave the reptilian a thumbs-up gesture.

The driver gave the bike some gas and the throaty sound of its engine revved higher. It began to roll across the floor, dragging Bradley along behind it. The level of acceleration wasn't significant yet, however, and he was able to crane his head around to observe his surroundings as he was slowly pulled toward the open glass doors. He got a look at Stuart, who was also now bare-assed and hooked in similar fashion to the other motorcycle. His friend turned a bleary gaze his way and a final moment of eye contact passed between them. Stuart mouthed the words "Fuck you" and turned his head away. Bradley sobbed in recognition of another hard reality—he was going to die with his only true friend hating him. What hurt even more was knowing he deserved every ounce of the man's contempt.

He turned his head as far to one side as he could manage and tried his best to hold it in that position. Curiously, he felt no pain other than a slight burning sensation, like when he scuffed a knee across carpet. In keeping a side of his face as flat as possible to the floor as it slid by beneath him, he was able to see a bit more of what was happening around him. Part of his shock-ravaged mind still wanted that, perhaps because it gave him an illusory sense of control. As long as he could see and anticipate what was coming, something primal and stubborn in his brain persisted in believing he could still avoid or ward off the worst of it.

The motorcycle passed through the open glass doors and out to the main part of the mall. After Bradley had cleared the doors, as well, the reptilian made a hard, sharp left, nearly tipping the bike. Bradley slewed sideways and smacked against the edge of a water fountain, resulting in another shockwave of pain.

They picked up speed slightly and rolled out onto the wide concourse outside the department store. Bradley's eyes rolled around in their sockets as he feverishly tried to absorb all the wild and unexpected sights inside the mall. Given his vision problems and his numbed state, his perceptions were like rapid-fire scrolling through Instagram or some other social media platform that relied on imagery. And each one of those images was more bizarre and horrific than the last.

The interior of the mall was characterized by an encroaching but intermittent gloom, broken by fires burning in metal trashcans and barrels, and lanterns and strands of twinkling Christmas lights strung about haphazardly. The storefronts stood open, and there was evidence of occupancy inside of them—bare mattresses and crude makeshift furniture. Decorations and other signs of obscene personalization adorned the walls. These varied from simple cryptic graffiti like "ANNIE CUNT" and "KILL EM ALL" to more elaborate things like bone chimes and a dreamcatcher fashioned with human hair and fingers instead of feathers. Open spaces between the storefronts were clustered with crudely made shacks, tents made from human skin, and dirty bedrolls.

The denizens of this place varied, as well. A minority looked normal, like Mark Hereford had. More straddled the genetic line, the way Captain Rat did. But the majority displayed mutations. Many of them looked barely more civilized than a pack of starving wild animals. That sensation of scrolling quickly through Instagram grew as he sped by them. A man with a penis growing out of his forehead. A woman with four breasts, upon which clung squalling tiny pink rats. A cyclops in a Lionel Ritchie shirt. Another reptilian who stood naked, and lacked any discernable genitalia. People with more than two arms or legs. People with no arms or legs. Something that looked like a human centipede. Conjoined twins and fetal twins and something that had physical characteristics of not just a man and a woman, but of an insect, as well. A figure that seemed more simian than human. Something else that looked like the famed Florida-based cryptid, the Bighead. Bradley, Stuart, Audrey and Chuck had once discussed taking a trip to Florida in search of the fabled creature. It would have been great content for the channel. But Celeste had vetoed that idea, adamantly declining to "go traipsing around in a fucking swamp in the armpit of America for a week."

He wondered where she was now.

Then he wondered if Stuart would get to see the Bighead, as well.

There was something wrong with his face. The burning sensation had stopped. Bradley tried to lick his lips, but part of them seemed to be missing. He tried to think of where they had gone. Could half of a person's lips just get up and walk away? Could a person live without half their lips? Looking at some of the freaks lined up to watch his progress, he supposed they could.

The denizens crowded close while still giving the motorcycle ample room to continue on its course. They spit on Bradley and hurled objects at him as he passed. They hooted and hollered and made hissing sounds. A few jumped up and down like monkeys. One person edged closer than the others and dumped the sludgy brown contents of a rusted metal bucket over his head. Bradley was pretty sure, judging by the smell and consistency that the slurry substance was a mixture of shit and piss. He blinked his eyes, trying to clear them. Some of it dribbled into his mangled mouth.

They approached an array of strange structures crowding the open area in the middle of the mall—winding, multicolored fiberglass chutes and slides, sections of which were covered with tunnel-like enclosures while the rest was open to the air. He realized that the interconnected pieces had once been a play area for children. Now, they were just one small part of a twisted and much larger nightmare funhouse.

The reptilian opened the throttle, giving the motorcycle more gas, and they picked up more speed. The friction against Bradley's face became noticeable again, but there was still no pain. The inside of his mouth rattled like a tin can filled with bloody teeth. He cried blood, gazing up at the twinkling Christmas lights. He realized that he would never see another Christmas, but that would be okay if he died soon.

The crowd hopped out of the way as the reptilian looped the bike around the concourse at the other end of the mall. Bradley's body slewed widely outward again. Seconds later, they were heading back the way they'd come, only now they were moving at an even greater rate of speed. This gave Bradley a chance to see the other side of the mall, and look at things he had missed before—except that there was something wrong with his eyes. He could only see out of one of them now. He tried to cry out, hoping someone would explain it to him, but his mouth felt so dry. He tried licking his lips again. He caught sight of what looked like a shredded sliver of reddish-purple beef liver. It seemed to be in the place where his tongue usually was, but that couldn't be right, could it? No tongue looked like that.

As the motorcycle rocketed down the concourse, Bradley realized that the driver was building up speed in preparation of taking the bike up one of those ramps in the playhouse area, and then apparently doing some stunt riding through the apparatus of chutes and curving slides.

Then he momentarily forgot about that as he caught sight of...

What had his name been again? The guy he'd come in here with? They'd grown up together. He should be able to remember his name. Stu something?

Stu something zipped past him, fastened to the other motorcycle by the same apparatus as Bradley. Bradley tried to raise his hand and wave, but he felt too weak.

More mall denizens scrambled out of the way as the reptilian brought the motorcycle back around to the concourse outside of Macy's, whipping Bradley's body against the withered remains of a large potted plant. Then the bike headed back the opposite way again, approaching what must have been nearly highway speeds.

Bradley's last semi-conscious thought was to wonder if maybe a police officer might pull the driver over for speeding. If so, he'd be saved.

His face sank lower, and suddenly, he could no longer breathe through his nose. With his only remaining ear, Bradley heard the thump of a tire hitting the base of a ramp and then he was rising up off the floor. The motorcycle thundered along one of the winding chutes, whipping Bradley's body against its curved sides. The reptilian rode with his head hunched down close to the handlebar, guiding the bike with a practiced command.

Then Bradley's head came apart.

By the time it was over, the rest of him had done the same.

Scug knocked on Annie's door. The rest of the occupants of the Westgate Galleria called her Annie Cunt, but she had always just been Annie to him. She lived in a space once occupied by a Suncoast Video store, though now the storefront was boarded over with plywood adorned by colorful spray paint art and profane slogans. The centerpiece of it all was a large rendering of a vagina, rich in realistic clinical detail along with other not-so-realistic touches, such as the outer labia lined with sharp teeth and the squirming maggots spilling out of the center.

Above him, on the mall's second floor, he heard motorcycles and cheering. Scug shook his head. He'd had enough of this place. He'd made the right decision. They were leaving. Tomorrow night. He had the urge to do it tonight, but sunrise was only a few more hours away, and he knew better than to guide his family through the outside world during daylight. They wouldn't make it a mile before being spotted.

Scowling, he knocked on the door again. While awaiting a response, he cast a glance back up at the ceiling again. It vibrated and rumbled. The motorcycle engines and cheers grew louder. Scug knew that none of his people were among the assembled throng. He'd told Gretch and Jax/Gax to round them up and, along with Klavo and Curd, begin making preparations to leave.

His scowl deepened. Scug didn't like fleeing, and that's what this was. He'd never run from anything in his life. But to stay here was to commit suicide. If that was the case, then they might as well have stayed in Philadelphia, emerging from the smoking, blackened ruins of the former home to be gunned down in broad daylight. Or worse.

Scug shifted impatiently. He turned his head from side to side, watching for any of the doctor's trusted lieutenants. Especially Captain Rat. Scug hated that skinny, pale fucker more than anyone.

He knew it wasn't over with Doctor Midnight. Scug had never seen the man allow insubordination, and he hadn't expected him to tonight. And yet, he'd allowed Scug and his companions to depart, with only a cursory—if severe—threat. The man must know that Scug wouldn't allow such a threat to stand. If, as he suspected, Doctor Midnight preparing to have him killed, then Captain Rat would most likely be the one assigned the task.

Scug turned back to Annie's door as it creaked open, and found himself staring into the double barrels of a rusty shotgun.

"Move it," he growled.

"Sorry, Scug. Heard all the noise and wasn't sure what was happening." The weapon was lowered, revealing an imposing figure. She was close to six and a half feet tall and weighed around three-hundred pounds. Her breasts were massive and unrestrained. She wore heavy combat boots, black pants held up by suspenders, and an unbuttoned Hawaiian shirt. The sides of her head were shaven clean, but she maintained a two-inch high black mohawk down the center of her scalp. Much of her exposed torso was covered in tattoos and there were more on her face and scalp.

When he didn't respond, she asked, "What is happening, anyway?"

He shook his head. "Assholes acting up. That's all."

"Makes sense, I suppose. The natives been getting restless lately."

"Assholes," he repeated.

"Aw, you can't blame them. Everyone likes a good show. Is it really any different than the movies your group has been making over there in the theater?"

"Yes. This is too much. It's going to bring trouble."

"It never has before."

"It will. That's what I want to talk to you about."

"So talk."

He shook his head. "Not out here. Too many eyes."

Annie studied him for a moment. Then she stepped back and waved him in with the lowered barrel of the shotgun. Scug stomped into her dwelling without further prompting. Annie immediately closed and secured the door behind them, a process that involved engaging the latches and bolts of multiple heavy-duty locks. When she was finished, Annie moved away from the door with the shotgun still balanced in the crook of her arm. She turned and indicated for him to follow with a tilt of her chin.

As he did with every visit to Annie's, Scug looked around, impressed by the size of the place. In terms of square footage, the former video store was just shy of being fully twice the size of most of the mall's other standard-sized spaces. The only larger space on the first floor—not counting the movie theater occupied by Scug and his clan—was the old video game arcade, and that was the domain of Captain Rat and his band of vicious followers. Annie and the Captain were among Midnight's top lieutenants, and both figures were almost as confoundingly mysterious as the doctor himself. Over the past decade, Scug had heard rumors about both. In Annie's case, she had supposedly worked in similar capacities with other necessarily underground criminal enterprises, but Scug didn't know anything about that. He'd interacted extensively with her over the years, and was on friendly terms. but had never pressed the woman for details about her past, because he simply didn't care.

The only thing he knew for certain was what Annie had revealed one drunken evening while the two of them were carving up a junkie who had made the mistake of trying to break into the mall. She'd told him about a woman in the outside world named Mabel, who was quite the connoisseur when it came to the preparation and cooking of human flesh. This woman had put Annie in contact with a group of wealthy elites who had similar predilections, and for a time, Annie had made good money supplying them with livestock to satisfy their cravings. Annie had told him then that human trafficking was her specialty. She made a living by moving people around the country. Currently, she procured victims for Midnight. Before him, she'd done it for others. She had a far-reaching network and was unmatched at making people disappear.

Scug hoped that was still the case.

Annie did not dwell alone in this place. The old video store was also home to her inner circle of sycophants and sex slaves, all of whom were female. Only a small handful of inhabitants who identified as men were ever allowed entry into Annie's sector of the mall, and even then, only temporarily. Some who entered never left again, at least not alive. Coming here alone was always a risky thing, just as it was when visiting Captain Rat or the doctor himself in their private lairs without bringing along some backup. Despite this, Scug never worried when visiting her. The two had formed a mutual respect and friendship over the last eleven years.

There wasn't much reason to think today would be any different, except that he was seeking advice and possibly even assistance on a level well beyond anything he'd ever sought before. There was also the very real possibility that Midnight was already moving against him, and that Annie was privy to that given her place in the hierarchy.

As he followed Annie deeper into the store's dimly lit interior, Scug was aware of numerous sets of eyes glancing his way. Women lounging around on moldering, low-slung sofas and makeshift divans tracked his progress across the room with suspicious, smoldering gazes. Some, like Annie, could have passed as an outsider. Others had more in common with Scug's clan, though they were no relation. There were lots of pale faces and black eye makeup, and they all wore stockings and lingerie or nothing at all. Another thing they shared in common was their general age range. Annie liked them young. Some of these girls were still teenagers, while the oldest among them were somewhere in their late twenties.

Scug passed within a few feet of one sofa, upon which a nude girl with platinum blonde hair lay on her back with her long, triple-jointed legs splayed in the air. Another young woman, this one a large-breasted redhead wearing only black stockings, was on her knees at the side of the sofa with her face buried between the legs of the moaning blonde. As he drew near, the redhead paused in her administrations and turned her face toward him. Smiling, she flicked a pointed, double tongue in his direction. The blonde stretched her leg out and slipped a foot beneath the hem of Scug's dress.

It took every bit of willpower he had to ignore this provocation. He picked up his pace and felt the woman's toes slide away from the bare skin beneath his dress. The blonde's mocking laughter echoed behind him. Scug wanted to drag her out of this place, skin her alive, and make a completely new outfit from her tanned flesh.

Instead, he walked on.

In a few more moments, they entered a narrow hallway at the back of the store and soon arrived at the door to Annie's private office, which, according to a faded, rusty sign on the wall, had formerly belonged to the store's manager. A horned female guard was positioned outside the closed door. Unlike the girls lounging around in the main room, there was nothing languorous about her. Clad all in tight black from head to toe, she had an athletic build and short, spiky blonde hair that turned to brown around the base of her protuberances. A handgun rested in a holster at her hip and a knife with a long blade was in a sheath attached to her belt. She stood ramrod-straight and her demeanor was all business. Her gaze betrayed no hint of emotion as she glanced briefly at Scug before shifting her attention fully to her boss. At a nod from Annie, she unlocked the door to the office, pushed it open, and stepped aside.

Scug entered first after another nod from Annie, who then followed him inside and closed the door. There wasn't much room to maneuver in the cramped space, some of which was taken up by an old metal desk and the chairs on either side of it. More of it was taken up by tall stacks of cash money piled up on two pallets at the back of the room. Those things in conjunction with the stockpile of assault rifles and ammo crates left little room for visitors, much less for the female gimp chained to a spot on the wall directly adjacent to the area behind Annie's desk. The slender but shapely gimp wore a head-enveloping black leather mask and nothing else. She did, however, have a piercing in each nipple—two metal rings connected by a slender silver chain. The girl's green eyes stared at him through narrow eyeholes. The zipper across the mouth was closed. She sat in a squat with her back against the wall, with nothing in her body language indicating distress.

Strange music played softly from an ancient boom box atop the desk. Scug had never heard anything like it before. It was sonic and hypnotic, lacking guitars or any other sort of instrument he recognized.

"You like it?"

Scug shrugged. "What is it?"

"The musician's name is Xander Harris."

"It is not like other music."

"It's a genre. Electronic or synth pop or some such shit. But I like it. The song is called Tanned Skin Dress."

"Tanned Skin Dress?" Despite his unease, Scug grinned. "I like that."

"I thought you might."

Annie settled into a large leather swivel chair behind the desk. It creaked and groaned. Jagged springs stuck out of its back, but she didn't seem to mind. She turned off the music and then summoned the gimp to her with a flex of her forefinger. The girl pushed away from the wall and scuttled across the floor. Then she lay her head in Annie's lap. The mistress drummed the fingers of her left hand along a side of the head mask and stared at Scug on the other side of the desk.

He stood stock still, unsure of how to proceed. He was unaccustomed to resolving things through conversation, and even more unaccustomed to asking for help.

Now, he had to try both.

Annie smirked. "Sit down, Scug."

Grunting, Scug sat.

Annie squirmed around a bit and leaned back in her big chair. She braced the double barrels of the shotgun against the edge of her desk, aiming them at a spot just above Scug's head.

"So what brings you here today? Something about our rambunctious populace, would be my guess."

"He told you already."

She nodded. "If you mean Doctor Midnight, yes, he did. But what you say here stays between me and you. Speak your mind."

"They're taking too many from outside. People who will be missed."

"Your own clan took someone tonight. From what I'm told, he will be missed, as well."

"But we weren't the ones who let him in. He shouldn't have gotten inside in the first place. For years, things were done more carefully. The system worked. You helped with that. Taking people from far away instead of close to home. Couldn't be linked back to here. That was good. We need to get back to that before it's too late."

"But you already believe it is too late, don't you?"

"Yes."

Annie pursed her lips and made a contemplative expression. "Hmm. Tell you the truth, I've noticed a lot of the same shit and it worries me, too. And if it worries me, you know it's a legit fucking concern."

"Tell that to Midnight."

Annie laughed. "You tried. How did that work out for you?"

"You know already."

"That I do. And I know it would go about the same for me."

"Probably."

"Did you also know that in addition to the outsider your clan killed, they also offed one of Captain Rat's flunkies tonight?"

Scug hesitated. "Who?"

"If you mean who from your clan, I'm told it was Curd, Klavo, and the kid."

"Lorok…"

She nodded. "They killed that three-armed dipshit. Sounds to me like he had it coming. And don't worry. They got rid of the body. Rat doesn't know. Neither does Midnight."

"Will you tell them?"

"Why should I? Nothing in it for me. I like yu, Scug. Plus, you came to me for help."

He nodded. "Yes."

"So…what would you have me do, then?"

"You move people. You told me once that you are a human trafficker. I want your help. I want to move my family out of here."

She grinned, making a sweeping gesture. "You fled the city and escaped to the suburbs. Now you want to leave the suburbs, too?"

"Yes."

"And go where, Scug?"

He shrugged. "Some place private. Some place where people will leave us alone."

"And you want me to help you."

He nodded. Then, after a long pause, Scug said a word he had never before uttered.

"Please."

Annie's smile vanished. "You know Midnight wouldn't allow that, right?"

He didn't respond.

She lifted the gimp's head off her lap and gave the girl a hard shove away from her. The girl yelped in surprise as she landed on the floor. The back of her head bounced off the wall. It was hard to tell through the mask's narrow eyeholes, but it sounded like she was crying. She said something that came out muffled behind the closed zipper over her mouth.

"You know you're not supposed to talk when that zipper's shut," Annie told her. "That's the rule. Done warned your ass about that too many times."

She pointed the double-barreled shotgun at the girl's head. The girl shrieked in muffled dismay and started rapidly shaking her head back and forth.

The shotgun roared and blew her head apart, shredding the mask along with it.

The door to the office burst open and the guard with the spiky blonde hair rushed in, weapon at the ready. Annie shouted reassurance and waved her away. The guard backed out of the room and closed the door again. On her way out, she said something but Scug couldn't hear what it was over the ringing in his ears.

Annie glanced at him and shrugged.

He did the same.

They both waited for a few moments, staring silently at one another and waiting for their hearing to return.

"Sorry about that," Annie said, "but I'm kind of like you in that I don't have a lot of patience with people who can't follow simple rules, even if they're really fucking great at eating me out. Like that bitch was. Also, I'm pretty sure she was a plant from either Midnight or the Captain, sent here to keep tabs on me."

Scug wasn't sure how a person who evidently spent a lot of time chained up in Annie's office could relay information to anyone else, but he didn't care. He was far more interested in the implications of what she was saying.

"You didn't want her to hear what you were about to say."

Annie smiled. "You're good."

He shrugged.

Annie set the still smoking shotgun down on the cluttered surface of the desk and opened the top drawer to take out a big bottle. She screwed the cap off the bottle and took a big swig from it before leaning back in her chair again. The bottle had no label, but he knew by the smell that it was alcohol.

"Here's the thing, Scug. You're right. The situation here has become untenable."

"I don't know what that is."

"Untenable? That means it's not working anymore and there's no real hope of fixing it."

"So you…agree with me?"

Annie nodded. "I do. I've been having the same thoughts you're having. I'm not one of the doctor's fanatics. All this talk of transformative energies, and transcendence, and the blending of the occult and science? It's all bullshit. I've stayed here because the situation worked for me. It was useful. But not anymore. It's my considered opinion that the time has come to move on to greener pastures. You know what I mean?"

Scug shook his head. "Not exactly."

Annie took another big slug from the bottle and wiped her mouth with the back of a hand. "Then let me lay it out for you."

She started telling him what she had in mind.

Scug listened.

It wasn't long before he decided that he liked what he was hearing.

Eventually, he smiled.

And hoped.

SEVENTEEN

Conor guided Lizzie through the dark landscape of the underground parking garage, occasionally steering her around chunks of fallen concrete with pieces of rebar protruding from them. Things scurried around in the darkness, making clicking, insectile sounds. Once she heard a wave of chittering noise that made her think of swarming cicadas, only with an element of something alien in it, a high-pitched warbling that set her teeth on edge. The sound cut off abruptly.

Despite the endless parade of depravity she'd witnessed and participated in thus far, the strange sounds left Lizzie unnerved. She pushed the unease aside, however. Nothing would sway her from this path. She needed to set aside instinctive fear and embrace her new reality.

Conor appeared blithely unconcerned by the presence of the unseen creatures. He was even whistling at a low volume, a repeating series of several notes that never varied. Lizzie had always thought of whistling as a habit of carefree individuals, but after a while she wondered whether there might be something purposeful about it in this case, something beyond idle noise-making.

"Can I ask you something, Conor?"

"Mm-hmm?"

"Is the whistling to keep them away?"

He chuckled. "Figured that out, did you? Amazing. You came in here high as a kite, strung out and reeking of booze. I honestly didn't think you'd be anything other than more fodder for the operating theater. But first impressions aren't always accurate impressions, I guess. Unless you're the doctor. He sees the truth behind every facade, even ones hidden away in the minds of people like you. Hidden away so well you're unaware they're even there until the doctor shines a light on them?"

Lizzie frowned. "How does he do that?"

"His third eye. The one inside his head."

"Third eye?" Lizzie's frown deepened. "But...I don't understand. You mean like some of the freaks I saw out there? Is that why he wears the mask? Does he have a third eye?"

The noises in the darkness increased again. Instead of responding, to her, Conor resumed whistling. After a moment, the sounds faded.

"Seriously," Lizzie said, "I don't understand."

Conor stopped whistling again. "You don't need to. Not yet. Understanding will come after you meet with the doctor. I could try to explain it to you, but it would sound so abstract. Better to see for yourself."

This only served to heighten Lizzie's sense of puzzlement. He sounded like a politician in the way he danced around a subject while never providing an actual answer. She considered pressing him on the matter, but decided not to press her luck.

They walked on, threading their way through the shadows. In the ensuing moments of conversational silence, their footsteps echoed. The clicking sounds returned, but they had a more agitated quality. They also seemed to be closer.

"Not much farther now," Conor told her.

Something grazed against the back of Lizzie's leg. She gasped in fright. The touch was wispy and feather-light, but there was something creepily insinuating about it—the whispered suggestion of a potential for great violence.

Chuckling again, Conor resumed whistling. As soon as he did, the unseen thing pulled away from her, clicking what sounded like mandibles as it retreated into the darkness.

Swallowing hard, Lizzie listened more intently to the notes Conor was making, committing them to memory. Then she pursed her lips and tried to repeat them.

"Very good!" His tone rung with genuine surprise. "You'll have the hang of this place in no time."

She saw a glimmer ahead of them—the soft glow of artificial lighting hidden behind something translucent. As they drew closer to the source, she spotted white sheets hanging from metal rods, which had been installed in a zigzagging pattern parallel to each other. The sheets formed a gently billowing corridor of cloth. She wondered about the source of the airflow. Whether it was artificial or blowing in from some hole in the crumbling structural frame of the place was hard to tell.

The corridor was too narrow for them to walk side-by-side, so Conor moved ahead of her to lead the way. Lizzie followed without hesitation. At no point did she consider turning and fleeing while his back was to her. She didn't want to run, but even if she had wanted to escape, the risk of encountering the scuttling, clicking things wasn't worth it.

Within the corridor, bare light bulbs had been screwed into sockets at the end of long cables dangling from above. Each bulb was spaced about twenty feet apart. Several of them were burned out, and the ones still working were decidedly low wattage, serving only to light the way, rather than dispel the darkness.

After what she gauged to be about ten minutes of walking, they arrived at the end of the cloth corridor. Beyond that point, a gray tent occupied a section of floor uncluttered by debris. It was massive—unlike the small two-person tent she'd camped out in her backyard as a child. This one stood roughly twelve feet tall and was wide enough to park several automobiles inside. More faint light was visible through the tan-colored fabric of the tent, spotlighting the indistinct outline of a figure moving around inside.

On impulse, Lizzie started toward the tent, but Conor stopped her with a hand on her elbow.

"Hold on. I have to announce you first."

"Like, seriously?"

He shrugged. "The doctor is a stickler for formality."

Moving away from her, he went to the tent and pushed through the open flaps. Lizzie heard muffled voices, too low and indistinct to decipher, but in another moment Conor reemerged and held a flap open, waving her inside.

"Come along."

Lizzie took a deep breath, held it, and then exhaled. She hesitated only an instant before shuffling forward. She felt a heady mix of trepidation, excitement and fear. She knew it was possible that a cruel joke was being played on her. Maybe they would kill her. Perhaps it merely amused the doctor to give her a false sense of hope and when she got inside the tent he would force her to participate in the sadistic mutilation of a third helpless victim. Although she hadn't been here long, she was pretty sure instilling that level of psychological torment in a person was the kind of thing he would relish doing, particularly after what they'd had her do to the man and then the woman earlier. However, while she couldn't dismiss the idea as a very real possibility, Lizzie strongly suspected that the doctor was precisely what he presented himself as, at least where she was concerned. He was a deeply deranged and eccentric man of mysterious means who, for reasons only he fully understood, occasionally opted to recruit acolytes from the ranks of new arrivals here instead of killing them or reconfiguring their bodies in grotesquely unusual ways. And she was nothing more or less than his latest recruit, albeit one still in need of evaluation—whatever that involved—and final approval.

As she neared the open tent flap, Conor nodded encouragingly while eyeing her with an eager expression and obvious sexual excitement. This didn't bother her. It wasn't like a creeper popping uninvited into her mentions on Twitter or some random perv leering at her on the street. She had a sense that his excitement had to do more with whatever was about to happen inside the tent than it did with her nudity. Judging by his expression and body language, it was raw, barely constrained, vicarious anticipation. He couldn't wait for her to experience whatever awaited her in the tent's confines. Whatever it was, she suspected her evaluation would involve far more than just answering questions or filling out forms, like in some normal job.

She stepped through the opening and stumbled, unsure of what she was seeing.

"What the hell…?"

Lizzie gaped. The woman she'd operated on earlier floated in midair in the center of the tent, held aloft by no visible means. There was no harness or strings. No straps were fastened to her limbs. She was just...floating, stretched out on her back as if she were lounging on an inflatable swimming pool raft. Her hands and feet appeared to drift languidly in invisible water. The octopus tentacles protruding from her vagina also appeared to float and writhe in that same slow, languid way. The eyes of the octopus, visible in the portion of its head sewn into place in the middle of the woman's abdomen, stared at Lizzie as she took a tentative step forward with an almost accusatory glare.

No, she thought. That's just me projecting human thoughts and feelings into the unknowable mind of a sea creature.

But the gaze still unnerved her.

The floating woman did not appear to be in pain. Indeed, the look on her face seemed euphoric, almost rapturous. Her mouth moved, slowly opening and closing over and over again. Her extended jaw made an elongated O of her mouth before reducing to a flat-line of pressed-together lips. This made her resemble a marine creature breathing through flapping gills, an appropriate impression in light of the new element included in her physical composition.

At the rear of the tent was a machine, emitting a low thrumming sound. Dozens of glowing tubes arranged in a circle rose from the surface of a rectangular metal base with vents in its sides. The base was the approximate size of a standard HVAC unit, a thing it strongly resembled, though the array of strange gauges and dials embedded in one side made it obvious its function was something other than circulating heat and cool air. The glowing tubes were of various widths and heights. Every so often the intensity of the glow would wax and wane in revolving, alternating patterns. Though the tubes produced no sound—that low thrum came from the base of the thing—there was something almost melodic in those light patterns, like watching the lights on a stereo equalizer go up and down with the beat of music. Curling wisps of steam drifted from the tubes, evaporating as soon as they hit the air.

The rest of the tent was vacant. Disconcertingly so, given its size. Lizzie frowned, glancing around. In fact, the ample space seemed quite a bit bigger than it should be based on her memory of the tent's exterior. Also, the interior was well-illuminated, but there was no sign of a light source other than the glowing tubes. She noticed that the level of light did not diminish or brighten as the tubes cycled through their patterns. It was as if daylight simply existed inside the tent.

There was no sign of Dr. Midnight, or anyone else for that matter. This, of course, stood in direct contradiction to what she'd been told. She had been brought here for an evaluation. To see the doctor. But where was he? She moved a few feet closer to the floating woman before turning in a slow circle again to confirm his absence. He couldn't be lurking behind the strange machine. Even without his high heels, Midnight was too tall to crouch down unseen behind it. But then again, size and spatial dimensions seemed different inside this place, so she supposed it was possible. Deciding to check and be sure, she slowly approached the unit. The floating woman didn't react as she walked past her. Lizzie's head started to hurt when she got within a few feet of the machine. The throbbing grew worse the closer she got. She quickly verified Midnight's absence and then backed away. The pain instantly vanished, as if a switch had been flipped in her brain.

Her curiosity mounted, but she was strangely unafraid. She gave the floating woman a wide berth again as she headed back the way she'd come, with the intention of poking her head out between the tent flaps to ask Conor what was happening.

But the flaps were gone.

It wasn't that Conor had zipped them shut. They were just no longer there. Vanished.

Lizzie whimpered—a small, quiet sound—not out of fear, but out of anticipation and awe. Then she took in her surroundings again, but this time she really looked.

She was not inside a tent at all. The flaps weren't the only thing that had disappeared. The canvas walls were gone, as well, replaced by the opaque glass of a large dome.

Alternate dimension, she thought, like that Labyrinth thing the crazies online are always ranting about? Or maybe some kind of alien ship or base?

Whatever the case, she had no control over the situation, so she decided not to worry about it. What would be...would be. Lizzie again returned to the approximate center of the enclosed space to better observe the floating woman and the octopus inside of her.

She wondered if Midnight was watching her. She saw no cameras, but that meant nothing in a place where reality itself could not be trusted. Yes, she suspected, he probably was watching her, undoubtedly gauging her actions and reactions to this new set of strange circumstances. She had no idea what he expected or desired of her, but she knew she couldn't just hang out and wait for him to finally show up.

He would expect her to do something.

But what?

She stood close enough to touch the levitating patient, but refrained from doing so. A tingling sensation rippled over her skin, warm and not altogether unpleasant. She assumed she'd entered the field of whatever force was suspending the woman in midair, but her own feet remained firmly on the ground. The motion of the octopus's tentacles grew more active as she moved into position between the floating woman's splayed legs. Lizzie inched closer still. The slimy tentacles reached out and caressed her bare flesh, pulling her gently closer.

See, she thought. It wasn't glaring at you at all. It's being nice.

The floating woman lifted her head and stared at Lizzie. She still had that same rapturous expression on her face, and her mouth still slowly opened and closed to repeatedly form that elongated O. Her skin shimmered in a way that made it look as if it'd been sprinkled with glitter.

"I'm assuming you can hear me, Doctor," she said aloud. "So…like, this woman is no longer quite human, right? And the octopus isn't just an octopus anymore either. They're not just two things that we stitched together. Not a conjoining of woman and aquatic creature. This is something transformed, right? A new thing entirely! A true hybrid."

If the doctor was monitoring, there was no indication from him.

The octopus, however, responded.

Lizzie gasped as a tentacle slid between her legs and pushed into her vagina. The sensation was surprising, but she didn't get a sense that the intrusion was delivered with violent intent. There was an insistency to it for sure, but not a harmful one. She winced, taking in a sharp breath. She worried that its suckers would damage her tissue—except that didn't seem to be happening. She felt them there, but they were subtle, more like bumps than suckers.

Ribbed…for my pleasure?

Cautiously, she exhaled and tried to relax. When she felt

more confident, Lizzie reached out and gripped the floating woman's thighs, holding on tight as the tentacle probed even deeper. Lizzie closed her eyes. She felt the appendage repeatedly swell and contract inside of her, sending wave after powerful wave of pleasure through her body. She cried out and arched her back as her nipples stiffened, the motion of her pelvis allowed the creature to penetrate her even more deeply. Then, another tentacle curled around her and brushed against her anus. After a moment, it entered her there, as well. Lizzie pulled even harder at the woman's thighs, smashing herself against the levitating form as ecstasy overwhelmed her. The floating woman thrust herself against Lizzie in response, arching her own back and opening her mouth even wider than before in a soundless gasp of orgasm. Dimly, Lizzie wondered if the probing tentacles functioned as pleasure receptors in some way. The woman reached up and pawed at Lizzie's breasts, making her squeal with delight.

All thought left Lizzie in that moment. She didn't think about staying alive or dying. She didn't remember Logan or Cam or Tara. She didn't think about her father and what he'd done to her. All she cared about as the bizarre coupling continued was the immense pleasure she felt—something beyond anything she'd ever imagined or experienced before. This was better than any high from any drug. She never wanted it to end. She could happily spend eternity locked inside this exquisite moment, forever having these most delicious sensations.

These were all feelings she knew would have repulsed her before today. Just the thought would have made her physically ill. And yet, Lizzie didn't care. Just like the floating woman, she wasn't the person she'd been anymore. And that was okay.

She was…transformed.

She became aware of someone standing right behind her, but she was unable to turn her head, locked in the throes of passion.

"Excellent."

She recognized the speaker as Dr. Midnight. She did not fear him. Her state of ecstasy was not diminished. If anything, it only intensified.

"Most excellent, indeed."

His rough hands took hold of her at the waist. The tentacle withdrew from her ass. The other appendage continued to pulse rhythmically. Lizzie tightened her pelvic floor muscles in response. Then she felt Midnight's stiff cock slide into the orifice the other tendril had just slipped from. Lizzie's eyes widened. She bit her lip and tried not to scream. The doctor was far bigger than the octopus had been. His hands slid up to her breasts, his fingers spreading wide over them as he wrenched her torso backward and put his mouth to her ear. From this proximity, she could immediately tell that he was no longer wearing the Richard Nixon mask. She tried to turn her head to face him, but he took one hand from her breast and stopped her. After a moment, he released her. Nodding to indicate understanding, Lizzie faced forward.

His breath tickled her ear as he continued to thrust into her from behind. "You are the one I've been waiting for all this time. My special one. The one capable of transcending and opening the rift into the Nothing."

"The Nothing?" Lizzie panted.

More tentacles surged forward, and wrapped around her, sliding over her abdomen and moving upward between her breasts. She glanced down and realized that these tendrils did not belong to the octopus. They felt subtly different against her sweaty flesh, and smelled different as well. The suckers lining their insides were much larger, and pulled at her skin in a more deliberate way. It was like being groped by a particularly ardent lover. But where were they coming from? Who did they belong to?

Then she realized…they were attached to Doctor Midnight. But how? How could he have possibly kept them hidden until now? Another wave of pleasure rolled over her, and Lizzie's thoughts grew hazy again. It didn't matter. Maybe they were retractable, or only visible here within this strange space. Maybe that was why he and some of his underlings wore masks—to hide that they weren't human. She didn't care. All she cared about was how he made her feel.

The doctor's tongue flicked out, teasing her earlobe. Lizzie sighed and writhed against him.

"You've never felt at home in this world, have you? Don't bother answering. We both know it's true. It's there in the way you've never quite fit in anywhere, and in that emotional disconnect that's always with you. You can't form real relationships with others of your kind because they could never understand you. So you numb yourself to the pain of severe alienation any way you can, committing slow suicide."

He thrust again, and then continued.

"What if I were to tell you that there is another way? A way to escape the rotten realm of your birth and experience joy unlike anything you ever imagined. Would that interest you?"

One of the doctor's tentacles slid over her left breast, taking her inflamed nipple into one of its suckers. She moaned in equal measures of pain and pleasure, turning her head to the side and catching a fleeting glimpse of green-tinged flesh.

"Yes. Yes, please. I'll do anything for you."

The doctor made a throaty sound. "Good."

Lizzie felt the octopus tentacle retract from her vagina. She gasped at the sudden sensation. A second later, it snaked behind her and wormed its way into her anus, wrapping its length around the doctor's pulsing shaft. Her eyes went wide, and she whimpered at the pain. Midnight shuddered against her, while that tentacle sucker pulled harder at her nipple. She licked her lips and allowed her head to loll around on her shoulders, nearly losing consciousness from the overwhelming sensation.

"The wait has gone on too long," the doctor groaned. "The process must begin soon."

She somehow found her voice. "What do I have to do? How do I... transcend?"

"When you arrived here, you recognized my masterpiece for what it was. You knew its name in your mind. That was how I knew."

She paused for a moment. "The Pillar of Souls?"

"Exactly. To transcend, you must scale the Pillar."

"What?"

Another of the doctor's tentacles came into her field of vision, hovering in the air like the head of an agitated cobra as it moved between the floating woman's splayed legs.

"You must climb the Pillar of Souls all the way to the top. Understand, it is more than it appears. You see it only as a tangle of bodies—welded flesh molded and shaped. But it is really a powerful signal tower capable of tearing holes between worlds."

Lizzie frowned. "But…how?"

The hovering tentacle extended to a length well beyond what Lizzie would have guessed was possible. Soon the tip descended, touching the levitating woman's sternum before sliding between her breasts. In another moment, it coiled around her throat and squeezed. The doctor groaned, his other tentacles rippling against Lizzie's skin.

"The Pillar transmits signals into the Nothing, producing vibrations that weaken the barrier between worlds—between all the different levels of reality. Those vibrations are amplified by human suffering. Think about everything that has happened this year. A global pandemic. Social and political upheaval. Riots. Racial violence. Authoritarian oppression. Economic woes. Natural disasters are occurring on an unprecedented scale—fires, droughts, hurricanes, earthquakes and more. Whole species are going extinct. There are more of you starving and dying and suffering than ever before. Conditions for finally tearing open the rift have never been so ripe."

"And then what?" Lizzie asked.

"Then? Then, we can finally go home. We can return to the Nothing. Will you scale the Pillar and do that for us? Will you open the way home for all of us?"

"I will," Lizzie promised. "Like I told you already, I'll do anything."

"Excellent." The doctor made another distorted chuckle. "Would you like to watch me destroy your creation?"

Lizzie looked at the floating woman's face. Her expression somehow remained serenely ecstatic despite the fact that her cheeks and the skin of her throat had turned a striking shade of purple as the tentacle continued constricting.

Lizzie reached between her legs and began to rub her clit.

"Yes," she moaned. "Do it!"

The doctor's long tentacle rippled and flexed again and popped the levitating woman's head off her shoulders like it was nothing more than a dandelion from its stem. Geysers of blood sprayed from the squished, pinched stump while the severed head shot across the room, thumped against the opaque glass of the dome, and dropped to the floor. Lizzie tossed her head back and unleashed scream after scream as the most powerful orgasm of her life racked her quivering body.

This time, she did lose consciousness.

When she came back to herself and was cognizant again, the doctor had disappeared. So had everything else. Lizzie was back in the tent again and Conor was there waiting.

"Are you ready?" he asked.

She nodded. "Take me there."

To the Pillar of Souls.

Where her ascension would soon begin.

EIGHTEEN

The human-spider hybrid made clicking, insectile sounds as it used its hairy spider legs to turn about on the floor. Incredibly, it sneered at her with an all-too-evident malignant intelligence. Nothing that looked like this monstrosity should be capable of coherent thought, let alone such a calculating malice. But then again, nothing that looked like this creature should exist at all. This wasn't a mutant or a freak. This wasn't some unfortunate series of birth defects. This thing, whatever its origin, was simply…wrong. It was a thing that should not be. And yet it was.

Its bloated head wobbled back and forth at the top of its elongated neck, like cornstalks swaying in a strong breeze. The prong-like appendage at the base of its bloated torso swelled in a way that was deeply unsettling. It was black and glistening, leaking some kind of fluid, but Audrey couldn't tell whether it was a stinger, a sexual organ, or some horrific combination of both.

The thing opened its mouth wider, and the insectile sounds grew frighteningly louder—a succession of distorted, warbling clicks and chirps. Audrey knew that spiders weren't technically considered insects, though as far as she was concerned they fell under the broader general umbrella of disgusting fucking bugs. She also couldn't recall any specific noises that she had ever associated with spiders. They were silent, in her experience. She supposed they probably did make sounds that weren't audible to human ears, but she doubted those sounds were anything like these.

She trembled, looking again into those intelligent eyes.

Could the thing be trying to communicate with her? After all, while it clearly had arachnid characteristics, it also had human traits, as well. Was it possible that what she was hearing was the human part of the creature ineffectually attempting to communicate via a spider's vocal chords?

Regardless, she had no intention of finding out.

Audrey raised the Sig Sauer.

Before she could pull the trigger, however, the thing skittered about again on its wispy, furry legs and crawled atop Celeste's corpse.

It's more interested in Celeste than it is me, she thought. Maybe it's peaceful?

No. Nothing about the creature radiated peace and harmony. But then another thought occurred to her. If it was about to devour Celeste's corpse, that would make a homicide investigation all the more difficult, in the unlikely chance that Celeste was ever actually found.

Common sense dictated shooting the beast and then fleeing, but the electrified exit door was to her back, and the monster was blocking her way down the corridor.

While Audrey debated what to do, the thing rose up on its numerous legs and positioned the prong-like appendage against Celeste's abdomen. More of that noxious-smelling fluid oozed from it now, as if the creature had turned on a spigot inside of itself. It gushed over Celeste's stomach and immediately began to dissolve the outer layer of her flesh. Steam rose from her body. The hallways filled with an acrid, burning stench. Seeing Celeste's flesh liquefy and sluice away in pink, fatty rivulets made Audrey nauseous. Given everything she had seen and experienced and engaged in tonight, she was surprised that there were still things that could turn her stomach.

As soon as the hole in Celeste's belly was of sufficient size, the spider-thing inserted the appendage and began to thrust in and out in a crude almost sexual manner. It made a weird, high-pitched breathing sound as it pumped away. The creature's thrusting soon reached a state of frenzy. Its long, bloated torso rocked back and forth. The gyrations grew faster, and its breathing became more labored. The beast's head whipped about as its fleshy stalk of a neck stretched even further, accompanied by more popping sounds as pieces of cartilage and tissue shifted. Then the head began to bounce off the walls of the corridor, as if the beast had lost control.

Audrey tensed, ready to skitter around it and flee but the creature's cries abruptly turned shriller. She cringed, reflexively clasping her hands to her ears. She accidentally struck the side of her own head with her pistol, raising a goose egg.

The spider-thing's torso shuddered as it suddenly withdrew the large appendage from Celeste's abdomen. Audrey glanced at the wound. It looked like a mass of red gelatin overlaid with shimmery glaze. The creature slowly heaved itself up and began to clamber down off the corpse. Audrey raised her gun again, tracking it, as the spider-thing slowly began to move away from the dead woman. As before, she was distracted from shooting it. This time, it was because she took notice of the wobbly way the monster moved as it scuttled sideways and collided with the wall. It appeared to be in a weakened state. It slumped there, making a mewling sound. Then, its struggling legs gave out entirely and the creature collapsed to the floor.

Audrey kept the gun trained on the unmoving form, but her hand began to tremble slightly from the weight of the weapon. She lowered it, and stared. The thing seemed dead. As dead as Celeste was. Whatever it had been doing—and that appeared to be having some kind of weird sex with Celeste's stomach—had apparently been too much for it. Could it have been laying eggs? She frowned, trying to remember what she knew about spiders. It was fuck all, basically. But wasn't there something in the natural world that died after having sex? Seahorses or praying mantises or some shit? Maybe this was like that. Maybe it had laid eggs inside Celeste's abdomen. The thought made her shudder.

Holding her breath, Audrey took a tentative step toward it, intent on verifying the thing's demise. She was almost overtop it, straddling Celeste's still smoking corpse, when a vivid image of the thing springing back to life and attacking her formed in her head. What if, instead of being dead, the beast was merely having a post-coital nap? And besides, how exactly was she supposed to verify life or death in this case? She had no clue where to touch the thing to feel for a pulse. No way she could put an ear to that swollen torso to listen for a heartbeat. Nope. That was a total non-starter. Even from a distance, the texture of its flesh looked gross and riddled with disease. No doubt the thing had stuff that would make COVID-19 seem like hay fever. She also sure as hell wasn't about to put her face close to the creature's mouth to check for breath.

She decided instead to just let the matter go and start searching for another way out of the building. She'd been lucky to last this long without being apprehended or killed by the mall's strange denizens. Being honest with herself, Audrey knew that she had squandered a lot of time that would have been more wisely spent in pursuit of an exit. Panic and shock had overwhelmed her. She needed to be smarter now, and take advantage of this one bit of good fortune while it was still available.

Letting out her breath, she stepped over Celeste's oozing corpse and carefully skirted the spider-thing, gingerly inching herself along the wall of the corridor. The thing looked smaller now—deflated, like a morning-after party balloon with half of its air leaked out. She realized this wasn't some vague or false impression. The creature's torso really did look significantly smaller than before, making the limp legs seem even more freakishly long now.

Audrey grunted.

Dead. It has to be…

She turned her head to glance back at Celeste, whose dead eyes were no longer facing straight up at the ceiling. The hybrid creature's frenzied rutting had caused her head to turn to the side, and she now appeared to be observing Audrey. An obviously false impression, of course, but a creepy one, nonetheless.

Her gaze returned to the spider-thing. She was close enough to touch the beast. She had the urge to poke it, just to be certain the thing was deceased. Grimacing, she reached out with Sig Sauer. Her hand started to shake again as the tip of the barrel neared the creature's deflated torso, hovering only a few inches above the mottled mound of flesh. She paused a moment, willing her hand to stop shaking, while at the same time tightening her grip on the handgun.

Then she heard a cracking sound. It was similar to the sounds the ligaments and joints in the spider-thing's neck had made as it stretched. Her gaze was still trained on the beast. Audrey was certain that it had not moved, but she stared at it more intently for another few moments, waiting for the sound to repeat itself. The only audible noise in the corridor was her own breathing. Once again, she was close to attributing a mystery noise to rats rooting around in debris, despite being wildly off-the-mark with that guess last time.

Just as she was about to move on, she heard the cracking sound again, louder now. It had come from behind her. Audrey whirled about and gasped. Celeste's corpse was bucking and spasming on the floor. Audrey put a hand over her mouth and slunk against the wall.

At first she couldn't fathom what was happening to the dead model. Celeste's limbs were splayed spread-eagle style, with legs kicked outward to their fullest extension and her arms thrown backward. Her body looked as if it were in the grip of an especially severe grand mal seizure. The muscles in her arms and legs vibrated and twisted as they began to bounce up and down on the floor. Her facial features contorted. Celeste's eyeballs bulged in their open sockets, as if something was pressing on them from behind.

Audrey didn't consider fleeing. She stood frozen, absolutely transfixed with disbelief. Celeste was dead. She'd killed her. She'd watched the light go out of her eyes, heard her breathing stop. She'd heard of involuntary muscular contractions or twitches in corpses, but nothing like this. Not even close.

Then, just as suddenly as they'd begun, the spasms ceased. Celeste's head lolled to one side, and then her corpse went still again.

"What the fuck…?"

The cracking sound came again. Louder this time.

Audrey shrieked as Celeste's left forearm shot straight up into the air and remained there. Then her right forearm did the same. The fingers of each hand began to stretch and twitch, lengthening until sharp black talons punched through her fingertips. The dead woman's mouth opened wide in a loud gasp. Her lungs sucked in air and exhaled.

Audrey shook her head. "No…no fucking way…"

Celeste was alive again.

She aimed the Sig Sauer at Celeste's head and started to squeeze the trigger.

For Celeste, her return to consciousness was like the flipping of a light switch. One moment, she wasn't there. She was gone, unaware of anything. She wasn't a lost soul drifting in a black void. There was no tunnel of light. No departed loved ones. No Jesus or Allah or angels or aliens. There was nothing. Then that switch got turned on and in the next instant she was back.

She opened her eyes and turned her head in time to see Audrey aiming the gun at her again. They were still in the same dark, dank hallway, so evidently not much time had passed.

She remembered…

Getting shot. She remembered that. She remembered those bullets punching through her. She remembered the pain, terror, and surprise she'd felt when that happened. Now what she felt was anger. Rage. She'd tried to make friends with this evil bitch and look what it had gotten her.

Fucking dead.

She remembered that, too—dying.

She'd been dead.

Only not anymore, apparently.

Celeste frowned. She'd always been especially proud of her fingernails, and regularly invested a lot of time, work and money into them. But now those nails were claws. She flexed her finger, experimenting.

Then she grinned.

She lashed out with her left hand and swatted the gun out of Audrey's hand. The weapon boomed and then flew into the darkness. Celeste heard the bullet ricochet off the wall. Audrey screamed, gaping in horror at what was left of her hand. It was mangled and shredded, ripped straight down the center, between her middle and ring fingers. Blood spurted from the wide gap between its two halves. Audrey held the wounded appendage in front of her face, shrieking in distress as her own blood splattered her cheeks and forehead.

I'm gonna tear that bitch apart.

Only then did it occur to Celeste to wonder how she'd managed to injure Audrey from so far away. She was still flat on her back on the filthy floor while Audrey was on her feet several feet away with her back against the wall. How had she managed to reach out that far?

She glanced over at her arm again and saw that it had stretched to twice its normal length. The physical change simultaneously terrified and fascinated Celeste. She seemed to have gained additional joints and segments that also hadn't been there prior to her revival. This answered the question of how she'd reached across such a distance, but everything else was still a terrifying mystery.

What the hell is happening to me?

As if in answer, another internal spasm made it clear her body was not finished changing. Celeste lifted her head and gasped when she saw the gelatinous, slimy mess that had been made of her abdomen. Curiously, there was no pain. The mangled flesh at the sides of the hole swelled outward in several places. Something inside of her was trying to push its way out. She squealed with confusion, her skin distending and then tearing as multiple hairy, spindly legs slathered in goo erupted from her torso.

Screaming, Audrey fled into the darkness, leaving a trail of blood in her wake.

Celeste reached up with both hands and grabbed hold of a pipe overhead. The metal squealed and flecks of rust rained down as she hauled herself up off the floor and stood uncertainly on her eight new legs. She experimented, goggling with wonder. Each limb exquisitely, sinuously flexible. She felt transformed.

The echoes of Audrey's pounding footsteps drifted down the corridor.

Celeste smiled.

Run, bitch. You won't get far.

She flexed her spider legs, and her smile stretched into a predatory grin as she realized how quickly they could carry her down the dark corridor.

Ready or not, bitch, here I fucking come.

She bolted forward, a dark blur slithering through the shadows.

NINETEEN

Lizzie, Conor, and Doctor Midnight stood at the base of the Pillar of Souls as the doctor's minions emerged from various points within the darker recesses of the underground garage. The solemn assemblage slowly entered the illuminated area enveloping the operating theater. The procession moved silently, almost as if they were in a trance. Except for Conor, their faces remained hidden behind plastic and latex Halloween masks. She saw celebrities both living and dead—Marilyn Monroe, Britney Spears, Kurt Cobain, William Shatner, Elvis Presley, Nicholas Cage, and more. There were world leaders such as John F. Kennedy, Adolf Hitler, George Washington, and Osama bin Laden. There were also a wide assortment of fictional characters from various films, comic books and media franchises—Captain America, Michael Myers, Batman, Mickey Mouse, the killer from the Scream movies, Chewbacca, a Klingon, and several different iterations of Jason Vorhees. Finally, there were various creatures from myth and legend—vampires, fairies, ghosts and the like.

There were still people strapped to many of the operating tables encircling the Pillar. As the masked minions passed by, some of the prisoners struggled against the straps binding them to the tables and cried out weakly for help. When it became clear no one would respond to these pleas, some of the captives on the tables sobbed in despair.

Upon hearing their moans, Lizzie felt a small flicker of compassion, a faint wish to relieve these poor, tortured souls of their suffering. This desire faded quickly, in part because she realized there was nothing she could do for these people even if she had wished to. Their fates were already written down on the parchment pages of a Deathbringer's journal, inscribed there millennia ago. She wondered to herself how she suddenly knew this piece of arcane knowledge, from seemingly out of nowhere.

Doctor Midnight made a low, almost inaudible sound of amusement. "The pathways of higher perception have been opened in your head."

She realized that he was right. So much was becoming clearer to her now. For example, she had a better understanding of the hierarchy of this place. The doctor and his kind ruled here. There were a small handful of humans like Conor and herself who served them. There were other humans, like someone named Annie, who were here in a partnership aspect. And then there were the others. Most of the creatures she had seen—the ones she assumed were genetic freaks of some kind—were simply the doctor's previous experiments. A small handful of others, like the man in the tanned skin dress—Scug—were more like the mutant counterpart to Annie, here out of an arrangement of convenience rather than devotion. And, Lizzie sensed, that arrangement was about to be broken.

"Yes," the doctor murmured, responding to her thoughts, "I am aware of Scug's betrayal. His insolence is being dealt with, even now. It is not our concern. We have far more important matters to attend to. The secrets of eternity are yours for the taking. You are ready to scale the Pillar."

The procession surrounded the Pillar of Souls, forming a circle. Each individual then raised their masked face to peer up at the Pillar. Lizzie thought they looked like worshippers gathered before the altar of some church.

"There are other versions of you," she told the doctor. "I see them on different levels of… the Labyrinth? I see them all in my mind, flashing by like faces in the windows of a train. I see your real face, Dr. Ominous."

"Do you indeed?" The doctor laughed out loud behind his Richard Nixon mask. "What you see lacks context. In the Labyrinth, space and time exist simultaneously. All things are happening at once. In the Nothing, space and time do not exist. And neither do I. The flow of time does not touch me. I exist outside the confines of the Labyrinth. Levels and alternate realities are nothing to me. I exist on all levels simultaneously, and yet on none of them. I am a ghost in the ever-shifting, unfolding cosmos. On some worlds, I am called by other names, including Ominous. I also wear other false faces that look real."

Lizzie frowned. "So I haven't seen your real face?"

He laughed again. "In a sense, no, you have not. In another sense…maybe?"

Lizzie looked into the eyeholes of the Richard Nixon mask. She saw two dark orbs with a small spot of red in the middle. They were nothing like the eyes she'd seen peeking out from behind the mask earlier.

She grunted. "Whatever."

She felt resigned, rather than annoyed or frustrated. The doctor was a man… a being… who, regardless of whoever or whatever he actually was, would always speak in confounding riddles. She knew that now. There was no point in pushing him for direct, clear answers.

Lizzie turned away from him and looked back at the Pillar of Souls. As her gaze traveled upward, she realized that the construct seemed significantly taller now, extending far beyond the roof of the mall and out into the heavens. She supposed this might be an illusion of some sort, but if so, it was an extraordinarily convincing one. She also wondered why this knowledge was denied to her when she seemed to know so much more about everything else. She mentally shrugged. One thing she knew for certain—the answers were up there somewhere.

"So, like…I just climb it?"

"Yes." The doctor nodded.

"Good thing I'm not afraid of heights."

Without another word, Lizzie strode across the dirty concrete floor on her bare feet. Seconds later, she stood face-to-face with the woman she'd tried talking to earlier, the one who'd begged her to end her suffering in the moments before Conor's intervention. She was sewn into the Pillar's outer layer of flesh at ground level, one of countless bodies interwoven with each other, limbs and torsos twisted and intertwined. The woman moaned at Lizzie's approach and then again as Lizzie touched her.

"Relax," Lizzie said, caressing the woman's cheek. "This is all written down somewhere, recorded on pages long ago. It's already happened, and it will happen again. It is always happening. And it is always happening to you. It's your destiny, so try to embrace it. Like I am with mine."

The woman's confused expression suggested solace would remain elusive. She moaned as Lizzie reached up and grabbed hold of the ankle of an emaciated old man whose gnarled foot was attached to the woman's shoulder.

"Good luck," Conor called.

Lizzie braced a foot against one of the woman's knobby knees and began to haul herself upward.

Audrey's eyes filled with tears as she ran heedlessly down the corridor, bumping and tripping over debris piles and a large trash can. She hit the latter hard enough to knock it over. Some manner of foul-smelling black and gray slop spilled out over the floor. She saw eyeballs and teeth floating amidst it. Her feet slid through the mess, knocking her off balance again. Audrey tried to maintain her footing by wildly pinwheeling her arms, but it was no use.

As she fell, instinct caused Audrey to twist and try to break her fall by getting her hands beneath her. When her mutilated hand hit the floor, the divided halves splayed apart even farther as they absorbed the brunt of the impact. More tissue and tendons tore. The agony lancing through her skull was molten. She screeched, nearly blacking out. She wanted nothing more than to simply sit there and cry until Celeste or one of the other things found her and killed her, but her will to live remained strong enough to override this defeatist impulse.

Audrey rolled onto her back and maneuvered herself into a sitting position. This brought another explosion of pain. Her jeans were soaked from both the trash can's disgusting contents and her own blood. Before getting to her feet, she needed to do something about her hand. Without the first aid kit in her backpack, there was only one real option. Using her good hand, she peeled her shirt off over her head and spent a moment considering how best to wrap the wound, all the while remaining conscious of not having a lot of time to get the job done. She wound up holding an end of the shirt in her teeth while using her good hand to press the halves of the bisected hand as close together as she could manage. The agony she experienced as she did this was the worst yet, making her scream despite the obvious need to stay as quiet as possible with a monster on her trail.

The pain kept coming, flooding her system in wave after nausea-inducing wave, but Audrey pushed through it, winding the shirt around her mauled hand until the makeshift bandage was as tight as she could make it. She tied it off around her wrist and sat there panting. Sweat bathed her forehead, congealing with the blood and dirt to form a paste-like sheen.

When her vision and nausea cleared, Audrey staggered to her feet. She swayed, and instinctively reached for the wall with her bad hand. She caught the error at the last second, and slumped against it with her shoulder instead, allowing her elbow to take the brunt. Then, with a loud grunt, she resumed her flight down the hallway.

Without the aid of some powerful narcotics, there was nothing she could do about the constant throb of her hand, but at least now she could move a little easier. She glanced behind and saw the trail of blood she'd left in her wake thus far, but that was it. No spider-thing. No Celeste. No mutants. She marveled at how well her eyes had grown adjusted to the darkness during the last few hours, but she longed to see the sun again.

Audrey set off in a loping, shuffling sort of jog. A few moments later, she spotted the open door that Hereford had led them through right before everything had happened. For the first time since Celeste's not-quite death, her thoughts turned to Chuck. Audrey pushed them away. It was heartbreaking and more than a bit weird to think about how completely and irrevocably everything about her life had changed in the intervening time since they had come this way. She hurried on past the door without even glancing through it. That way was not an exit. It led deeper into the mall itself, and therefore, deeper into the den of deviants.

A short way up ahead, the corridor branched off to the left and she nearly ran into a spiked wall before realizing she needed to change course. Getting her feet turned in the right direction without taking a spill wasn't easy, but after wobbling precariously a moment she managed to regain her footing and keep moving. She gave a cursory glance at the spikes. They were fashioned from metal poles, and they'd been driven through the wall at various heights. Human skulls dangled from some of them. A pile of dust on the floor beneath them indicated that there had once been more.

She tried to imagine where the change of direction might be taking her relative to the mall's interior. All she had seen however was quick glimpses through the van window when they first arrived. Audrey figured she must now be circumnavigating the department store and heading deeper into the guts of the mall. That meant more risk in being discovered and captured or killed, but it also meant encountering more doors, and thus, more potential exits from this rotten place.

Only a few hundred yards after the hallway shift, she spied one of those doors on her left. At first glance, it looked like it might be something other than merely another Macy's entry point. For one thing, it was on the wrong side of the corridor. Also, it was larger and had more of an industrial look to it than any of the other doors she'd passed. A spot on the wall directly above it marked a space that had once held a sign, but whatever it had read was now long gone. She had no idea what that might indicate or where it might lead her to, but she heard a low, slithery sound from somewhere behind and above her and realized she was about out of time. Celeste—or possibly something else—was closing the distance and would be on her within moments if she didn't try something now.

She pushed her hip against the door's metal push-bar and sighed with relief that it was unlocked. The door swung inward, creaking quietly. Audrey staggered into a space so dark, that her night vision was useless. While her eyes had grown accustomed to the darkness of the corridor, this was something deeper and almost palpable. She spent a few seconds she couldn't afford to waste waiting for her sight to adjust and—when it did—then assessing where she was and any new possibilities that might be available now. Directly in front of her was another short stretch of corridor, at the end of which was another door similar to the one she had just fled through. Audrey's spirit soared and the pain vanished for a brief instant. She suspected this second door might lead to somewhere outside. The hope was dashed a second later when she saw that the door was blocked by a rusted engine block from some old car or piece or large equipment.

"Fuck…"

She saw a flight of concrete stairs and a metal handrail to her left. Audrey headed for those instead. Clutching the railing with her good hand, she ascended step by careful step. She was a quarter of the way up when she belatedly realized she should have tried blocking the door she'd come through with something. There wasn't time for it now, though, so she kept climbing instead. It was possible this flight of stairs led to the roof of the building. Once she got up there, there might yet be another opportunity to block the path of whoever was pursuing her.

After she had limped up a few more stairs, the palm on Audrey's uninjured hand began to tingle. Chalking it up to shock and exhaustion, she pressed on. It was only when the tingling turned into a burning sensation that she stopped and removed her hand from the railing. The stinging grew worse. She held her hand close to her face and squinted. It was greased in some sort of frictionless, viscid substance. She glanced down at the railing and realized that it was coated in the material, as well. Within another few seconds, the burning intensified. She hauled herself up another two steps before the pain became too much to go on.

She knelt on the stairs and looked at her hand again. The top layer of skin on her palm was now a seared, gooey mess that reminded her of what had been done to Celeste's abdomen. Head reeling, Audrey closed her eyes and let her head slump forward until her chin touched her chest. She fought back tears—feeling the absolute heights of hopelessness and despair. If she'd had the strength, she would have flung herself back down the stairs right now, hoping her neck broke during the tumble. Her entire body shuddered as silent sobs overtook her.

She was still crying when she felt something prod at the bottom of her right foot. Then, an instant after she felt the pressure, the unseen thing prodding at her foot jabbed sharply upward. She screeched in pain and opened her eyes in time to see something sharp and black protruding from her foot. It was slick with her blood and some other, shiny substance. Then it retracted and was gone.

Audrey felt no relief in that moment. Whatever it was attached to stood on the floor below, shadowed in the darkness. The fact that it had been able to reach up this far and still stab her told her all that she needed to know. She knew her time was at an end. Her sobs grew louder as the thing that had once been Celeste skittered into view at the bottom of the stairwell. In addition to the two arms and two legs she had always possessed, Celeste now had four goo-slathered furry legs that had sprouted from her torso. Several of them scraped along the wall and the railing, making a horrible, unnerving sound. Celeste smiled as she hurried closer, an expression made grotesque by the genetic changes to her face.

Resigned to her fate now, Audrey stared at the Celeste-spider with detached, loathsome curiosity. The former Instagram model had been made into something new as a result of the hybrid creature's attack on her, a process apparently initiated by something it had implanted within her. That much was obvious. She remembered how the spider-thing had pumped away, as if it were fucking her. Thinking of it as a reproductive act, however, didn't feel quite accurate. It was more akin to the passing of a virulent contagion from one life form to another—an infection that twisted and transformed the flesh of its host in a variety of bizarre, incomprehensible ways. It probably varied on an individual basis. The creature that had attacked Celeste, for example, had been without human limbs, but Celeste's non-arachnid limbs still appeared functional.

If she had more time, perhaps she could have figured out why.

But she didn't have more time.

Her time was up.

Celeste stopped and grinned, poised directly above her now. She had lost her top and bra at some point during the transformation. Her breasts hung down nearly low enough for Audrey to reach out and touch.

"Guess your days of getting thousands of likes on Instagram are over, huh?"

"That's still more than you ever got." Celeste's voice was coarse and grating, and entirely unlike how she had ever sounded on video.

"Listen to you," Audrey said. "Hell, just fucking look at you. You're a monster. You're fucking disgusting. If Bradley could see you now, he'd—"

She screamed as Celeste fell upon her and wrapped her spider legs around her body, pulling her close and holding her tight. Her face was mere inches away from Audrey's, allowing her to peer directly into a hole where her nose had once been.

"I may be a monster," Celeste snarled, "but at least I was pretty once."

"Just kill me and get it over with, bitch."

"I was going to, but now I think I might cocoon you in webbing instead and save you for a snack later on. I'll try, at least. I'm still not sure what all I can do. I'll have to practice, I guess."

Audrey squirmed harder as Celeste pressed her lips against her mouth.

"What are—"

A gurgling scream followed as Celeste began to chew Audrey's lips from her face.

Audrey was still alive when the cocooning process began, but she could no longer scream.

TWENTY

Once his clan was assembled in the movie theater, Scug took a head count to make sure they weren't missing anybody.

Then he told them the plan. When he was finished, he looked at them all. He hated seeing the fear on their faces. They hadn't looked this way since fleeing Philadelphia. Some of the younger ones had never known terror and anxiety like this before.

"Questions before we move out?" he asked. "We're meeting Annie outside."

"Can we trust Annie?" Gretch asked.

"We can't trust anyone who's not family," Scug replied, "but she wants out, too. She's done."

"Midnight," Jax said. "Captain Rat. The others. They'll try to stop us."

"Yeah," Scug agreed. "They'll try."

"There's more of them than there are us."

"Yeah."

"What's the plan for that?" Curd asked.

"You, Klavo, and Lorok did it once already tonight." Scug smiled. "Kill every single thing that gets in our way."

Lorok raised his massive war hammer and hooted. Jax and Gretch joined in the cry. Gax shouted from Jax's shoulder. Then the rest of the clan raised their weapons and did the same.

Scug's smile grew broader. Nodding, he started up the aisle.

One by one, the others fell in line behind him.

"Sneak if we can," he reminded them. "If we can't sneak and it comes to a fight…leave nothing alive."

Amazingly—horrifically—Stuart was still alive after being dragged around the walkways of the mall's second floor multiple times.

He suspected this wouldn't remain the case much longer. The motorcycle he was chained to was picking up speed again and appeared to be on the verge of heading up one of those ramps leading to the system of twisting slides and covered chutes of the children's play area. He'd seen the aftermath of what had happened to Bradley after his rider took him that route. Even without his glasses, Stuart had witnessed enough to know how grisly it had been.

Strangely, he was no longer scared. He supposed that maybe it was shock. He was in terrible agony—which was no surprise given that most of the skin on his back was now scraped away and smattered all over the mall's second floor—but despite that, he felt a bizarre sense of calm.

Then his serenity sputtered as the unexpected happened. The guy riding the motorcycle let off the gas and allowed the bike to roll to a complete stop. Stuart's naked form slid forward several more feet before also coming to a stop. Then the driver put the kickstand down, cut the engine, climbed off the motorcycle.

Stuart frowned, trying to understand what was happening. As far as he could tell, his driver apparently had a bone to pick with someone in the crowd of onlookers, because he waded into their midst, grabbed a scrawny guy with a wild mane of scraggly gray hair by the collar of his filthy old sheepskin jacket, and dragged him kicking and screaming out into an open space. Once he had the man where he wanted him, the biker punched him in the face, a jaw-rattling haymaker that sent multiple teeth flying out of his mouth. The object of his ire dropped to the floor, but the biker was far from done with the man. He repeatedly kicked the unfortunate, causing the smaller man to curl up in a protective fetal ball. The tactic did him little good because his assailant immediately switched to kicking him in the face instead. The heel of the biker's boot flattened the man's bulbous, purple-veined nose. More shattered teeth fell out of his mouth. His jaw looked on the verge of coming unhinged.

Stuart had no idea what this was about. All he knew was he was getting an unexpected temporary reprieve; one he wasn't even sure he wanted. The pain hadn't lessened despite the fact that he was no longer being scraped across the floor or dragged by the sharp hook wedged deep inside his mutilated asshole. Quite the opposite, in fact. The pause allowed his brain to focus intensely on the various ravaged parts of his body. The agony began to intensify rather than abate.

Survival no longer existed as even the faintest of hopes in his thoughts. Though basic human instinct compelled him to try pleading for mercy again, Stuart resisted the urge. He was resigned to death now, almost eager for it—a mental surrender that hurt almost as badly as his body did.

He'd been a happy guy until today, content with his lot in life. It hadn't mattered that he wasn't fabulously wealthy or adored by legions of hot women. In partnership with his long-time best friend, he'd played a significant role in building a successful internet content brand. They didn't get rich, but they made enough money to live comfortably while doing exactly what they wanted. A lot of people—hell, most people—never got anywhere close to that point. As a not insignificant bonus, he'd even gotten laid with girls way out of his league a few times as a result of his association with Lost Places. He'd made people laugh. He'd made them happy. He had, in some small way, distracted them from whatever horrible shit was going on in their own lives. He'd helped get them through a bad day at school, or at work, or at home. That was a hell of a lot more satisfying than slaving away in a warehouse somewhere or working in retail, or being a fucking Uber driver.

It was all over now, though. The dream was dead. Stuart Carlson had motorboated his last bouncing pair of plus-sized boobies. There would be no more jokes about the quality of the pushin' relative to the size of the cushion. The jokes were lame and older than time itself, but they had made Bradley laugh every time, regardless. His best friend was dead too now, a fact that pained him despite Bradley's attempts to use him as a human shield. Those things had wounded him in the moment, but he could forgive him now. A lot of people did shitty things when faced with fucked-up, scary shit. It didn't mean you forgot all the good times that came before the scary shit.

I forgive you, dude. It was fun while it lasted.

The biker finally ceased beating and kicking the man he'd pulled out of the crowd. However, instead of remounting the bike and starting the engine again, he wandered away in an apparent daze, weaving and staggering his way through the crowd until he disappeared from sight.

In his absence, Stuart expected one of these other scummy pieces of shit to take his place astride the bike, but that didn't happen either. In fact, a large segment of the crowd melted away after that, apparently having lost interest. He wondered if something was happening somewhere else in the mall. As the minutes continued to pass, even more onlookers dispersed, leaving him completely unattended as far as he could tell. He considered crying out for help, but then remembered his situation.

Whimpering, Stuart turned his head about and spied a keyring still dangling in the motorcycle's ignition. The notion that he might be able to climb up on the bike and speed the hell out of this nightmare zone was tantalizing, but then he remembered his pulped legs and the hook in his ass. He couldn't even sit up, never mind haul himself upright, climb onto a motorcycle, and ride away.

Nope, he was still completely fucked. Sooner or later someone would come along and finish the task abandoned by the apparently manic biker. Until then, all Stuart could do was lie here and suffer as he waited for the end. His eyes filled with tears that he did not bother to blink away.

The scariest thing was how quiet the mall's interior had become.

Eventually, he sensed a new presence standing above him. Stuart blinked hard a few times and saw the face of a young girl staring down at him. She looked normal save for the conical shape of her head. He knew that in the less socially aware eras of the past they had called people like her pinheads. He wasn't sure what they were called now. Regardless, slur or not, the name was apt.

The girl wore only a dingy pair of boy's briefs. Her breasts were withered-looking things that hung off her scrawny chest like tumors.

She held something in her right hand, but he couldn't see what it was and had a hunch she was purposely concealing it.

He cleared his throat. "What are you hiding?"

The girl squatted next to him, exposing rotten teeth as she grinned. She opened her hand and showed him three slim firecrackers wired together end to end with an extended fuse.

Stuart frowned. "What the fuck?"

Giggling, she grabbed hold of his limp penis and pulled at it until she had it stretched out several inches. Her hands were damp and cold. Shuddering, Stuart begged her to stop, but the girl pinched his flaccid member hard and held on tight. He tried rolling away from her, but the condition of his body prevented it.

Still giggling, the girl pushed the first firecracker through his dickhole. His former sense of resignation was completely shattered now. Terror overwhelmed him. Snot bubbles came out of his nose as his pleas for mercy grew ever more desperate. Ignoring him, the girl continued shoving the firecrackers down into his urethra. The insertion was itself incredibly painful, but the anticipatory dread he felt was far worse.

At last, with the task completed, the girl reached into her dingy briefs and took out a pink plastic lighter. She made eye contact with Stuart and grinned in her goofy way again as she flicked the lighter, producing a tiny column of orange flame. He shrieked as she pulled at his dick again and touched the flame to the fuse. Then she quickly stood up and backed away, watching the fuse burn. Her eyes grew wide as the flame singed the hairs on Stuart's doughy thigh. Despite not wanting to see the awful thing about to happen, Stuart couldn't help lifting his head to gape in wide-eyed horror.

The tip of his dick blew apart in a cascade of fleshy red bits as the first firecracker exploded inside of him. The horrendous pain he felt in that moment was exceeded only by the agony he felt in the next as the other firecrackers exploded, sloughing away more large chunks of his penis.

He was too consumed by agony and renewed shock to take much note as the girl once again rummaged around in her underwear and produced another length of firecrackers.

These got inserted in his nose.

His ears came after that.

It was a long time before he died.

TWENTY-ONE

The asymmetrical nature of the Pillar's human exterior made scaling the structure a risky proposition from the start. No human body was exactly like another even under the most optimal circumstances. People came in wildly varying shapes and sizes and were not meant to fit together in this manner. The bodies forming the Pillar's fleshy outer layer had required an extreme amount of stretching and twisting in order to fit and connect, a process aided in many places by flayed open arms and legs.

As Lizzie climbed, the stench of necrotizing tissue was almost too much for her to handle. Her eyes watered and her gag reflex was triggered repeatedly. Determined, she pressed on. These were inevitable betrayals of physiology. She would not allow simple physical discomforts to sway her from this task. Soon she would be beyond such things, no longer a slave to the failings of the flesh. Soon, she would transform. Her moment of ultimate transcendence was coming, and thanks to the opening of her inner eye, she already knew exactly how glorious it would feel.

Knowledge of the reward awaiting her did not, however, make her oblivious to the frustrations of the difficult physical process of climbing so massive and unique a structure. In meticulously piecing together the human outer layer, the doctor and his minions had utilized adjustable scaffolding and harnesses, whereas Lizzie was using only her hands and feet. Several times she slipped and nearly plummeted back to the floor, but each time she'd managed to hold on by desperately flailing and grabbing on to random pieces of human anatomy.

When she was about thirty feet above the floor, Lizzie slipped again, and saved herself by jamming her hand into a woman's open mouth. The still-living victim tried to clamp her teeth down on Lizzie's fingers, but she yanked her hand free before that could happen and grabbed a handful of the woman's filthy hair instead. Lizzie hung there for a moment, looking into the woman's glassy eyes. Then she smiled. Like the other living pieces of the human jigsaw puzzle, the woman was connected to a system of tubing designed to feed her a steady stream of nutrients and antibodies to sustain her as long as possible.

Laughing, Lizzie ripped the tubing from the woman's arms. "You won't be needing that anymore, bitch."

She had another close call at fifty feet. By then, she was beyond the point where the Pillar extended through the massive hole in the roof of the underground parking garage. At that height, she should have been just about even with the mall's first floor. Instead, Lizzie suddenly found herself enshrouded in a cloud of radiant light—golden in hue, like the glow of the sun on a clear summer day, but it projected no heat. She realized that she could no longer discern much of the physical world around her. The more time she spent within the cloud of light, the more euphoric she began to feel. She was so enraptured by the sensation that she lost focus at a crucial moment.

Balanced on the shoulders of a man below her, Lizzie reached overhead for another handhold without taking a moment to first determine its viability as a climbing aid. Her hand closed around the cock and balls of a deceased elderly man. The rotting flesh of his groin began to tear as she pulled herself upward again. Startled, Lizzie yelped as the dead man's genitals tore free of his corpse. She lost her footing and began sliding down the side of the Pillar. Her face slid through putrescent flesh. Her fingers clawed desperately, shredding some of the sewn-together sections of flayed skin. The Pillar's collective screams joined with her own.

Then the bottoms of her feet slammed down upon the bowed head of a bald woman. Lizzie pitched backward, teetering. In the last instant before she would have fallen, a withered gray hand reached out from a tangled mass of limbs and grabbed hold of her wrist. The unexpected savior held her there a moment before pulling her back toward the column. Lizzie's feet still rested atop the head of the person whose neck she'd just broken. Taking a deep breath, she quickly steadied herself and used her free hand to find secure purchase elsewhere. Shivering, she exhaled. She made no attempt to resume her ascent, focusing instead on allowing her panicked state of mind to ease.

"Climb!"

The voice came from within the tangled mass of limbs. Lizzie peered into the intertwined bodies in search of the speaker's face, but all she could see was a single red-rimmed eye leaking pus.

"Thank you," she said.

Lizzie began to haul herself upward again. She estimated she'd lost at least fifteen feet of progress during her unplanned descent, a result of carelessness and loss of focus. The cloud of radiant light had receded, and she could perceive the world around her again. Despite the height, she heard faint murmurs from below. There were undoubtedly some among Midnight's faithful who didn't believe she was up to the task. Or quite possibly they resented her status as his chosen one. She understood how both camps felt. They'd been here for years, some of them, while she hadn't even been here a full day. In their place, she would probably feel the same way.

But she was not in their place. She was here, scaling the Pillar, doing the thing only she could do. She knew that because her inner eye had shown her already, that world that existed on the other side of the rift she would soon open.

The place the doctor called the Nothing.

Lizzie redoubled her efforts, climbing faster than before while also intensifying her focus. In a few more minutes, she made up the ground she'd lost. The cloud of radiant light materialized again, from seemingly out of nowhere. She could still see the human fabric of the Pillar, but nothing else.

The first otherworldly vibrations began after she'd climbed another ten feet beyond that point. She felt them resonating in her teeth and in her bones. Lifting her head, Lizzie stared up the length of the Pillar, which now seemed to extend miles above her—a column of thousands upon thousands of tortured, living bodies. Even with the knowledge granted to Lizzie by her third eye, this baffled her for a moment. The doctor couldn't possibly have taken this many victims from the area surrounding the mall, not even with years of dedicated effort. She knew that he employed Annie and others to bring in more raw materials from afar, but even that couldn't account for the impossible number of souls. There were more victims here than in all the concentration camps of Nazi Germany.

Then her inner eye opened again, and another truth was revealed. Construction of the Pillar had occurred not just here, in the rotten guts of a dead mall, but throughout multiple planes of reality. She was climbing through different dimensions, and in each of them, workers had contributed to the Pillar.

The vibration intensified the higher she climbed. Lizzie had to cling tightly to keep from falling again. Then, the radiant light yielded to the red-tinged sky of an alien world. Another glance up the length of the Pillar revealed a purple sphere high above her, emitting a constant series of sparks. Occasionally, more powerful bolts of electricity that looked like flashes of lightning erupted from it.

She knew at once that this was it. This was the Nothing. She'd done it!

And yet… she sensed that she wasn't meant to stop climbing. The rift between her world and this indescribable place was not yet fully open. To complete her task of transcendence, she had to keep going.

Steeling herself against the increasingly violent vibrations thrumming up and down the length of the swaying Pillar, Lizzie reached over her head again and grabbed a slender ankle.

Before she could ascend even another inch, however, something wet touched her cheek. A droplet of something foul. Assuming it was merely the bodily secretion of some diseased unfortunate sewn into the Pillar's fabric, she wiped it away with her free hand and started pulling herself up again. She was two feet higher when a larger splat of the same rancid fluid hit the crown of her skull. The stench was awful, and the substance had a consistency that reminded her of the yellow custard they used to serve in her middle school's cafeteria.

She felt wind on her face. It only made the stench worse. Another droplet splattered against her. Then another.

Retching, Lizzie lost her footing but maintained her hold on a man's wrist as she swung outward from the Pillar, swaying slightly in the rising wind. She looked up and saw numerous swollen, yellow globs of liquid sliding down from somewhere beyond the charged purple sphere. It drenched the bodies above her.

"What the…?"

More and more yellow globs appeared. They became a trickle, and then a torrent, cascading downward. As more of it splatted into her face, Lizzie realized what the substance was.

Pus.

A waterfall of pus.

And something swam within it.

Strange creatures emerged from the liquid. They were black and insectile but varied greatly in size and shape. Some of them possessed large claws or mandibles, while others had beachball-shaped heads and wide mouths lined with teeth that looked capable of biting off a man's head. The clawed creatures raked at the flesh of the Pillar as they slid downward, shredding it and unleashing streams of blood. Abdominal cavities were torn open. Guts and organs spewed from these chasms, joining the gooey torrent of human and alien disgorgement.

A human eyeball plummeted downward and adhered to Lizzie's cheek. She shook the bloody orb loose with a hard toss of her head, but more pieces of shredded viscera streamed down upon her. Half a kidney slapped against her forehead. A loop of glistening intestine collided with her shoulders. Lizzie closed her eyes and held tight to the wrist. It was the only thing keeping her aloft. There was no getting away as the rain of blood and guts buffeted and enveloped her. Bodily fluids and alien goo soon covered every inch of her naked flesh. Rather than feeling repulsed, however, she felt elation. The rift between Earth and the Nothing was opening.

She had succeeded.

Heavier clomping sounds from above signaled the arrival of even more fearsome creatures. She kept her eyes shut. The howling wind tossed her about like a ragdoll. She held on because there was nothing else left to do, until the swaying of the Pillar became so violent that she lost her grip.

Instead of falling, however, Lizzie was swept along on a tide of yellow pus and liquefied human flesh. She felt her own skin begin to melt as a delayed solvent reaction resulting from her skin's contact with the alien substance began to melt her body. In a few more moments, she felt the pus eat into the bones beneath her flesh. The process was a painful but necessary one. This was an integral part of her transformation, the shedding of her human shell. She was part of something bigger than herself now. Something more important and meaningful than all life on Earth, a world that would now be a playground for their kind. She was no longer Lizzie. This was her last thought as the tide of rotten organic matter and alien life forms crashed through the rift between worlds, plummeting into the underground parking garage of the Westgate Galleria, and instantly flooding it.

Some while after that, she opened her eyes and knew her transformation was complete. Her new tentacles flopped about on the damp floor of the parking garage, now no longer flooded but empty of human life. Skeletons lay scattered everywhere. Bones and plastic Halloween masks were all that remained of Midnight's minions.

But Dr. Midnight was still there, waiting for her.

They embraced, twining tentacles around each other as they communicated without sound.

The time of leaving has arrived. We will go out into this world and wear our false faces as we infest its communities one by one, slowly taking over. Are you ready?

She smiled in her new way.

She was ready indeed.

TWENTY-TWO

"She's not here," Gretch moaned.

They stood outside, in the movie theater's back lot. This area was occupied only by several vacant, rusted garbage dumpsters and a pile of wooden pallets that had clearly sat there since the mall's initial closure. There was little moonlight or stars overhead, but dawn was not far off.

"She will be," Scug said. "Be patient."

They'd hidden the younger members of the clan, except for Lorok, behind one of the old garbage dumpsters. Because he was physically stronger than the rest of the children, Lorok stood guard over them, occupying a loading ramp that overlooked the space. His massive hammer was slung over his broad, warty shoulder. Scug was struck by how much he resembled his father, Noigel, in that moment.

"She's not coming," Gretch insisted. "We're fucked."

Scug raised his hand, intent on backhanding her, when the ground trembled beneath their feet. The sound came next—unmistakable. It reminded him of Philadelphia, when explosions had rattled their home. Instinctively, he reached out and grabbed on to Gretch, pulling her close and shielding her. She clung tightly to him, crying.

"Not again," she murmured. "Please. This isn't happening again."

Jax and Gax seemed to be worrying about the same thing. Both heads glanced around frantically, searching for falling debris—but there was none.

Scug realized that whatever the nature of the disturbance, it was happening inside and beneath the mall, rather than out here. He cautiously let go of Gretch and stood listening as the pavement trembled again. Some monumental form of upheaval was taking place down in the bowels of the mall—in Midnight's lair.

He feared what they were feeling was a prelude to the destruction of the mall. Just like Philadelphia, he was powerless to stop it. The only difference was the house in Philadelphia had been their home. This was just a place they had lived, for a while.

"Let it fall," he said. "Hope that stupid pillar goes with it."

It occurred to him that whatever was happening inside the mall was good for him and his family in more ways than one. If the mall was under siege, or if a disaster had struck, then that meant that Midnight would be too distracted to worry about them. The emptiness of the lot around him seemed to verify this.

But where was Annie? What if something had happened to her?

Scug balled his fists. They couldn't just hide out here until sunrise. Sooner or later, they'd be found. Captain Rat's people would hunt them down. Indeed, they might be searching for them right now. But neither could they sneak off into the darkness. There would be no place to hide before daylight, and that increased the likelihood of them being found a hundred-fold. And they couldn't go back inside. Not with whatever was happening in there.

Was it possible that Doctor Midnight had discovered their plan? Did he know that the two individuals responsible for consistently keeping him supplied with flesh—Annie Cunt and Scug—were sneaking away in the middle of the night? What if Annie was already dead?

Scug started pacing. An uncomfortable number of additional moments ticked by. He was close to giving in and suggesting they all hide in the dumpsters when he heard the sound of a heavy latch being disengaged and drawn backward. He turned around and saw one of the boarded-over door sections at the entrance to the cineplex swing outward.

"Here she is!" Gretch clapped with glee.

But it wasn't Annie.

Captain Rat emerged into the open air, flanked by two dozen of his followers.

Scug tensed as they fanned out to either side of him in their usual predatory way. All of them were smiling.

Up on the ramp, Lorok unslung his hammer and growled.

"Wait," Scug said.

Captain Rat and his forces inched closer in an unhurried but implicitly threatening way. Each of them carried a weapon of some kind. Scug saw baseball bats, swords, machetes, boards, and golf clubs. The Captain had his sledgehammer, as usual, and Scug guessed there was probably a firearm hidden in a pocket of the long black trench coat the man now wore.

"What do you want with us, Rat?"

The Captain scratched his pointy chin and chuckled. "I heard a rumor you and your clan might be trying to leave this place for good."

Scug grunted. "So what? It's nothing to do with you."

"Well, that's where we'll have to agree to disagree." The Captain lifted the head of his sledgehammer and thumped it hard against the asphalt. "You see, Dr. Midnight is going to be gone soon. In fact, he may already be gone."

"Then we have no business with you."

"Ah, but that is not so, yes? With Doctor Midnight gone, that leaves me in charge of things. I'm the new landlord. And I don't like tenants skipping out without paying the rent."

"What rent? People get lured inside. We bring them to you. That's the arrangement."

"That was the arrangement. But not anymore. You and your people belong to me now. You're my property. My slaves, only there will be no emancipation for the likes of you. No. I advise you to fall in line and keep your simple-minded kin in check. Do that and things might work out okay for you here, yes? But if you rebel or pull any kind of underhanded shenanigans, things won't work out for you at all. Am I making myself clear?"

Several of the Captain's followers laughed and slapped their weapons against open palms. Scug eyed them one by one, letting his gaze drift over the crowd. He stopped at a hunchbacked adolescent with a misshapen head.

Captain Rat tapped the sledgehammer against the pavement again. "I asked you a question, Scug. I would advise you to—"

Scug lunged, clearing the distance between them before any of the Captain's followers could react. He slammed into the hunchback, knocked him to the ground, and clamped his jaws down upon the boy's waxen throat, ripping and chewing, and shaking his head back and forth. Within seconds, he tore the hunchback's throat away, and spat the bloody scrap on the ground. Blood sprayed from the ragged hole. The boy kicked and gurgled.

Scug sat up and looked at Captain Rat. He grinned with bloodstained lips.

"There's my answer, Rat. Kill them!"

Scug's clan attacked, wielding weapons of their own. Gretch had two long butcher knives that she'd salvaged from the mall upon their arrival here eleven years ago. Jax hefted a club with nails driven through it. Both of them dropped an opponent each before Rat's men could even mount a defense. Klavo swung a meat cleaver. Curd charged with a mop handle spear. Then Lorok waded into the fray, swinging his hammer back and forth in a wide arc. He knocked two more opponents off their feet, crushing their ribcages and sending them flying through the air.

Captain Rat shrugged. "So be it. I am more than happy to send you into the great beyond, Scug. This will be fun, yes?"

His followers had now gotten over their initial shock, and they pressed the attack back on Scug's clan. Scug caught glimpses of the fray in between his own kills.

Jax defended himself while Gax called warnings to his brother. He swung the club with frenzied berserk abandon, heedless of where or who he struck. Luckily, the rest of the family knew to avoid him in this state. The nails in the club impaled and tore and slashed through flesh and bone and organs.

Gretch slunk low, sliding between a man's legs and slicing him open from groin to asshole, before springing upright again, spinning, and cutting another opponent's throat. Blood from both kills sprayed her in an arcing shower.

Two of Rat's minions attacked Curd simultaneously. One approached from the front while the other crept up behind. Curd thrust his spear into the first man's stomach. Then he wrenched it free, spun, and pinned the second attacker by stabbing him through the foot with enough force to embed the wooden mop handle in the asphalt. The first attacker dropped to his knees, holding his abdomen. The other shrieked, trying to yank the spear free. Curd reached out and squeezed the man's head between his large hands until it collapsed.

Klavo moved fast and silent. He disemboweled an opponent, flung his meat cleaver at a second, and then used the looping intestines of his first victim to strangle a third.

Lorok lumbered about, swinging wildly, knocking opponets aside in a frenzy of bone-crushing blows.

But despite these little victories, there were simply too many of them. Scug realized his clan would be overwhelmed within moments.

Just as he was about to tell the others to run, the belching blat of a diesel engine roared. Headlights pierced the darkness as a big rig tractor trailer barreled around the corner of the movie theater. The driver picked up speed and the truck burped exhaust as it rocketed toward the group. Then the horn blared, drowning out everything else.

The Captain's followers stared, frozen in surprise as the big rig raced toward them. Even Rat himself looked stunned.

Taking advantage of the panic and confusion, Scug ran at Rat and leaped upon him, knocking the sledgehammer from his hands. They tumbled to the ground together and rolled about on the pavement as Scug tried to get his hands around the man's pale, slender neck. Rat slipped his grasp, however, and bit Scug's cheek, tearing away a ragged chunk of flesh.

"You taste like shit," Captain Rat said. "Perhaps I will feed you to the rest of your clan."

Roaring, Scug drove his knee into Rat's groin, but his opponent's long, pointy teeth pierced his skin a second time, digging deep into his forearm. The truck horn blared again, sounding as if it were right overtop of them. Growling, Scug ripped his own arm free, willfully allowing his skin to be torn. Before Captain Rat could react, he grabbed the man's head in both hands and smashed it into the asphalt.

The truck slammed into the rest of the attackers, smashing and crushing them beneath its wheels. The clan scattered just in time, avoiding the speeding behemoth.

Scug slammed Captain Rat's head into the pavement again and again and again. He giggled when one of the man's eyes popped out, and shouted with glee as his skull cracked, and then shattered. Grunting, Scug dug his fingers in through the broken scalp, heedless of the sharp bone fragments that sliced his fingertips. Straining with the effort, he pulled with all his might until slowly, agonizingly, Captain Rat's head came apart and his brains splashed out onto the pavement.

Panting, Scug stood up and squashed the brains beneath his boot. They squirted across the asphalt like jelly and curds. Still not satisfied, he ground them beneath his heel and then stomped on them again.

The truck swung around the lot and idled to a stop beside them. The air brakes hissed. The driver's side door opened, and Annie swung out and clambered down.

Scug nodded at her. "Thanks."

She stared at what was left of Captain Rat. "You had enough, or do you want to pulverize him some more?"

Scug turned and spat on the corpse. Then he glanced down at his bleeding arm. He knelt, ripped two scraps of cloth from Captain Rat's clothing, and wrapped one of them around his wound. He pressed the other to his injured cheek.

"You're hurt," Annie said. "Want to get those bites looked at?"

"I'll be fine. I've had worse. Our kind…we heal."

"Fair enough. I know a doctor who could treat you, no questions asked. But he's a good distance from here."

"I'll be fine," Scug insisted.

Annie shrugged. "You ready to blow this popsicle stand, then?"

Scug shook his head. "I don't know what that means."

"It means are you ready to leave?"

"Yes."

"Are any of your people hurt?"

Scug glanced at each of them. "Everyone okay?"

They nodded, one by one.

Scug turned back to her. "No."

"Well, okay then. Everybody get in the back of the truck. We've got a long way to go."

"Where are we going?"

Annie smiled. "I'm taking you home. Like we agreed."

In a bit of a daze, Scug guided the others over to the trailer and helped them climb inside. Before Annie closed the door, he looked at them all gathered in the rear of the container—Jax and Gax, Gretch, Curd, Klavo, Lorok, and the younger ones. All of them were safe.

As he sank to the floor and rested his back against the side of the trailer, Scug began to realize just how physically tired he really was.

No. More than tired.

Exhausted.

Sighing wearily, he closed his eyes and fell asleep.

EPILOGUE

The journey southward took a full day, the travel time extended by the need to occasionally stop and open the trailer container so Scug and his people could get fresh air. Annie spent a few minutes talking to him during each of these stops, telling him about where they were and how much farther they had to go.

A place called West Virginia.

Annie had told him that they'd take Route 30 to Interstate 83, and then Interstate 81 southward to Interstate 64. From there, they'd head west. Scug didn't know what any of that meant, but he pretended to understand.

The long periods locked away inside the trailer were difficult for all of them. It was hot and suffocating and sweaty, and not unlike that final night in Philadelphia, when they'd cowered in the sewers beneath the city, hiding in the piss and the shit.

Many miles before they reached their destination, Scug knew they were no longer traveling along the nation's major freeways. The big truck was chugging along at a much slower rate now and the thrum and hiss of surrounding traffic was non-existent. The road they were on was much rougher, too, pitted with potholes that caused jarring lurches for Scug and everyone else in the container. Even this stretch of the journey went on longer than he expected, taking well over an hour before the truck slowed again and started down an even rougher, rutted path. The sound the tires made on asphalt stopped, making Scug think that they must now be on a dirt road somewhere.

After just another couple miles, the truck slowed even more, almost to a crawl, and soon it came to a complete, shuddering stop. The rumble of the engine ceased, and they heard the creaking of a cab door opening.

Then came a loud clanking sound as the door was unlocked and unlatched. It rolled upward and Scug had to squint against an intrusion of the brightest sunlight he'd ever seen. Other members of the clan held hands up to block the light.

Annie laughed, looking up at them. "All right, this is it. End of the road."

Scug grunted as he stepped down to the bumper, and then jumped down to the ground. He waited for his vision to adjust. When it finally did, he gaped.

The landscape was far different than what he was used to. He had never seen anything like it, other than in pictures. The urban and suburban landscapes that had characterized his surroundings all of his life until now were nowhere in sight. Instead, he saw that they were up at the top of a gently rising hill overlooking countless acres of rolling greenery and forests. Mountains towered to the sky in the distance.

Nestled at the top of the hill was a house so grand it was almost stupefying. A long porch stretched from one end of the structure to the other, with banisters and tall pillars and a swing at either end. The house had two additional stories, and the middle story featured a balcony nearly as long as the porch beneath it. A two-story barn stood nearby.

A closer, more lingering look at the house revealed signs of decay. The white paint of its exterior was faded and peeling away in many places. Some of the windows had boards in place of glass.

The chains holding up the swings were rusted brown. Scug thought the house and barn might be hundreds of years old. The rest of his clan nonetheless stared at it with expressions of wonder as they emerged from the trailer and joined him on the ground.

Scug looked at Annie. "What is this?"

She hooked her thumbs inside her red suspenders, smiling as she stretched them outward. "This is your new home, Scug. Long time ago, back before the Civil War, slaves worked all this land you see, making money for their master."

"Is that what you are to us now? Our master? Are we your slaves?"

"Lord, no!" Annie laughed heartily. "We're gonna be partners, Scug. Partners in crime, that is. I'm setting up a big operation down here, and you're gonna be a vital part of it. It's the perfect place for something like that, too. No real law for miles and miles around. Besides, the real master of this place wouldn't have it any other way. You see, there's a reason I thought of this place for you and your kin. It's perfect in more ways than one."

Before Scug could ask what she meant by that, the front door of the house creaked open and a man in an exquisitely tailored velvet suit stepped out onto the porch. The suit had a matching vest and the man wore a bolo tie around his neck. The heavy trod of his boots made the porch planks creak noisily as he came forward in an unhurried manner. The sun's position in the sky caused a shadow to fall across the porch.

Scug watched with narrowed eyes.

As he arrived at the edge of the porch, the sunlight hit the man's face. He had a misshapen head and more than the usual number of fingers on the hand gripping the silver lion's head at the top of his cane.

More people followed the man out onto the porch. Children in fine clothing and a lean woman in a sundress. All were deformed in some way.

Scug felt a lightness within unlike anything he'd ever known.

Annie was right. This place was perfect.

For the first time in many years, they had a real home again.

* * *

Somewhere in the cold Midwest, many states removed from Scug and his family's new home, two young boys aged twelve and thirteen walked the streets and alleys of their small town. The streets were wet from a recent rain and the air bore the sharp chill that always came with the advent of fall. They talked about video games and girls at their school. They were heading home after a trip to the town's one drugstore for some candy and cans of pop.

As they waited for a light to turn green at an intersection, one of the boys spotted a garishly illustrated flyer stapled to a utility pole. Curious, he wandered over to it.

"What's this?"

His friend came over to stand beside him. He slowly read the words on the flyer out loud.

"Two nights only. The Flaherty Brothers Traveling Freakshow and Carnivale. Featuring Dr. Midnight and his Bizarre Bazaar of Dark Wonders."

The kid who'd first spotted the flyer said, "They spelled carnival wrong."

"I think that's like an old school way of spelling it."

"Date on there is next weekend. Weird time of the year for a carnival. Wonder if our parents will let us go?"

His friend smirked as he ripped the flyer off the utility pole, folded it up, and shoved it into a pants pocket.

"Easy peasy, lemon squeezy. We just won't tell them about it and go anyway."

The two friends high-fived and laughed about it. They walked along together a short while longer, until splitting up to head toward their respective homes. The older of the two took out the flyer after he got home and retreated to his bedroom. He smoothed it open and studied it for a long while as he dreamed about how much fun he and his best friend would have at the carnival.

He couldn't wait to meet Dr. Midnight.

ABOUT THE AUTHORS

BRIAN KEENE is the author of over fifty books, mostly in the horror, crime, and fantasy genres. His 2003 novel, *The Rising*, is credited with inspiring pop culture's recurrent interest in zombies. He has written for such media properties as *Thor, Doom Patrol, Justice League, Doctor Who, The X-Files, Aliens,* and *Masters of the Universe.* Several of his novels and stories have been adapted for film, including *Ghoul, The Naughty List, The Ties That Bind*, and *Fast Zombies Suck.* His numerous awards and honors include the 2014 World Horror Grandmaster Award, 2001 Bram Stoker Award for Nonfiction, 2003 Bram Stoker Award for First Novel, the 2016 Imadjinn Award for Best Fantasy Novel, the 2015 Imaginarium Film Festival Awards for Best Screenplay, Best Short Film Genre, and Best Short Film Overall, the 2004 Shocker Award for Book of the Year, and Honors from United States Army International Security Assistance Force in Afghanistan and Whiteman A.F.B. (home of the B-2 Stealth Bomber) 509th Logistics Fuels Flight. Keene serves on the Board of Directors for the Scares That Care 501c charity organization.

BRYAN SMITH is the multiple Splatterpunk Award-winning author of more than thirty horror and crime novels and novellas, including the cult classic *Depraved* and its sequels, *The Killing Kind, Slowly We Rot, The Freakshow, Kayla and the Devil, House of Blood, Dirty Rotten Hippies, Kill For Satan, Last Day,* and many more. His novel *68 Kill* was adapted into a motion picture directed by Trent Haaga and starring Matthew Gray Gubler of the long-running CBS series Criminal Minds. It won the Midnighters Award at the SXSW film festival in 2017 and was released to wide acclaim, including positive reviews in The New York Times and Bloody Disgusting. Smith also co-scripted an original Harley Quinn comic for DC Comics.